THE CROSSOVER PARADOX

Other books by Rob Edwards

Justice Academy Series:
The Ascension Machine

THE CROSSOVER PARADOX

BY

ROB EDWARDS

ISBN: 978-1-951122-28-7 (paperback)
ISBN: 978-1-951122-41-6 (ebook)
LCCN: 2021947204

Printed in the United States of America.

Shadow Dragon Press
9 Mockingbird Hill Rd
Tijeras, New Mexico 87059
www.shadowdragonpress.com
info@shadowdragonpress.com

CHAPTER 1
SUDDEN ARRIVAL

My name is Grey and I'm a student superhero.

Technically, Grey isn't the name on my ID, but since that name is also fake, I'm not sure why I should be limited by it. Grey is who I chose to be, and so far, he's been the most successful me I've ever been. The first year I was Grey, I made a lot of friends, enrolled in college (although that was under yet another name) and stopped an alien invasion.

Identity. It's a complex issue.

At the end of that first year, during the summer break, most of my new friends went back to families and homeworlds. Me, I don't really have either of those. My family and I, um, parted company when I was eight. As for a home, I spent the better part of a decade drifting from space station to space station, seeing the galaxy from a variety of orbital boxes. I survived. Prospered, on one level. Although I did get into a whole lot of trouble.

The most important thing to me during that summer break was not to fall back into old habits.

# # #

"There he is! Get him."

Well, so much for *that* hiding place. The gantry swayed as the two Cholbren climbed the ladder near my feet, and I power-crawled away as best I could. Far below us, the Cholbrens' boss shouted encouragement. To them, not me.

1

This was getting me nowhere. Really nowhere; I was rapidly running out of gantry, and there was no ladder at the far end. Just a long drop to the sloping roof of the Kirby class star cruiser docked below. Another gantry swung from the ceiling across from me, but it was a good twenty meters away. Earlier in the holiday I'd have just snapped out my grapnel gun and swung across, but the propellant cannister was long-since out of gas, so now I had no way to bridge the gap. A quick glance back, and the golden shoulder fur of the first of the Cholbren just crested the top of the ladder.

Can't go up, across or back. That only leaves one direction.

I pulled the grapnel from my belt, hooked the claw onto the gantry. No propellant, but I still had plenty of cable and the inertial reel on my belt should, in theory, slow my descent. We hadn't covered it in Grapnel Gun Basics at the Academy, maybe it was an Advanced topic, but I couldn't see a reason for it not to work. *No choice anyway.*

The second Cholbren topped the ladder. The gantry shifted, tipping slightly as the first Cholbren passed the mid-point. "Mr Bowrider wants a word with you," he growled.

"Popularity is a curse," I said and threw myself off the gantry.

I fell, faster than I hoped, but slower than I might, the cable paying out smoothly. When I hit the roof of the cruiser, it was with enough force to blast the air from my lungs, but not enough to break bones. By reflex, I clicked the gun control to release the claw and retract the cable. Immediately, I started to slide. There was just enough curve to the canopy of the cruiser to restart my acceleration ground-wards. I let the grapnel gun go, it clattered behind me, the cable still retracting.

Picking up speed, and spinning as I slid, I scrabbled for handholds. I caught at one edge, a safety grip designed for extra-vehicular work. *Too fast.* My fingers slid across the hard edge; I couldn't secure my grip. All I did was add a little extra spin to my fall. The world whipped by in a whirl, as I slipped and clattered along. I bounced off something, suddenly airborne. When I landed it was on the smooth plexiglass of the main bridge window, I caught a glimpse of a startled Zalex crewman working on the bridge, but I spun by too fast to catch his response.

The front of the Kirby dropped away sharply after the end of the bridge section, I had to slow my descent before I hit that. I abandoned the idea of handholds, instead fought for drag, stretched myself as wide and as flat as I could, put as much surface area against the ship as I could manage. My slide slowed as the incline grew shallower. I was running out of spaceship, though. If I couldn't find a way to stop before I went over...

Now I needed a handhold, something, anything, to grab onto, but the sleek nose section of the cruiser was not obliging. I slowed, slowed... and then the world dropped away, as I reached, and plummeted over the edge.

I fell five meters, then came up sharp as my belt cut into my waist. That was going to leave a bruise. But my grapnel gun, still rattling along behind me had caught on something above, left me dangling ten meters above the docking bay floor. I hit the control on the reel to pay out cable, let it drop me to the deck. I lay panting, bruised and battered, on the cold deck of the docking bay, the Kirby loomed above me, its name painted across its hull in meter-high lettering. *The Sudden Arrival.* I liked it.

Booted feet pounded the deck. That and shouting told me the chase wasn't over yet. I cut the cable, no time to unsnag it, and clambered to my feet. *Where to now?*

Perhaps I could lose myself amongst the cargo pallets stacked against the near wall. I set off at a hobble, as the Cholbren boss and two more of his minions gave chase.

I grabbed the edge of the first pallet I reached, used it to swing around the corner.

There, looming out of nowhere was a wall of green muscle, a Brontom warrior, four arms braced, a grim set to his jaw.

I tried to stop, leaning back enough that I fell, my momentum carried me up to his shins, just as the Cholbren chasing me also rounded the corner.

The Brontom swung, connected, and the gang leader fell to the floor, unconscious.

Standing behind the Brontom, five station security officers braced their stun bolters ready to cover him. The Cholbren's minions staggered to a halt, hands raised in surrender.

I looked all the way up to the Brontom, grinning above me.

"Seventhirtyfour!" I said.

"Hey, Grey," he rumbled.

# # #

Station Security took over the problem for me. They cuffed the three at ground level and coaxed the two Cholbren off the gantry above. I let them worry about it, my work here was done. For once it hadn't needed to be a huge on-going caper; it made a nice change of pace.

"So, who were those guys?" Seventhirtyfour asked.

"Just some random mobsters. Part of the Bowrider smuggling operation out of Bantus. I recognised one of them, so I spoke to Security and offered to help bring them in. Funny, this time last year I was running from Station Security, now I'm actively working with them."

4

"We'll make an upstanding citizen of you yet, Grey."

"One thing at a time. I'm still working on 'superhero', 'upstanding citizen' sounds more like a post-graduate course."

We watched the last of the Cholbren get jostled through the exit, on his way to the station brig.

I cast a sideways glance at Seventhirtyfour. "I have to ask. You know I have to ask, right?"

In the long and glorious history of victories achieved by the proud Brontom warrior race, Seventhirtyfour's battle to hide his grin was not one. "Ask me what, Grey?"

I gestured broadly, taking in his outfit. He'd spent our first year in jeans and an x-shirt, but he'd clearly decided it was time to step it up. Most of the outfit was made of some tough but close-fitting material in a shade of deep purple, accented with dark blue on his arms and legs. It was armoured, or at least padded, in strategic locations. The upper shoulder pads and combat boots were chunky and black, good quality, but from a different aesthetic. At the centre of his chest, a golden circle with "P(k)" drawn in. "I mean, that. What's that?" I asked.

"It's my costume, Grey! I'd hoped to have one by the end of first year, but things kind of got in the way, you know?"

"Sure, I remember."

"Even some freshers arrive with costumes and names in place. I couldn't have turned up as a second-year with nothing. It would have been embarrassing." He bit his lower lip. "You'll be fine, of course, it doesn't really apply to you, but for me, you know?"

I laughed. "I really should come up with something, I guess." I was all in for the Academy, what it stood for and what it could offer me, but there was no getting away from it, the code names and costumes were still a bit silly.

5

"You'll come up with something, Grey. I know you will. Oh! You haven't seen the best bit." He pressed a button on his collar, and a hood, no, a mask, folded out and over to cover his head and the top half of his face. "There? See. That's so cool. And I've worked the Psionic Crown into the mask, too. Another toggle engages that when I need it. I don't know if this is the final version, but I needed a starting point. What do you think? First impressions? Be honest."

"It looks great. You might want to fine-tune the colours to go with your skin tones, I'm not sure if that blue works with your green, but yes. I like it. It's a good start. Kind of classic."

Seventhirtyfour beamed. "Thanks, man. It is, isn't it?"

"Do I want to ask why you have PK here?" I tapped his emblem.

"Ah! That's about my name. I'm thinking of going with Probability Kid." He gestured broadly with his right hands for emphasis. "It works because of my precognition, and with my name being numbers and P of k being the probability of 'k'. It does work, doesn't it? You know we Brontom aren't great with names."

"Sure, Seventhirtyfour. Although, 'kid'? Don't you want something cooler? Captain? Doctor? No, not Doctor. 'Probability Man'?"

"I can't call myself Captain, it might be years before I earn my commission. And as for 'Man', Brontom don't technically have genders, although most of us do identify with one. I think having 'Man' in my name might confuse people."

I nodded. "That's a fair point. Okay. Well, we can think about it, we have time. But, yeah, Probability Kid, I like it. Is that what you want me to call you?"

"On missions, yes please, but when it's just us, or

around the Academy, Seventhirtyfour is still fine. Or." His face fell a little, I could see even with his mask up. "Yeah, about that. I have some news."

"More exciting than your new name and costume?"

"No," Seventhirtyfour said. "Unfortunately, not. Come on, let's head topside. There are some people I want you to meet. Or, well, there are some people you probably *should* meet, anyway." He pressed the button to stow his mask and we headed off to the hangar-level lifts.

"What's wrong? Did something happen over summer?" I asked.

"No. No, summer was great. Got to visit with my old vat mates, check up on how they're doing. They're deploying out again next month, but that's the life of a Brontom clone warrior, you go where you're needed."

"You certainly do. Thanks for showing up today. How did you find me?"

He rallied a little, waggled his eyebrows. "I have my methods."

Seventhirtyfour was a mutant Brontom; not only was he a few centimeters taller than he should be, but he had psychic powers too. "You had a premonition about me? You're getting better at that."

He rumbled a soft chuckle. "No, actually. I saw the station alert on the security feed and figured I'd find you in the middle of it. It's good to see you, Grey."

"It's good to be seen."

The lift arrived and we stepped inside. Seventhirtyfour gestured through the top of the control field, and the elevator dutifully ascended.

As it slowed to a stop, Seventhirtyfour squared himself up to his full height. "Okay, Grey, here goes." He stepped out of the lift and as he did, hunched his shoulders, dropped his head a little. "There was one development over summer. My superiors were impressed with my report and decided the Academy might be a useful place to put other Brontom mutants."

He ducked into a cramped coffee shop, made all the smaller by the presence of three more Brontom clones. I'd never seen so many in one place before, four Seventhirtyfours in all. At first glance, identical apart from their uniforms and Seventhirtyfour's slouch which made him notably shorter than his duplicates.

We slid into their booth as Seventhirtyfour made introductions. "Grey, I'd like you to meet Nine, Two and Three. Sergeant, this is Grey."

The Brontom whose chest emblem was a large red 9 looked down at me. "Four has told us a great deal about you, Grey. It's a pleasure to meet you." Even his voice was the same as Seventhirtyfour's.

He extended his lower right hand, and I shook it, somewhat bewildered. "Likewise."

"They have signed up as new students at the Academy this year," Seventhirtyfour said.

"Oh, great. Are you precognitive like Seventhirtyfour is, Nine?"

"Please, call me *Sergeant* Nine, it's my rank, but also my chosen 'hero identity'."

"Clever."

"Two has been designated 'Twin Strike', and Three as 'Triple Threat'. To answer your question, no. Our... our mutations," he stumbled over the word, "are all different. My apologies, it is not a subject we Brontom speak easily about."

"Oh, I'm sorry, I didn't mean to offend," I said. Offending a group of full-grown warrior clones was *incredibly low* on my to-do list.

Sergeant Nine shook his head. "No apology necessary.

We must adapt, particularly if we are now to study how best to use our... individual... abilities. My body temperature runs higher than it should, and if I focus..." He held out his upper left hand. A small yellow flame danced in his palm. "Like so."

"Cool," I said.

One of the cafe wait staff, a Polifan girl, wings furled in the cramped space, approached our table. Nine hastily closed his fist to extinguish the flame.

The conversation dissolved into a round of drinks orders, and the girl left to collect them.

"You're going to love the Academy," I said. "There's always something going on, most of it... strange. It keeps you on your toes, right, Seventhirtyfour?"

He nodded but said nothing. He was being noticeably quiet.

I tried another conversational line. "I'm looking forwards to trying out some new classes this year. I've applied for some pretty exciting ones. Have you selected your courses for this term yet, Twin Strike?"

The Brontom with crossed swords on her chest emblem cast a glance towards Nine before answering. "I am beginning with combat and reconnaissance classes to assess the relevance to standard Brontom tactics," she said.

"Sure. Okay. Have you considered branching out a bit? There's so much more to learn, things I'd never even have thought of before I went. I can see the combat classes being appealing, but there's a load of other options."

Triple Threat said, "I will be assessing the survival and combat engineering instructionals. We have most of the bases covered between us."

They were missing the point of the Academy to my mind, but that was something I hadn't realised at first either. They'd learn. Or not.

I looked at Seventhirtyfour, to see if he'd leap in and save the conversation, but he sat close-lipped looking kind of miserable. It was up to me then. They weren't biting on Academy small talk, and it's pointless discussing the weather on a space station. That only really left Galactic News. "They say piracy is on the rise again out east," I tried.

"Brontom command is aware. To comment further could impact operational security," Nine said.

"Ah." That was it, I was out.

I finished up my coffee in silence, none of the others seemed inclined to lead the chat.

"Well, it was great to meet you all," I said, at last. "And I'm sure Seventhirtyfour will enjoy having some more Brontom around the place. When you know which accommodation block you're in, be sure to tell us, and Seventhirtyfour and I will come over for a visit."

"That will not be necessary," Sergeant Nine said. "I have spoken to the Academy administration, and Four has been reassigned to billet with us."

"Seventhirtyfour? I thought we were—?"

"I'm sorry, Grey," Seventhirtyfour shrugged his four-shoulder shrug. "I was looking forward to sharing again, but I have... my squad needs me more."

"Oh."

"Brontom work best when together. It is our design," Nine said. The other three nodded in unison.

CHAPTER 2
WELCOME HOME

The flight from Meanwhile Station to the Academy was uneventful. I'd hoped to spend the time catching up with Seventhirtyfour, I suddenly had a lot of questions to ask, but Sergeant Nine seemed set on treating the trip like a military operation and sat his squad together. I was disappointed, but there would be time to check in with Seventhirtyfour later. Nine couldn't keep him bottled up permanently, right?

We disembarked, and I followed everyone else out through the terminal building. The Academy's climate was warm, tempered by a sea breeze blowing across the nearby beach. The sky was wide and blue, and the sun welcomed us warmly. Did I pause before stepping out into the quad to check that the sky wasn't doing anything strange? Yes. I don't know if I'll ever trust places without a proper ceiling, but I'd developed coping mechanisms, and stepping into the quad didn't immediately send me into a panic attack. This time.

It helped when I had distractions, and the first day of term at the Academy could distract anyone. The colourful costumes, a few thousand excited happy students from a dozen different species. I spied a few familiar faces among them, exchanged waves and greetings. My chest swelled. The space stations of the galaxy might be my natural habitat, but the Justice Academy was my *home*.

As the crowd moved around, I caught a brief glimpse of Dez. I couldn't hear her clearly over the general hubbub, but she looked to be engaged in a sing-off with a Frantium student. Dez's reptilian tail tapped in time to the beat as she wailed into her microphone, her rival retreating before her. I waved, but she didn't respond, too wrapped up in her song. No doubt she would crush it and her opponent. I couldn't help smiling, even as the flow of the crowd hid her again.

"Grey!" A bolt of light flew over the heads of the assembled students, gliding to a halt above and in front of me. Pilvi's hair glowed white, and her eyes blazed as she grinned. Like Seventhirtyfour, she'd decided to lean into the whole costume thing. Hers was a sky-blue body suit with white shoulders, gloves and boots. A single yellow stroke cut across her body, from her left shoulder to her right hip. "What do you think?"

"Could you...?" I gestured down towards the ground.

"Oh! Sorry, yes." She floated down, but didn't quite land, I noticed. "Better?"

"Much, thanks. I like the new costume, very nice. A beam of light through clouds?"

"Yep. It honours where my powers came from, and who I was." She spun in the air. "It's so good to be back here. Can't wait to get started. I've spent the summer practising my flying, I think I'm going to ace the flight skills course."

"Given your approach to your studies, I don't doubt it, Pilvi."

"Call me Säde."

"Sarday?"

She laughed. "Not even close. Shorten the vowels. Säde. It's an old Finnish name meaning 'beam'; like a beam of light. I thought it made a good superhero name. Don't tell

12

Dez before I do though."

"Wouldn't, if I could."

"Oh there's... sorry Grey, I need to go say hi to... I'll catch you later."

"Sure thing. I—"

Pilvi hurtled skywards again, I kept my gaze down.

I shook my head. "Seventhirtyfour is Probability Kid, Pilvi is Säde," I muttered to myself. If everyone was picking codenames this year things were about to get confusing. "Seventhirtyfour, Probability Kid. Pilvi, Säde."

A burst of green flame illuminated the front of the Hall of Justice emanating from whoever was in charge of corralling the first years. They began calling out names. I had my accommodation sorted already, so I didn't need to hang around for that. Instead, I forged on through the crowd, looking for the last two members of my team.

I spotted Avrim's grey-feathered wings first. He tended to keep them furled in company, but they were out now, he held them in an arc, wingtips forward.

"Avrim!" I called out.

He beckoned me forward.

"Hey, Grey," he said. "Don't step on Gadget Dude. He's decided that the middle of the first-day ruckus is the perfect place to do a spot of kit-bashing." He nodded to the ground in front of him.

Gadget Dude, the blue Zalex of our group, sat cross-legged on the ground, protected from being trampled by the curve of Avrim's wings. Surrounded by a spread of motors and circuit boards, Gadget Dude hummed happily to himself as he combined pieces together seemingly at random.

Avrim rolled his eyes. "There's no talking to him now, he's in the zone. But I'll tell him you were here."

"How was your summer?" I asked.

"Pretty good. Visited the family cabin on Artamantis, spent a couple of weeks there sailing the thermals. Just feeling the wind on my wings."

"Sounds nice."

"Yeah. Quite the change of pace after Nymanteles. I didn't get shot once."

I grimaced. "Sorry again about that. How is your shoulder?" I asked.

"Fully healed, thanks. Your leg?"

"Same." Our trip to Nymanteles had been... fraught. I looked down at Gadget Dude. "What is he making? Did he say anything?"

"No idea. I've never any idea. Sometimes not even when he's finished. No doubt it will be astonishing, at least until it breaks," Avrim said dryly.

"No doubt. Good to see you both. I'm going to stow my things in my room. Oh! I meant to ask. You're still Avrim, right?"

"What?"

"I've spoken to Seventhirtyfour and Pilvi so far, and they're both using codenames this year. Seventhirtyfour is Probability Kid and Pilvi is Säde. Just checking you're still Avrim?"

"I'm still Avrim. I've not worked out what my 'thing' is yet, hard to find a codename without a thing."

"I know what you mean."

I left Avrim to continue his watch over Gadget Dude and headed to my dorm. My room this year would not be as grand, but I'd been looking forward to having Seventhirtyfour across the corridor again. Instead, I'd be sharing with strangers. I gave a wave to a couple of them as I forged through the shared kitchen. I'd do the introductions thing later.

#

The comm light on my console was blinking when I got in. I slumped into my desk chair and gestured to accept the call. The woman who appeared on screen was around sixty. She wore an expensive business suit, her steel-grey hair pulled back from her sharp-angled face. From the window behind her, I could see it was night wherever she was calling from.

"Mrs. Gravane, hello, this is a surprise," I said, sitting up straight again.

"Mr. Grey. I trust you are well. I'm afraid this is not a social call," she said. "I have news. I don't know that it directly affects you, but I feel you should be made aware."

"Is this about Mirabor?" I asked.

My relationship with Mrs. Gravane was a complicated one. I'd spent a good part of the previous year impersonating her son, Mirabor. First, because he asked me to, then later when she had, to cover her son's kidnapping. I'd eventually mounted a rescue mission to the world of Nymanteles only to discover Mirabor had faked his own abduction. Oh, and he'd used an alien device called the Ascension Machine to give himself and others superpowers that were slowly driving him insane. Exhibit A, he'd started calling himself 'Doctor Gravestone'. He and his alien Vadram allies were intent on some dastardly scheme or other. My friends and I had stopped all that and captured Mirabor so that he could get treatment. Mrs. Gravane had been grateful and gifted me with a scholarship so I could continue my studies.

But I'd told you all that already.

"Yes," she said. "Nine days ago, there was an attempt made to break him out of the facility that had been caring for him. An attempt that only failed because my son had been transferred to another location only that morning."

"Is Mirabor okay? Where is he now?"

"I am told he remains well, and secure. As to his location, the fewer people who know, the better." To most, her face would have been an impassive mask, but I'd seen her worried for her son before. The slight frown, the way she refolded her hands on the desk—a fidget she would never have displayed in normal circumstances.

"Of course, I get that. That's worrying news. Is there anything I can do to help?" I asked.

"Continue with your studies, Mr. Grey. I have no intention of calling you away for little adventures this year. However, I felt it important that you knew of the attempt because all three of the perpetrators exhibited powers. While I do not believe an attempt to extract my son should have any implications for you, the confluence of superpowers and your association with Mirabor... I felt it was my duty to warn you."

"Thank you, Mrs. Gravane. Can you tell me who I should be on the lookout for?"

"I have the file in front of me now. Two of them were well known to Galactic Police. A cyborg Welatak who goes by the name 'The Incapacitor'—" Mrs. Gravane sighed. "Really? Very well. 'The Incapacitor' can disrupt technology and caused much of the facility's security grid to deactivate. A Germile who, for reasons that elude me, uses the name 'Big Bang' kept most of the facility security forces occupied, letting the third member of the team infiltrate the hospital and reach what had been Mirabor's room."

My console pinged as two new files arrived—detailed descriptions of The Incapacitor and Big Bang. "Thanks," I said. "Do we have nothing on the last one?"

"Very little. She was spotted several times during the assault, but the descriptions were largely unhelpful. Human, female, dark hair, early- to mid- twenties. The only consistent factor is that she laughed frequently. All of the people who reported seeing her said she was laughing."

"Laughing?"

"Yes. Apparently, this has led to some referring to her as 'Laugh Riot' but I'm not sure we should condone such a thing."

"No, probably not. It's an odd team," I said, skimming through the profiles. "Incapacitor and Big Bang look like mercenaries. How would they know Mirabor? Has, I mean, awkward question, but has the Gravane Corporation ever hired them before?"

"Certainly not!" Her indignation flashed away quickly, then she admitted, "We have been known to access certain legally ambiguous resources on occasion, but never any with powers."

"Okay, so their link to Mirabor is either through the Vadram, or this third member, Laugh Riot." I jotted a note down.

"I know that look," she said, holding up an admonishing finger. "I did not bring this to your attention for you to investigate, Grey. I do not authorise such an investigation. I simply felt it best to inform you, should these events somehow reflect upon you."

I shrugged. "Okay, Mrs. Gravane. I shall leave it alone. Thank you for the warning."

"Then, warning delivered, I must return to other business. Study hard. I expect a return on my investment."

"Yes, ma'am."

After she hung up, I stared at the two profiles. Not the start to the year I'd hoped for. But maybe Mrs. Gravane was right. There was no reason that these three would come after me, right?

CHAPTER 3
TRUTH HURTS

"Lying," said Veritas. She stood in front of the class and let the word hang in the air. Silence can make a point better than a lot of words.

I've known many Polifan over the course of my travels, some were downright scruffy and disreputable. Not Veritas. She leaned into the whole angelic look, choosing a floaty white dress to complement her snow-white wings. When she lingered in front of one of the wall lamps, it emphasised her blond hair to give her a halo of light. Deliberate artifice? I assumed so, but I didn't ask.

Her face lit with a dazzling smile and she picked me out of the crowd with an open-handed gesture. "Mr. Grey, perhaps you'd like to come up and take this lesson."

"That's okay, Professor. You can take it, but I'll fill in any gaps you miss," I drawled.

"Gracious of you," she said with a slight bow.

The events of my first year made me something of a celebrity. People knew I'd spent a lot of time lying about who I was and why I was at the Academy. I'd avoided Veritas back then, her power to compel the truth was a little inconvenient when your whole life is a lie. But now that my life was an open book, almost an open book, I'd signed up for her Ethics class. Didn't mean I'd sit at the front of course. Nobody did. The radius of her truth power was generally understood, which was why the front three rows of chairs stood empty.

"We talk a great deal about 'Truth' in the life of a super-hero," Veritas said, her wings flexed in time to the rhythm of her speech. "And yet, look at the literature, almost all superheroes in the early days lived their lives as lies. The very notion of a 'secret identity'? An understandable pre-caution, perhaps, but difficult to square with the idea of fighting for Truth and Justice."

"Also, a lot of hard work," I added. It got a laugh.

"You certainly burned a few calories running away from me," she said. It got a bigger laugh.

"Putting aside Grey's more mendacious tendencies," Veritas began. For some reason, a few of my classmates gasped at that. Perhaps they were offended on my behalf, though it seemed a reasonable description to me, perhaps they just didn't understand the word. Either way, Veritas continued, "I want us to tackle this question. In what sit-uations is it okay for a superhero to lie? What crosses the line? As with so much we talk about in this class, the answer is more complicated than you might think. Who wants to start us off?"

A woman in the back row raised her hand. "Combat situations? Most strategy is deception, right?"

"An interesting point, Miss...?"

"Um, I guess, just 'Fusillade'?" She sounded a little older than a typical first-year but like someone trying out her hero name for the first time.

Veritas smiled her matronly smile. "Welcome to the class, Fusillade. You make a good point, but how would we square that with the concept of a fair fight? Anybody?"

"What's the merit of a fair fight?" asked a Germile stu-dent, Bolsta. She was standing by the door, too massive for the seats, and I don't think Germile bend in a way that allows sitting even if she wasn't. "If we want to stop a villain from hurting innocents, shouldn't we be putting them down as quickly as we can? It's not a training bout, no need to give them a sporting chance."

Veritas held up a hand. "Now that's a fascinating topic, for another day, I think. Let's stay with lying. Do we all agree that it's okay to lie as a combat tactic? Show of hands?"

Most people seemed to agree, but there were a few holdouts. I raised my hand.

"Interesting," Veritas said. "Let's get a dissenting opinion. How about... Bloodshock? Why is lying bad in combat?"

Bloodshock was a blue Zalex, like Gadget Dude, but that's where the comparison ended. He was one of the dark angsty types I didn't get on with, heroes with costumes featuring black trench coats, edges and angles. "If fight darkness, can't be darkness," he said, his voice pitched low and gravelly.

"But what if the only way to beat someone more powerful than you, is to lie and tell them, I don't know, you've already defused their bombs?" asked Fusillade.

"Find other way," Bloodshock said. He clenched his fist in front of his face to show off the spikes on his knuckles.

"What if there is no other way? Grey? Is it true you beat that guy on Nymanteles by lying to him?" Fusillade asked.

I sat up in my chair, I hadn't expected to be drawn into this one. "Yeah," I admitted. "Then I punched him, so it was a bit of a two for one deal. But it's true I'd never have gotten close to Doctor Gravestone without lying to him first."

Fusillade nodded emphatically. "I knew it. See, Bloodshock?"

Bloodshock turned his face visor towards me. "Grey always lie. Not hero."

"Okay, let's keep this in the abstract, shall we?" Veritas

21

said. "It's a good start though. Let's break into groups to discuss it further. Use the talking points on page fifteen to lead the discussion."

# # #

At the end of the class, Veritas called for me to stay behind. I stood back by the fourth row of chairs, and she respected my choice by staying on the dais.

"My apologies, Grey. I shouldn't have called on you at the start, it gave the others a chance to follow suit."

I shrugged. "Who, Bloodshock? Don't worry about it, Professor, I've been called far worse by people whose opinions matter to me more."

"All the same, it was inappropriate. Sorry."

I shrugged. "Hey, Professor?"

"Yes, Grey?"

"Was lying to Gravestone the ethical choice? I don't think I had an alternative, but that doesn't make it right, does it?"

Before answering, Veritas perched on the stool behind her podium, hands resting in her lap. "It's a big question, Grey, one much bigger than an after class Yes or No. We will spend most of this semester discussing it, in one form or another. There are different philosophies, different ethical frameworks to apply. Do you want me to say you were right? Read up on utilitarian ethics. Want to beat yourself up about it? The human philosopher Immanuel Kant would provide you with plenty of ways to do that. Do you want to know what *you* really think about it? Step closer and tell me."

Why had I asked? I stared at the imaginary line between us. Step across it and I couldn't lie to her, or myself. I backed up. "Thanks, Professor."

Her wing beats slowed, and she raised a hand. "But

you're not asking the right question," she said softly. "Let me give you a different one to ponder. Can you be a good person without making ethical choices?"

"I—"

"Welcome to Ethics 101, Grey, you're going to do fine."

# # #

I had to hustle to make my next class. It was scheduled in the biggest lecture hall on campus, occupying most of the twelfth floor of the main tower block, eight floors above Veritas's classroom. The closer I got to it, the more crowded the stairwell became. Students from all three factions—Powers, Tech and Skills—loitered on the stairs and in the corridor outside the lecture hall. They were all talking in a hushed but excited hubbub, augmented by the usual cacophony of strange sounds that any large gathering of Academy students generated.

I spotted Seventhirtyfour in the throng and I elbowed my way towards him. He wasn't alone; Pilvi, Avrim, Gadget Dude and Dez surrounded him. I looked around for Lucy too, but if she was here, she was lost in the crowd. It was an eclectic group, even for the Academy: a glowing, hovering human, a winged Polifan, a short blue Zalex and a... whatever reptilian species Dez was.

"Guys!" I called, squeezing between two power-armoured tech students. "What the hell is this all about?"

"You made it," Seventhirtyfour rumbled happily. "I didn't know if you even knew about it."

"Professor Gale's class? I saw it was popular when I applied for it, but I didn't realise it was this popular. What's the deal?"

"It was overbooked," Dez said, her voice perfectly modulated to cut through the racket, despite coming from down at waist height. "Most popular class in the Academy's history. I wanted in but there's a waitlist for the waitlist. I thought I'd try my luck and see if anyone dropped out."

"A unique idea that occurred to absolutely nobody else," Avrim drawled. Avrim, a Polifan like his Aunt Veritas, looked uncomfortable, keeping his wings tightly held in to avoid getting them crushed in the crowd.

"These people all turned up on the off-chance?" I asked.

"The people who got in are presumably here as well," Seventhirtyfour sighed. Was that a tinge of jealousy?

"I don't get it. Why is everybody so excited about a class in 'Crossover Etiquette'? It looked interesting enough when I applied, but not mobs-in-the-hall interesting."

"Not course. Professor," said Gadget Dude.

"Professor Simon Gale? Oh, come on, Grey," Pilvi said, "I know you're not the superhero scholar that Seventhirtyfour is, but even you must have heard of him?"

"Or his secret identity, Apogee?" Seventhirtyfour added wistfully.

"If it's a secret, why would I have heard of it?"

"Did you not even read 'Superheroics: A History'?" The Brontom shook his head, disappointment radiating off him.

"I've been meaning to get to it."

"Apogee is the most famous alumnus of the Academy," Dez said. "He was in the very first graduation class 22 years ago. He saved the population of Ngembe III from a rampaging space kraken."

"Helped evacuate a Polifan colony world when a super volcano erupted," said Avrim.

"Stop death cyborgs in Turriff Pass," Gadget Dude enthused.

"And that's just his solo adventures. He's worked with all the greats. The stories he'll be able to share!" added Seventhirtyfour.

I nodded. "Okay, I get it, the dude's a big deal."

The level of noise from the crowd rose, a ripple of excitement propagating from over by the stairs. The woman next to me said, "He's here!" I recognised her from the previous class, the first year who'd introduced herself as Fusillade.

I couldn't see the Professor, but I could mark his progress by the reaction of the students swelling the corridor. I caught my first glimpse of him as he reached the lecture hall door. A human male in his early forties, in good shape for his age, but not astonishingly so. He had dark hair, greying at the temples, and was wearing a tweed suit and glasses that made him look like he came from another century. He was talking to the students closest to him, but I couldn't hear from across the corridor.

He unlocked the door and stepped into the lecture hall. A small fraction of the assembled horde of students began filing in after him.

"Well, that's it then," said Avrim. "I mean, I suppose we could wait, but there doesn't seem much point."

"It was really him!" said Seventhirtyfour. "But yes, I should probably head back. I told Sergeant Nine I was going for a run. He'll get suspicious if I'm away too long."

"None of you are actually in this class?" I asked.

"It was a lottery, Grey, you see the odds, right?" said Dez.

"Um." I took a step towards the lecture hall. "I... well..."

"No!"

"I didn't realise I'd signed up for something that was such a big deal. One of you should take my place. Seventhirtyfour?"

"No, Grey, this is clearly my punishment for fibbing to my CO. I should know better."

"Dez, then?" I said.

"Just get in there before they give your space to someone else," she said.

"And they have the nerve to call it the 'Justice' Academy," Avrim said, before shooing me towards the door.

"Okay, guys. I'll catch you later at the Gamma Bomb? Good to see you again, guys."

Gadget Dude pointed sternly at the door. "Go, Grey!"

Embarrassed, I slunk off.

The lecture hall filled quickly, I ended up closer to the front than I preferred. In moments, the rest of the seats were filled, and a few stragglers found themselves standing on the steps against the wall.

The Professor stood behind the podium on the stage, a shimmer in the air in front of him suggesting he was using a teleprompter for notes. "Good afternoon, class, welcome to Crossover Etiquette. I am Professor Gale. Over the next ten weeks, we will be discussing the intricacies and challenges presented by working with other superheroes whose powers and tactics you may not know. We will study ways you can minimise the time you spend inevitably fighting your fellow heroes before teaming up to defeat the real threat, whatever that may be."

He stepped out from behind the podium and began to pace the stage, his rich voice easily carrying to the back of the room.

"In later sessions, we will consider how to determine who should take the lead. Strategies for when and how to switch opponents in group combats. We will apply the fundamentals of the art of crossovers to use your abilities to complement those of your heroic allies, whether their abilities are similar, or diametrically opposed, to your own. During the course, we will revisit on several occasions a principle that I call the Crossover Paradox. A philosophy that has stood me in good stead over the years and simplified many a thorny encounter.

"Be warned. This course will be both serious and intense. Those of you here to enjoy an encounter with a 'celebrity superhero' or to spend hours listening to war stories, I must disappoint you. We have a lot of material to cover, and it is more important to me to equip you with techniques that may save your lives than to bask in my own faded victories. I am here entirely as Professor Simon Gale. I am not here to entertain you in my other identity."

He paused at the centre of the stage and grinned. "Well, perhaps just once. Apogee."

A wind rose from nowhere, blew across us in the audience, and swirled around Gale. It lifted him from his feet, carrying him a meter into the air. He stretched out his arms and a warm red light shimmered around him, then coalesced into a deep crimson body suit spreading over his tweeds, replacing them. Golden boots, wristbands and shoulder guards snapped into existence with a chime of ringing metal. A crimson domino mask, the last element to manifest, completed his uniform.

It was absolutely the most superhero thing I'd ever seen.

"We are only doing this to stop you pestering me about it for the next ten weeks," Apogee said, floating above the stage, lights glinting off the metal parts of his uniform. He smiled warmly as he chided us. "You have fifteen minutes to get it out of your system before we start the course proper. Who has a question?"

A sea of hands sprang up.

#

It is something of a tradition after the first day of classes each year to have a major party, notionally based in the main student bar on campus, but it tended to spill out and take over the surrounding area. The bar had had a face lift for the start of term and had been renamed; no longer the Gamma Bomb, it was now The Fortress of Epictude. Giant crystals jutted from the walls, floor and ceiling, none sharp enough to cut, but I bumped into more than one at an unexpected angle. I suspected there would be a few drunken bruises come the morning.

The lights were low, the music loud, the students laughing, dancing, and shouting to be heard. It was good to be back.

It took me a while to find any of the gang, and when I did it was Dez who'd staked a claim on a small table near the stage. She gave me a wave when she spotted me, and I snagged a nearby stool and pulled it up to join her.

"Not singing?" I shouted.

"Nah. First night is always a night for freshers to sing. I had my chance last year; it's someone else's turn this time. He's pretty good. A Welatak. Means he can really hold the long notes."

Welatak are an amphibious, grey-skinned people. They have to wear saline suits when not in the sea, or their skin dries out, but they breathe oxygen and can hold it in their lungs for a long time, releasing it with impressive breath control. The Welatak on stage was belting out a rock ballad, his saline suit coated with silver and gold glitter, making him sparkle as he sang.

"Not bad," I said. "You're better."

"I know." She grinned, her forked tongue flickering between her teeth. "Hey, so how was the big class? You made everybody jealous. Seventhirtyfour would have turned green if he wasn't already."

"Really good, actually. Intense. He did a fun Q&A to start, but when he got into the main part of the lesson, he posed lots of interesting questions. Hopefully, we'll get some answers to go along with them eventually."

"Ah yes, one of those types. Well, be sure to tell Seventhirtyfour it was terrible." She looked at her empty glass. "Now you're here, you can save the table, I'm going to the bar, do you want anything?"

"I'll take a beer, sure."

"I'll be right back." She looked at the wall of students pressed together between her and the bar. "I'll be back eventually," she amended.

I sat and enjoyed the music.

Avrim and Gadget Dude appeared before Dez returned. Gadget Dude was using a remote control to pilot a tray of drinks; it floated over the heads of the crowd, only wobbling occasionally. He brought it down to a shaky landing on our table, spilling less than half of each of the drinks in the process. He seemed happy. I grabbed a beer from the tray before it took off again.

"We just saw Seventhirtyfour," Avrim said. "He's on his way over. Looks like he snuck away from his army crew again."

"Dez is at the bar getting drinks," I said.

"Line them up," Gadget Dude declared happily.

"Were you in my Aunt's class today?" Avrim asked.

"Yeah, why?"

"She was supposed to meet me earlier, but she didn't show. Did she say anything to you?"

"Only a few book recommendations."

Avrim shrugged. "OK."

As the Welatak on stage segued from loud and shouty to soft and croony, Seventhirtyfour and Dez arrived at the table, another round of drinks between them. "I switched piquet duties with Triple Threat," Seventhirtyfour said. "I'm not on duty for almost an hour. Let's party! Non-alcoholically in my case."

"What is the deal there? Are they ever going to let you off the leash?" Avrim asked.

"Of course. Probably. Sergeant Nine just needs to come to terms with the Academy not being a Brontom boot camp. He's kind of operating on high alert, treating it like unknown territory. Once he's completed his threat analysis, I'm sure he'll loosen up."

"Riiiiight." I caught the scent of ginger from Avrim's wings; Polifan wing scent usually mirrored their emotions, ginger was a sure sign that he found the whole thing hilarious.

"Can't you just tell him?" Dez asked, bouncing up onto her stool to strike a defiant pose. "Just say 'I'm a trainee superhero, not a soldier.'"

Seventhirtyfour's brow furrowed. "I don't follow you."

"Just tell him you're not in his army anymore and you don't have to follow his orders. You made it all through last year without them."

"Dez, I'm a Brontom. I am a soldier. I am in our army. I'm not out to study at the Academy, I'm stationed here. Granted, Nine is taking things to the extreme. This isn't what I expected when they stationed more Brontom here, but that doesn't mean he's doing anything wrong. I'll make my case at the right time, but for now, I don't get to choose."

Dez deflated somewhat at that and stopped hopping up and down. "Oh."

"Can we help?" I asked. "Is there something we can do to get Nine to loosen up? Get him a bit more in the Academy vibe?"

"Just give it some time, Grey. The Sarge has the potential in him to be more chill, he has the same chill genes I do, after all. We just have to give him time to find them."

"Sure thing, whatever you say." I raised my beer in

salute. "To everybody finding their chill and an awesome second year."

"Drink to that!" Gadget Dude's voice came from under the table where he was taking apart his hover-tray and rebuilding it into something else.

"Hear, hear," said Seventhirtyfour.

"Cheers!" Avrim clinked his glass against mine.

"Let's change the subject," I said. "Has anyone seen Lucy yet? She has come back this year, hasn't she?"

"Yes, she was in Aerial Combat this morning," said Avrim. "Though I'm not sure if she'll stick with that class."

"Oh?"

"Yeah, she seemed a bit up in the air about it." Avrim guffawed at his own joke, banging the table, bouncing the empties. The scent of ginger was strong.

"You know Avrim, I think I prefer you grumpy and pessimistic," I said.

Red-faced, he wiped tears away. "I'm so proud of that one."

Dez shushed him and turned to me, a twinkle in her eye. "Any particular reason to ask about Lucy?"

"Well, you know," I said, my face feeling suddenly warm. "Last year, we kind of, almost, I thought maybe there might be—but things last year were so complicated."

"True." Again, Gadget Dude's voice came from below.

"I thought, this year will be saner. I thought, maybe I might like to see if there's something there," I rubbed the back of my neck, gaze lowered.

"Yeah, you did," Dez teased.

Avrim's comm chimed. "Hold that thought, I need to take this, but I don't want to miss out on any Grey-hazing." He stepped away from the table and the band's speakers.

Seventhirtyfour looked forlorn. "Grey, I don't want to disappoint you—"

"About what?"

"Pilvi told me that Lucy arrived at the Academy a couple of days ago, with several new students from Nymanteles. Seems the Academy is popular there since we saved them from the Vadram."

"We were very inspirationally heroic," Dez said.

"We were. Only, one of the new students she arrived with; Pilvi said he was Lucy's boyfriend. I'm so sorry, Grey." Seventhirtyfour put a hand on my shoulder.

"Oh. Right. Well, that makes sense. I mean, she's from there, she must have known—and then there was her heroics—and, well, I'm happy for her. Of course." What was this feeling? I didn't like it, a sort of weird hollowness in my stomach, but I wasn't hungry.

"Don't give up yet, Grey. Maybe Pilvi got it wrong," said Dez. "Where is Pilvi anyway, I thought she'd be the first one here tonight."

"That's a good question, where is Pilvi?" I craned my neck around trying to catch a glimpse of her in the throng. In any other crowd, her glowing white hair would have stood out a long way off, but with the various lighting effects amongst the student body, all being scattered weirdly by the Fortress's new crystal décor—there was no sign of her. "Does she seem okay to you guys, I had an odd conversation with her yesterday, she seemed a bit off."

Avrim re-joined us, face pale. His hand shook, and his eyes burned with anger. "That was Captain Hawk," he said. "My Aunt Veritas. They just found her in her classroom. She's dead."

"What? She can't be!"

"Only, he didn't say 'dead'. He said 'murdered'."

CHAPTER 4
CONTEMPLATING TARTARUS

"I'm sorry, Avrim. You'll have your chance to say your goodbyes, but for now, we need to let Professor Croft and her team work in peace." The area around Veritas's fourth-floor lecture hall was taped off. Teachers stood at each barrier to ward off the curious, but when we arrived as a group, the headmaster, Captain Hawk himself, came out to speak with us. "Be sure that we're doing everything we can, and we will keep you updated on any and all progress we make."

"I'm not here to say goodbye," Avrim said. He stood so tautly he all but vibrated. His wing scent was sharply acidic, it rolled off him in a visible haze, seeming to boil the air around him. "I am here to understand what happened. How was she murdered? How *could* she be murdered in a building full of superheroes?"

Hawk held up both hands defensively. "I regret the way I told you, son. I was off-balance. I was very fond of your Aunt, and I know that she wouldn't want you focussing on that. You need to grieve. Get some rest, I can give you a full update in the morning."

"You can give him an 'update' now," I said. "You can't just tell him this happened and then send him to bed, for pity's sake. You must know something. How do you know it was murder, for a start?"

Gadget Dude tried to take Avrim's hand, but the Polifan

shook him off.

"How did she die, Hawk?" Avrim asked.

"Sister Fashionista, might you see if Professor Croft can spare a moment to join us?" Captain Hawk asked the Polifan teacher assigned to guard this end of the corridor.

"Of course, Captain." Fashionista stepped into the classroom and returned moments later with Professor Croft.

Croft, I knew well; she taught Criminology and Evidence Analysis and had one of the sharpest analytical minds I knew. A human woman in her early fifties, she was one of the few among the teaching staff who eschewed codenames and costumes. Instead, she wore a dark suit, her greying hair tied back in a short ponytail. Croft nodded to me as she approached, but spoke to Avrim. "You want the facts of the case?"

"Yes, please," said Avrim.

"Alright, I warn you, it's grim telling."

"I can handle it."

Croft nodded, and touched her wristpad, presumably to check her notes. There must have been pictures there too, but she didn't show us. "Subject was physically assaulted, wounds consistent with blunt force trauma, either from a hefty blunt instrument, or her assailant had augmented strength. The first blow shattered the subject's radial and ulna bones in her left wing, rendering flight impossible. A blow to her head cracked her skull, but not fatally. COD was strangulation. The cable from a Grapnel gun wrapped around her throat and pulled with some force judging by the bruising. Death was quick, but not instant. Some defensive wounds indicate the victim fought back, but only briefly."

Avrim nodded, very quietly. "I see. Anything else?"

Croft shook her head. "We have barely begun the

investigation. We will know more by the morning, I assure you. There were no cameras in the classroom itself, at Professor Veritas's request. But we have fair coverage out here in the corridor." She gestured behind us. "That may tell us more. We've secured the security tapes."

"When did it happen?" I asked.

"We won't know until the autopsy, but shortly after her last class today. That would put it at about 3 pm."

"I was in that class," I said.

"We know. Did you see anything suspicious in the area?" Croft asked.

"No. She seemed her usual self when I left her. Not worried or upset. And I didn't notice anyone hanging about when I left." I tried to think, had there been anything? I'd been in a hurry to get to Gale's class, had I missed something?

"Who was with her when you left?"

"Nobody, Professor, I was last out. I stopped to ask her a question about something we'd talked about in class."

"What?"

"The ethics of lying," I said. I knew how that sounded.

Croft nodded. "Well, Grey, I might have more questions for you in the morning."

"Anything and everything I can do to help, of course," I said. "Could you answer a question of mine?"

She pursed her lips. "Shoot."

"You said she was... strangled... with the cable from a grapnel gun? How are you so sure?"

"We found it. In situ."

"What... what model was it?"

She flicked through her notes on her wristpad. "A PS 10N. Do you think that's significant, Grey?"

"Probably not. It's a common model. I have one myself." I tapped mine, clipped securely to my belt.

"Hmm." She turned back to Avrim. "I should get back. Have you any other questions?"

"No. Thank you, Professor."

Croft put a hand on Avrim's shoulder. "There really isn't much for you to do now. Get some rest if you can. I'll call you in the morning with more." She headed back into the murder scene, tapping on her wristpad to bring up her sterile field as she did.

Without a word, Avrim turned and left. We followed silently on behind him.

# # #

We went down one floor, but then Avrim stopped in a deserted lounge area, near the entrance to the main gym. I could just make out the sound of the start of term party, still in full flow below us, but the music and laughter were muted, incongruous.

Avrim stood by the window, looking out across the campus. His wing scent was a tangled mess. Gadget Dude stood by him, close, but apart. For once the Zalex had nothing in his hands, just stared at this friend in silence.

"Avrim—" Dez started, her voice soft, but Avrim held up a hand and she trailed off.

We waited in silence for several minutes before Avrim finally spoke, still staring out of the window. "We're going to find out who did this," he said.

Seventhirtyfour nodded sharply. "Of course, we are."

"You know we'll help however we can," I said, "but Professor Croft has the skills, access and experience. I don't know what we can add."

Avrim said nothing. His silence cut me.

"But, yes, obviously we will help," I said.

Nobody spoke. Seventhirtyfour, Dez and Gadget Dude all looked to me.

I cleared my throat. "Sure. Okay. First principles, then. Motive, means, opportunity. Did your aunt have enemies?"

"Not that she ever mentioned to me. Some people were wary of her because of her power, but who could hate her enough to want her dead? She was nice to everyone, respected boundaries, never abused her abilities."

"She didn't," I said, remembering. "But accidents happen, someone could have let a truth slip around her that her killer couldn't afford to be known?"

"That's possible," Dez said, "but I don't think it helps us. We're looking for someone with a dark secret that nobody knows? There probably aren't many people who match that description, but how would we know who they are?"

"Let's put a pin in that for a moment. What about relationships? Is... was Veritas involved with anyone here on campus?" I asked.

"She never told me. Never asked me about my relationships either," said Avrim. "Like I said, she was the sort to respect boundaries."

"We need to know, now. Dez?"

"Yes, Grey?"

"Can I put you in charge of looking into that? See what rumours you can unearth. About that, and any enemies she might have. Check your sources though, there are going to be a lot of rumours flying around over the next few days and most of them will be made up."

She nodded, and I moved on.

"Means is the tricky one, lets deal with that last. Opportunity. I'll talk to people who were in that class. As many as I can remember, anyway. See if any of them remember seeing anything suspicious. If we can get the time of death from Professor Croft that will help establish the window, but most teachers don't stay in their classrooms after a lesson, so the fact that she was killed in the lecture hall... to me it makes sense that she was attacked soon after the class finished."

I looked around the group and there were no dissenters. Avrim still had his back to us, but his wing scent was settling into something metallic and determined.

"So, method," I said.

"You asked about the model of grapnel gun," Seventhirtyfour said.

"I did. If it had been an unusual make that might have told us something. But the 10N is the second or third most popular model on campus. There are probably a couple of hundred personal models and at least twenty or so practice models in the Maintenance class store cupboard. We should check to see if any are missing."

"I do," said Gadget Dude.

"Thanks. We had a description of the injuries," I looked over at Avrim again, but ploughed on when he didn't object. "We need to work out how strong you need to be to break a Polifan's wing bones. That is something we can use to narrow the field, a little. Pilvi—" I stopped, where was Pilvi? We would need our scientist on this case.

"I'll look into that," said Seventhirtyfour. "The Brontom combat protocols database has all sorts of weird things like that in it."

"Will Sergeant Nine let you get involved?" Dez asked.

"Yes," said Seventhirtyfour, his voice stony. I realised he'd missed his deadline to report back for duty. I hoped he wouldn't get in trouble for that.

"Great, thanks, Seventhirtyfour. Anything else I'm missing?"

"Security footage?" asked Gadget Dude.

"Croft said she had it secure, and with her in charge, I'm certain it will be thoroughly checked. But Avrim, when you talk to Croft tomorrow, see what you can get from her. As next of kin you'll get more leeway than I would. We could offer our services to scrub the footage, extra eyes wouldn't hurt."

Avrim nodded.

"Okay. Look, I don't know how much we can achieve tonight. Do what you can, but, seriously, getting some rest might be the best thing if you can manage it. We'll need all minds sharp to work this tomorrow. I'll set up an investigation board and run it." Of all of us, I'd had the most training with all things criminal both at the Academy and before. "Report your findings as you get them, and if anyone has any bright ideas for things we should follow up, don't be shy about sharing them."

"Sure, Grey," said Seventhirtyfour.

"Yes, boss," said Dez.

"Avrim, anything to add?" I asked.

He turned back to us at last, spread his wings to their fullest extent. "We're going to find this person, whoever it is, and we're going to make sure they face justice for killing her," he said.

"Yes, we are," I said. He wouldn't have accepted anything else.

# # #

I probably should have taken my own advice and headed to bed, or at least gone back to my dorm room to get started on the murder board. Instead, I headed up.

The top floors of the Hall of Justice are closed to students, containing the tech the building needed to function, from lift mechanisms to servers for the virtual arcade. I threaded my way between the machinery to a hatch which gave access to a narrow walkway circling the building.

It was a long way down.

People sometimes misunderstand my phobia. Heights don't bother me; the outside doesn't bother me. It's not having a roof that freaks me out, and the floor above overhung the walkway enough to not trigger me. Did it make sense? Not really, but that's phobias for you. I push the limits when I can, but sometimes I just run into a wall of nope.

I wasn't quite done with my climb yet. I stepped up onto the guardrail, it creaked as I did so. This high up the slight wind was enough to sway the building, not so I could see it, but the building felt it all the same and let out occasional groans of complaint. That same wind picked at my clothes as I edged along the guardrail, a drop of hundreds of meters to my back. I tensed my knees and jumped, upwards, so my hands could close around an exposed beam above me. I let myself hang a moment, swaying above the quad, then hauled myself up onto the beam and sat, back to the concrete of the building, lowering my head so I fit under the overhang.

It was the most isolated location on campus that was still *on* campus. It was a great place for a spot of brooding, and while I'm not, I think, a natural brooder, there are moments when a good brood is the only sensible response to events.

The quad sparkled below me. I couldn't make out details from this high up, but enough of the student body glowed that the party, still raging at ground level, rivalled the stars above. The Dome, home to the superhero sport PowerBall was dark and quiet, but beyond the edge of the main campus, separated from it by a swathe of the local jungle, the grim and solid Tartarus shimmered beneath its forcefield. I'd explored every inch of the campus, except there. The superhero jail.

The whole planet was Academy owned. There was

no police force here beyond a militia from the teaching staff that Hawk could call on when he needed it. On the rare occasion that a crime needed investigating, Hawk would call on Prof Croft as both the lead investigator and the head of the Criminology department. But crime at the Academy was incredibly low. Most of the people who came here wanted to learn to uphold the law; sometimes disagreements about how to do that could lead to scuffles. The factions didn't help, Powers vs Tech vs Skills. All the same most crime was trivial.

Tartarus was an option of last resort, and nobody had been sent there in the time I'd been at the Academy. It existed as a precaution, the kind of thing you wanted to have but never need, rather than to need and not have. With a few thousand new adults, some with incredible powers and some with incredible egos, it would be idiotic not to have a place to restrain them if things went terribly wrong.

As they had.

Someone was going to Tartarus over Veritas's murder.

I was worried it might be me.

I hadn't murdered Veritas, of course. I leave out plenty of things in this story, but I wouldn't skip an important detail like that. I didn't need Seventhirtyfour's precognition to know the finger of blame would get pointed at me eventually, however.

Motive. I was famous for lying and noted for having a difficult relationship with Veritas in the past. That's not a motive, but it wouldn't take much imagination to conjure one from there.

Method. The grapnel gun is one of my signatures. And the murder weapon was the same model as I use. Me and a few hundred other students, of course, but when you also figure in my 'motive'? Pretty damning.

41

Opportunity. I was the last person to see Veritas alive. Sure, I claimed she was alive when I left, but where's the proof?

It was only a matter of time before I'd be suspect number one. I had faith Prof Croft wouldn't fall for it, she knew me better, and her forensics would be rigorous. The court of public opinion was another matter entirely.

I hated the part of me that wondered if that was significant. Talk about incredible egos. I made a useful patsy, but what if Veritas had been killed to somehow get to me? I would never voice such an idea to Avrim, I wouldn't make his tragedy, Veritas's death, all about me. I couldn't quite suppress the tiny voice at the back of my head: Could this be linked to the attempt to break out Mirabor Gravane? How? Why?

"Sorry to bother you, I didn't know anyone else knew this spot."

The voice kicked me out of my reverie, and I tensed in shock, never a good choice when you are balancing on a narrow beam. My heart filled my chest as I slipped from the beam and I fell, flailing for a grip.

Apogee, floating a few meters away, held out his hand. The wind whipped around me, stopping my fall, gently pushing me back onto my perch. "And I'm even more sorry about that. Are you okay?"

Adrenaline surged through me, making my fingers tingle and my heart pound but, "Yeah," I said. "You surprised me."

"And you, me. I've never seen anyone else up here, certainly not at this time of night. It's a poor place to daydream."

"Duly noted," I said. "Although it was more of a brood than a daydream."

He chuckled. "Ah, well it *is* an excellent place to brood,

42

that's true. I shall leave you to it."

"No, it's okay. I'm done. Any more would be self-indulgent." And then because I felt the need to explain, "I'm a friend of Avrim's, Veritas's nephew."

"Ah. I was sorry to hear the news. We were in the same graduating class. I won't say I knew her well, but the Academy was a smaller place back then, everybody knew everybody at least a little."

"I didn't know she was a graduate," I said.

Apogee floated over and joined me on my beam, I shuffled over to give him more room.

"Oh, yes. The only Polifan to graduate in that first class if I recall. There had been a couple of other Polifan students but they—" he paused. "Wait, you were in my class today, weren't you?"

"Yes, sir. I'm Grey."

"Really?" He gave me an appraising look. "I've heard some stories about you."

"All good, I hope?" I said, but I doubted they were.

"Mmm," he hedged. "You're planning to investigate the murder?"

"In our own way. I'm sure Professor Croft will get there first, but if we can help, we will."

"Good. It's important to stand by your team." He sounded wistful.

"I'll leave you to your ledge, sir," I said. "I'm done here, and I need to get some rest to start fresh tomorrow."

"Of course, Grey. See you in class."

I left him staring out over the jungle. Or was he contemplating Tartarus, too?

CHAPTER 5
AWKWARD CONVERSATIONS

Setting up the murder board the next morning took no time at all, we had a dearth of information, it barely dented my office supplies.

The one thing I could add was a list of names, students who had been in the Ethics class. Depending on the time of death when we got it, they were either a list of potential witnesses or our most likely suspect pool. Either way, we'd need to talk to all of them, and my list was woefully incomplete. From memory, there had been around twenty students in Veritas's class, but try as I might I could only remember a handful.

Bloodshock, the edgy Skills student who'd called me out. From what Croft had told us last night the murder scene had sounded a little too clean for someone with his gimmick, but that wasn't enough to rule him out.

Then there was the fresher, Fusillade. She was probably human from what little had shown under her helmet, but that was about all I knew. Had she been on campus long enough to have a reason to kill Veritas?

Skybeam, a second-year Zalex tech student. Loud and clunky armour, but maybe he could run a silent mode? It didn't seem likely. But then none of the suspects we had seemed likely.

The Germile student standing by the door. Her name was... Bolsta, maybe? Yes, that was it, a third-year Powers student, I'd played against her in a few Power Ball matches, though the rest of her team all graduated the year before. Her ability was some sort of psychic power to boost her allies' abilities. As a Germile she was tough and strong. Strong enough to break Polifan wing bones? I'd know more when Seventhirtyfour reported in.

I knew the names of three other students, but little extra information about them. I added them to the list: Kid Kinesis, Gold Laser and Xoxoroxox.

That left about a dozen potential witnesses—or suspects—that I knew nothing about. Prof Croft would have the full list, but I suspected I'd need to ask her a favour before the end of this, and I'd rather save that until I really needed it. For now, I'd start with the students I could remember, and hopefully, they'd point me at others.

I checked my wristpad. An hour before my first class of the day, The Art of the Chase. Time enough to get started on my list, at least.

I stopped at the door to my room, hand hovering over the lock pad. Going out that way would mean walking through the communal kitchen. Maybe my housemates wouldn't have questions. Maybe word about the murder wasn't even out yet. But I wasn't ready to get caught up on long explanations with strangers. I retreated and opened the window. Much more like it. I could grapnel across to the next accommodation block over, drop down from there to the edge of the quad. It was a short jog across to the Dome. I'd start my search there.

I checked the sky. Blue and empty. I swallowed hard. *It'll be fine.*

I pulled my grapnel from my belt, sighted the roof opposite and pulled the trigger.

The investigation had begun.

# # #

It was hard to believe this was only the second day of term, so much had already happened, the Academy hadn't had a chance to find its normal before being completely overturned. Word was out. That much was clear. The day after a big Academy party was often quiet, but today everybody seemed especially subdued. Students gathered in small groups, cliques forming along faction lines quicker than they had the previous year. Lots of hushed conversations that I was clearly not invited to, not that I wanted in.

Still, while the Dome wasn't busy there was at least a semblance of normalcy. A smattering of students up in the stands watched half a dozen teams practice on or above the main Power Ball pitch. The pitch was too crowded for an actual game to break out, but some teams worked on basic ball control, penalty shots or the puzzles on the puzzle platforms.

I wondered if Seventhirtyfour would want our team back together this year or if he'd have to play with the other Brontom. It didn't seem a good time to ask him on several levels. We had a couple of weeks before the first games of the season.

A hard tackle on the pitch crashed into the guard rail, and the spectators whooped and jeered. I climbed the steps by the closest stand to get a better vantage, scanned the area for anybody on my list.

On the far side of the pitch, I spotted Bolsta. She was holding up a Power Ball drone, presumably explaining its features to the gaggle of freshers around her. The aim of Power Ball was to score points by knocking the drone into goals, but the drone had a shield which made hitting it hard unpredictable.

I could wait for her to finish, but I only had an hour. Instead, I moved back down the stands and circled the pitch to get near her group. I let myself in through the nearest gate and stepped onto the pitch. On a puzzle platform above me, a Welatak student clacked in delight as he solved a puzzle.

"...times when power is required, but they are the exception," Bolsta said to her group, "more often it's about control. You could be the mightiest monster on the pitch, but if you don't know where that drone is going when you hit it, you're no help to anybody."

I caught her eye, and she nodded.

"Looks like we have *another* visitor," she said. "You played, right, Grey?"

"Not the full season, there were certain complications, but yeah. By The Numbers, go team! We did okay."

"Better than this sorry lot will, I expect." Her crowd shifted and mumbled. Bolsta threw me a bat. "Let's give them a demonstration."

"I'm not really here for that," I said.

Bolsta lowered her voice to a growl. "I know why you're here."

Without another word, she launched the drone towards me.

I resisted the urge to hit it; instead, I caught the drone, leading its flight with my bat, decelerating it, turning my whole body, dragging the drone with me until it came to a complete stop. I tapped the drone gently on its top, it dipped a little before its antigrav bobbed it back up again and I tapped it once more, bouncing it down and up on my bat.

"Impressive move," Bolsta said. Her freshers gave me a smattering of applause.

"Thanks," I said with a grin.

"Totally useless in an actual match, of course."

"Totally," I agreed. "And yet it's about the only move I

48

ever properly practised."

"Hrm."

I caught the drone with my off hand and tossed it back to her. "I wanted to talk to you about the end of the Ethics class yesterday."

"About Professor Veritas's murder?" she asked.

"You've heard the news, then."

"Everybody has heard," said Bolsta. "What do you want?"

"I'm just checking with everyone from class, to see if anyone remembers seeing anything."

"You and your little crew are investigating, are you? I already spoke to Professor Croft."

"Can I ask what you told her? I wouldn't bother you but, well, Avrim. You know, Veritas's nephew? He's a friend of mine, and he wanted me to help out."

"I know why you're asking." She rolled her massive shoulders, her whole body shook. Germile are physically powerful, their posture lends itself to walking on all fours, but their massive forelimbs worked fine as arms. She tossed the drone into the air then brought her bat around with her other hand to give it a mighty thwack. The drone pin-wheeled off around the pitch, accelerating as it went. She looked at the reinforced wooden bat; she'd broken it with the force of her strike. "Somebody fetch the drone, then you lot practice passing it to each other," she said to her students. They beat a hasty retreat.

Bolsta dropped the ruined bat. She was strong. Certainly strong enough to break a Polifan wing. It hadn't occurred to me before, if the killer was in my class, sooner or later my investigation would bring me to them. As Bolsta's arm muscles tensed, that realisation gave me pause.

"If you don't want to talk..." I said, trailing off.

"I'll talk. I told Croft. When I left, the only one of my classmates still in the lecture hall was you, Grey. I didn't see anyone else near the classroom, but that Zalex kid, the one in the blue mech suit?"

"Skybeam?"

She shrugged. "Maybe. I saw him paused by the stairwell, but that's at the end of the hall."

I made a note. "Interesting. Anything else unusual?"

"Only thing odd I saw was the student who stopped to talk to the Professor after they'd argued in class. You."

"Argued? There was a bit of banter, maybe a little back and forth, but it was all quite friendly to my recollection," I said.

"You're telling me what I remember?"

From the corner of my eye, I saw Bolsta's group had begun knocking the drone about between them. The few closest to us were paying much more attention to me and Bolsta than the drone, though.

"No," I said, "I know better than to contaminate an eyewitness account with my own biases."

"I should think so," said Bolsta.

"Where did you go after class?"

"Here. My team got close last year; this is my last chance before I graduate. I was putting up posters to get people to come for try-outs."

"Did anyone see you?"

"Plenty of people, I'd think."

"Right." I'd already run out of questions. I didn't feel much like a master detective right then. Wasn't I supposed to have a case-breaking gotcha question all lined up by now? "Thanks for your help. Do you remember who else was in the class?"

She rattled off a few names; I recognised most, but there were two new ones, Captain Dynamic and the Blue

Claw. I added them to my list.

"Thanks, Bolsta," I said.

She bent her elbows to dip her head in acknowledgement. "You tell Avrim, I'm sorry for his loss," she said, no trace of her earlier hostility.

"Thanks, I'm sure he'll appreciate it."

# # #

I left the Dome, pausing before heading out into the quad. The main thing I'd learned from that first interview was that I wasn't clear yet what I was trying to find out. Our investigation was going to struggle until we could get a better understanding of what happened. I got why Captain Hawk and Professor Croft had kept us away from the scene, but it meant we were starting behind on this case. We wouldn't be able to properly assess the crime scene, we didn't know what facts about the attack we were trying to confirm or explain. We were going to be behind Croft and her team all the way. But one thing Professor Croft had drilled into us in class, everything is evidence. And, sure, we might not know much, but the only way to correct that was to ask questions. So that's what I'd do.

I set out across the quad, heading for the main Hall of Justice. It was possible that all the people I was looking for were already in class or hadn't even left their dorms yet, but I wouldn't know unless I looked. I ducked my head down and powered across the wide-open space, keeping an eye out for the people I passed in case they were any of my candidates.

What I needed was backup. Someone to find the questions I missed or to keep the witness talking while I stalked around being cryptic. But who? Avrim would want to help, I was sure, but that brought problems to the interview. Gadget Dude? Dez? They would both bring a different energy, but would it work with mine? I needed Seventhirtyfour. I missed Seventhirtyfour.

A rush of air buffeted me, and in a flash of light, Pilvi was there.

"Grey. Is it true, what they're saying? Is Avrim's aunt...?" she said.

I kept walking, wanted to get inside. "Yes."

Pilvi followed, hovering, glowing. "That's awful, how is Avrim doing?"

"About as well as you'd expect. I've not talked to him yet this morning, but last night, he was pretty raw. He's set on working the case ourselves, so we're going to do just that." The door to the Hall swished open. I stepped into the vast bright Atrium. Safely inside, I rounded on Pilvi. "And where the hell were you?"

"What?" Pilvi's light blinked out and she dropped to the ground, stumbling on her landing. "Grey, I had no idea anything like this was going to happen. How could I?"

It wasn't fair and I knew it. "You never even checked in with us," I said.

"It's the start of a new term, Grey, I'm taking a lot of new classes, ones that I would never have considered last year. I'm meeting new people. I got invited to a party last night and I went. Why are you acting so weird about it?" She put her fists on her hips and the glow of her hair intensified.

I ignored her question. "If you can spare time from your exciting new friends, we need your help."

"And you'll have it. Of course, you will. What do you need?"

"Talk to Seventhirtyfour, see if he has information on the amount of force the murderer used. I'll send you specs on the grapnel gun. I need you to start working up a pro-file of their power set, or what tools they used."

"Sure," she said, then paused. "I'll need to book some lab time. I don't have any science classes this term. But I can talk to Professor Alembic, she'll let me use the facilities, I'm sure."

"You don't have any science classes? You?"

"I've had a lifetime to study science, but I've only had these powers for a few months. I need time to understand them, Grey. Look, I'm sorry, I have class. But I'll check in with Seventhirtyfour and get the profile started."

"Thanks," I said, but I couldn't keep the hollowness out of my voice.

"See you around, Grey." She burst into light and launched herself back outside.

What was wrong with me? Why had I been so snippy with Pilvi when she'd only stopped by to offer help? My stomach churned and my heart felt heavy. Stupid. I'd find her later and apologise. Maybe.

I pushed down the feeling and shook it off. This wasn't helping find Veritas's killer.

CHAPTER 6
CROSSING PATHS

I found Fusillade in one of the power-training gyms. There are dozens of them around campus, heavily reinforced and segmented into smaller spaces so that students could practice more destructive abilities safely. This gym had six training chambers, only two of them occupied. Fusillade was in the one closest to the door. From further in I could just make out the buzzing of an electrical burst being fired at a target.

Fusillade stood just outside of arms reach from a dummy target, one hand raised. She snapped her fingers and a small explosion, loud but without much force burst in front of her. The target dummy seemed unphased.

"Impressive," I said.

Fusillade started, but then laughed. "Hello," she said, "It's Grey, isn't it?"

"That's right."

Her helmet covered most of her face and eyes, but it left her mouth and chin exposed. She smiled at me. "Are you here to ask me questions about class yesterday as well?"

"I'm afraid so. Have there been many?"

"Professor Croft first thing this morning, a couple of people claiming to be investigating it, and a dozen more just being curious. Which category are you in?"

Other people were investigating? I shouldn't be surprised really; this was the kind of case that a lot of students came to the Academy to learn how to solve. "I'm investigating too, as it happens."

"That's alright then," she said with another laugh. "What can I help you with?"

"I'm just trying to get a picture of everyone's movements after class yesterday. To see if anyone saw anything suspicious."

"And have they?"

"Not yet, but you're only the second person I've talked to."

"Oh, well, still early then." She thought for a moment. "I don't have anything special to say really. I didn't hang around after Professor Veritas's class, I wanted to see if I could catch a glimpse of the famous Apogee, so I ran up to his classroom."

"That's right, I saw you there," I remembered.

"You did? Okay. But other than that, I don't know what to say. I'd not even heard of Professor Veritas before yesterday morning when I signed up to her class in Registration. She seemed a nice sort. I can't think why anybody would kill her."

Behind me, I heard the distinctive hissing-clomp of steam-powered armour, as another student entered a training alcove.

"That's on our list of things to find out," I said with a shrug. "Okay, I guess that's it for now. Did you know any of the other students in the class?"

"No, this is only my second day on campus, it's all new, I've not made friends yet."

"Give it time, this place has a way of absorbing people. I'd never planned to be here long-term, but here I am at the start of my second year."

She shrugged. "I'm used to not making friends, I've

always been a bit of a loner. And then I got these powers in a freak accident and... I just thought the Academy could be a place for me."

"Your powers are those explosions?"

"Yes." She held her hand up towards the target and snapped her fingers in rapid succession. A ripple of small explosions followed the motion. "I'm hoping that with practice I can throw them. That's what I'm trying to practice anyway. No luck so far. I can see there are uses for close up explosions, of course, but I reckon further away would be better." She chuckled. "Even close up, they aren't 100% reliable."

"You're way ahead of me," I said. "I'm Skills all the way."

"Can I ask you something? About the Academy?"

"Sure."

She paused for a moment as a speedster student zoomed past behind me. The place was starting to fill up, it must be about time for the morning break.

"What's this place like? Normally? Yesterday was hyper and today is... tense. Neither is normal, right?"

"That's true. But normal? I don't think there is such a thing. The Academy is a madhouse, I'm not sure it could be anything else with so many different people, powers and cultures in one small space. But it's also kind of magical. As I say, it absorbs people. It's easy to find a home here if you let it happen."

"That sounds nice. I didn't know if I'd fit in when I came here. I'm older than most first-year students by a few years, I only got my powers recently. I didn't know what to expect."

"Not this," I said. "It's... well for me, it's the first place that's felt like a home in my life that I can remember. I know people at the end of term were so excited to go back and visit their friends, families and home worlds. Me? I kind of resented having to take a summer holiday. I was so looking forwards to getting back here, being around my friends again, just living a quiet life studying superhero stuff. I had enough stress last year; I was looking forward to some peace and quiet. So far, it's not been like I was hoping either."

I ran a hand through my hair, tried to shake off the funk. "But it will be. It'll be awesome, you'll see."

"Sure, Grey." She snapped her fingers at the target, but this time there was no explosion. "I guess that's my cue to take a break. Thanks for talking with me, Grey."

"You're welcome, Fusillade."

# # #

It had taken longer than expected to find my first two witnesses. I had time, but not much, not enough to continue my hunt. Instead, I found a quiet corner near my next class and commed Gadget Dude. "How's it going, man? Did you find anything when you checked the grapnel guns?"

"One missing," Gadget Dude said. "Tom said not checked locker since summer."

"So, we have a possible source for the weapon, but no idea when it was taken. Well, it's something. I don't suppose the cabinet had any security?"

"Who steals grapnel gun?"

"Yeah. Oh well, thanks."

"Other thing, spoke to Croft. Offered help with video. Been watching."

"Outstanding! What did you see?"

"Not much. Class end, most leave. Skybeam pause by stair. Grey leave. Skybeam leave. Nobody else on vid stream for hour."

"Right, that lines up with what my witnesses have said so far. Sounds like Skybeam is my next priority. If there was nobody in the corridor, how did our murderer get to the room? No windows in the lecture hall. Invisibility? That's a thing, right? Can people teleport?"

Gadget Dude paused, head cocked to one side. It was hard to tell from the image on my wristpad, but he looked intrigued.

"Don't... think so..." he said, slowly.

"Focus, Dude," I said. I couldn't help laughing. "Okay, let's put a tentative line through that, then. What about the video feed itself? Could it have been tampered with?"

Gadget Dude's face scrunched up as he considered it. "Did notice some odd blurring. Will check."

"Great work, Gadget Dude. Thanks. Have you seen Avrim today? How is he?"

"Looks tired. Not slept. Tried help with vids but fidgeted. Frustrated. Then left."

"Right. Keep an eye on him. I'm worried."

"Same, Grey."

# # #

After class, Prof Croft caught up to me in the quad. I'd known it was only a matter of time, but I'd hoped for a different venue.

She gestured to a bench. "Take a seat, Grey."

I perched on one end, had to fight the urge to grab on to the seat for security. Croft sat next to me, close, despite ample space on the bench. Together we took a moment to watch the flow of brightly costumed students, criss-crossing the open space in front of us. Notably giving us a wide berth.

"Outside where you know I'm off balance," I observed. "Sitting close enough to make me uncomfortable. Positioned between me and the closest door inside, subtly suggesting my only escape is through you. All deliberately done to exacerbate any nerves I might be feeling."

She smiled. "All suggesting what, Grey?"

"Applying pressure can run the risk of creating false signals from the innocent and can cause the guilty to shut up. You only ever do it to shake someone's confidence and when the evidence is particularly damning. You're here to interrogate me as a suspect, not a witness."

"Well done," she said in her most teacherly voice. Coincidentally reinforcing her position of authority over me.

"Impressive to see it in practice," I said. "Efficient of you to make it a lesson and casework. Although, for the record, I'm innocent."

"Tell me about Veritas, in your own words," her tone shifted from teacher to investigator. She might switch several times during the conversation, trying to keep me guessing.

For once, I had nothing to hide. "I stayed behind after class to speak with her about some stuff that came up last year. I needed an ethics perspective for what happened on Nymanteles. We talked for maybe five minutes, not even that, probably. Then I left to get to my next class."

"Which was?"

"Professor Gale's class. Crossover Etiquette." She would have known that already. She was throwing me a gimme to get me in the habit of answering.

"Was anyone else present when you left the class-room?"

"No."

"Did you see anyone else near the classroom?"

"No."

"Did Veritas give you the answer you were looking for?"

I paused, considered. "I don't know. Maybe? You know

how she could be, more likely to answer a question with a question."

"And that annoyed you?"

"Why would you think that?"

Croft tsked. "Don't do that, Grey."

"Sorry."

"How did Veritas seem when you left her?"

"Alive." I bit back, regretted it instantly. "She seemed fine. Cheerful. She was having fun, I think. Teased me a little."

"What books did Veritas recommend?"

"None, as far as I can remember."

She leaned even closer. "Why did you tell Avrim that she had?"

"When did I—oh, yes. I told him that in the bar. I don't know. I didn't want to tell him what I'd really been talking to his Aunt about, I suppose. She did suggest I read some Kant at one point, I think."

"You lie to your friends a lot, don't you?"

"Last year, a lot. Yes. Now, no more than anyone else, I'd think."

"You consider yourself a good liar?"

What a question. "Yes."

"If you wanted to, could you lie to me in this interview and expect me to believe you?"

"Yes."

"And how would that look? What techniques would you use?"

I ticked off some pointers. "Keep it believable. Choose the emotion to play against it. No unnecessary details." At which point I shut up and smiled.

"Do you think that helps your case?"

"No. But I have confidence in you as an investigator. You'll find the truth. And for once the truth is on my side. I liked Veritas. We weren't close, but she was okay. I had no reason to kill her. I didn't kill her."

"And if evidence *is* pointing towards you?"

"Then you haven't finished your investigation yet. I'll wait."

She slapped her knees and stood up. It broke the spell and the general hubbub of the quad, that I'd tuned out during the interview, came rolling back in.

"Well, I think that's us for now," she said cheerily.

"That's it?"

"That's it. You forgot the other reason to use the pressure interview technique," she said.

"What's that?"

"When you need to interview a wise-ass student with a tendency towards flippancy. It shuts them right up. Mostly." She gave me a piercing glare. "I'm still gathering information, Grey. It's far too early in a case like this, to be calling anyone a suspect. It doesn't mean you're off the hook... but that's all I need from you at this stage. I know where to find you when I need more."

"Yes, Professor."

She took a step away, stopped, and half turned back to me. "Oh, you're wrong by the way. I spotted your lie."

She strode off before I could respond. What lie? I hadn't lied to her. Had I?

# # #

I returned to my search. I found Blue Claw in the library and Xoxoroxox in the same canteen I stopped in for lunch. Neither had anything new to add; Blue Claw had jammed their first day with so many classes I had to remind them which one Veritas's had been and Xoxoroxox was more interested in asking me if Dez was looking for backing singers. It was too early to rule out any of my potential suspects but unless they were incredibly good actors, I didn't think either of them were long for my list.

Neither were able to fill in the gaps on my attendance list, even. Xoxoroxox spent five minutes trying to think of the name of one student, but we eventually worked out he was trying to think of me. Powers students. What can you do?

I continued my search upwards through the tower. I was at the door to the stairwell on the 10th floor when I heard Lucy call my name.

"Grey, wait!"

"Lucy, hi," I said. The boy standing next to her was too close for my liking.

"Hi, Grey," she said. She ran fingers through her hair, pushing it back behind her ears. Her jewelled headband glittered in the hall lighting. "I heard the news, how are you? How's Avrim?"

I shook my head. "I've not seen him today, but Gadget Dude said—well, Avrim's about as well as you'd think, in the circumstances."

"Of course. You have the team investigating?"

"It's what Avrim wants. I don't know how much difference we can make, but if we help at all, that's a good thing."

"Right."

We trailed off into an awkward silence.

"I should—" I said, pushing the stairwell door ajar.

"Hi, I'm David," the boy said at the same time. He held out a hand, but I was already pushing on the door, so I couldn't shake it.

"Oh!" said Lucy. "Yes. This is David, he wanted to meet you."

"Sure."

"Good to meet you, man," said David. "Hero of

Nymanteles. I mean after the Brontom dude and my Lucy of course." He laughed a stupid laugh.

"Not forgetting the Nymanteles militia," I agreed. "I didn't do so much."

"Humble, too. Lucy said you were a good sort. My Sky Diamond, she's a great judge of character."

Lucy lowered her gaze, putting a hand up to her face. "David, I think perhaps—"

"Yeah," I said, "I need to get on. Got a case to work."

"Sorry, sure, of course," David said. "Or, hey, maybe we can help? Three heads are better than one, right?"

I couldn't think of anything I wanted less, but nor could I think of a good excuse to get out of it. "Why not, Lucy?" I said, hoping she could come up with something.

She bit her lip. "I don't know."

"Great then, where to, boss?" David asked, beaming.

"I guess, up to the next level then."

# # #

We worked our way up the Hall of Justice tower, looking for anyone from my witness list. I expected David to be a bumbling buffoon, but in fairness, once we started the task, he kept quiet and on the lookout. I was far too focused on my task to engage with him, though I did have to bite my tongue several times to stop myself from asking Lucy things.

We searched floor sixteen, the last of the teaching levels, without finding anyone on the list. As we took the stairs to the next level, I said, "I want to complete a full sweep before backtracking to the busier levels. Why don't you two head back down to keep watch on the canteens, or the Atrium? People will have to show up there eventually."

"No, man, I'm learning too much. You have a weird way

of looking at buildings, Grey, I wouldn't have looked in half the places you peeked into."

"You can get a lot from the Building Infiltration course," I said. That and spending a decade dodging station security, but I saw no reason to mention that.

"Let's go, David, Grey can cover this ground quicker by himself. And we're more likely to spot people on the list down there."

David pulled open the door to the next floor. "What's left to search?"

"The top few levels are old labs," I said. "Most of them aren't used any more, since newer, better-equipped labs were built in separate buildings. Oh, well, and above that is the service area, but we won't find students in there. Or here, probably, I can't think the last time I saw a student up here, other than me."

There was a clatter of metal followed by the sound of several items of glassware breaking from behind the door to the closest lab. I paused.

"Okay, that was weird," I said, quietly.

David's eyes lit up. "We should investigate!" he whispered.

Lucy sent me a look.

"Do you have any powers, David?" I asked. "Anything that would help if the mysterious noise in the spooky abandoned lab turns out to be a ghost, or an alien monster, or something?"

"Skills and proud of it, just like you, man!"

"Great."

I looked both ways up the corridor and drew my grapnel gun before I opened the door. The lab was dark; the lights were off, and the blinds pulled down. The light from the open door was enough to show the near end of several lab benches, but the far ends were lost in darkness. In the middle of the room, a metal tray lay face down on the floor. The smashed remains of several glass beakers caught the light as I moved. There was no way they got there like that without help. Not just as I got there, certainly.

"Hello," I called, taking a step into the lab, and fumbling to find the light controls. Lucy and David followed behind me, but my focus stayed locked on the room.

Somewhere at the back, I heard someone breathing.

"David, perhaps you should go back and look for a teacher," Lucy said.

"No way, babe."

"I'm just going to turn the lights on, if that's okay?" I said.

"Don't do that," said a male voice from the darkness. The voice was distorted, through a speaker maybe. He was on the other side of the lab from where I'd heard the breathing. Two of them?

"I'll keep the lights low; I just don't want to step on any broken glass." Some species were extremely light-sensitive, I didn't want to hurt whoever was in there, but I needed to see. I gestured through the control field, but nothing happened.

"You have to press the button," the voice said. "But I wouldn't if I were you."

"Why not?" I asked. I found the physical switch and flicked it.

"Because of the gas," the voice said.

There was a fizzing pop as the panel sparked and shorted out.

CHAPTER 7
EXPLOSIVE DEVELOPMENTS

The explosion knocked us flat.

Everything happened at once. Lucy pushed David back out of the lab, shouted something at him I couldn't make out through the ringing in my ears. A pair of spotlights mounted on the shoulders of a power suit lit the room, and three other shapes—I couldn't see more than that as I tried to focus—jumped out from behind transparent blast shields.

One of the shapes, shorter and darker than the others, shouted something like, "Don't let recover!" It charged right towards me.

The shape resolved into Bloodshock, just in time for me to block his flying kick. The black-clad Zalex somersaulted away from me, landing in a backwards skid, his long coat billowing behind him. I didn't have time to admire the form though, as the second shape, a human student I didn't recognise, also dressed in black, stepped into the gap and swung a baton at me. I tried to sway away from the strike, but I was still disoriented, and the baton struck my left shoulder, a glancing blow but enough to numb my arm.

"Lucy," I called out.

She must have known that I was about to tell her to run because she just said through gritted teeth. "I can take the other two."

I didn't have time for a reply as the baton was coming in again. I grabbed for my attacker's wrist, fumbled the grip a little but held back this attack. I stepped in and applied a knee to the situation. He twisted his hips and I caught him on the thigh.

The other two, a Cholbren woman and whoever that was in the battlesuit advanced on Lucy. She stood her ground, in a defensive stance; Sky Diamond was not an unarmed expert, but she knew enough of the basics to hold her own in a fair fight. The battlesuit wasn't fair though and—

"Ow!"

Bloodshock struck me on the calf. I felt his spiked knuckles break the skin, a sharp pain before he rolled away, a flash of red across his hand.

"We have them on the back foot, keep pushing," shouted the Cholbren. She struck again and again; all Lucy could do was block and retreat.

I wasn't in a much better state. The Baton guy struck at my head, shoulders, arms, I kept him off me as best I could, but I could never counter-attack; every time I forced an opening, Bloodshock would swoop in and slice me. His cuts weren't deep, but I was hyper-aware of warm blood trickling down my leg, draining strength from my stance, and when I lost that, that would be it.

That's when the power armour chose to enter the fray. He stepped in towards Lucy, reached back his hand—

—and clubbed the Cholbren woman across the back of her shoulders. She collapsed, unconscious.

Lucy, Sky Diamond, whooped in glee, the jewels on her headband glittering. "Got him," she said.

The power armour turned towards my assailants. "Bloodshock," he said, the voice tinny through his speakers. "Look out, this isn't me doing this."

Baton guy and Bloodshock both goggled, so I punched baton guy in the throat. He doubled over, gasping; I swept his legs out from under him.

The armour stepped on Bloodshock, pushing him to the floor and keeping him there, not applying enough weight to crush him, but more than enough to stop him from going anywhere.

"Lucy! That was awesome. I thought you couldn't take control when someone else was already piloting?" I said.

A smile lit her face, but there was still a furrow of concentration. "That *was* true, but I came to the Academy to get better with my powers, after all."

I laughed, more from relief than anything else. My knees buckled, and I caught myself on the corner of a lab bench. "Whoa, I feel weird. Those knuckles of yours, Bloodshock, they're not poisoned, are they?"

Bloodshock did his best to spit at me, but the geometry was against him. "Gloat if want. Won't get away. Others know. Will stop you!" he said.

"Stop me? You attacked us, you maniac," I said.

"Oh, give it up, Grey." The guy in the armour, Steel Spartan, said. I recognised him, now I'd had a chance to take him in. "We know what you've been doing, going around leaning on witnesses to make sure they don't say anything. Trying to cover your tracks. It won't work. The truth will always beat your lies."

"Wait, you think *I* killed Veritas? I didn't kill her; I'm investigating her death. We're investigating," I said, gesturing to include Lucy. The strain of keeping control of Spartan's armour was starting to show.

"Oh," said Spartan. "Um. Bloodshock? He's not lying. I mean I guess Sky Diamond could be controlling the output on my voice stress analyser, or maybe he's just that good at lying, but... I don't think so. I think he's telling the truth."

"Grey always lie. Everyone know," Bloodshock said, though even he sounded less sure of himself.

"Of course I'm telling the truth!" Although for the record, beating a voice analyser isn't so hard, if I'd known he had one. But that's probably not the point. "We're not the bad guys here, you're the bad guys!"

"We heroes. We solve case. You murder Professor."

"Grey, I think I need to let go of the armour," said Lucy.

"Do it. Spartan's going to talk, right?"

"Yeah, okay," said Spartan. "Can I check on Channis and Penumbra? And somebody should turn off the gas taps before we get an even bigger explosion."

"See to your friends, I'll get the taps. Bloodshock, try not to cut anyone."

Lucy sagged with relief, and Spartan set about checking on his unconscious friends. Bloodshock climbed onto the corner of a lab bench and knelt there, sulking, his coat draped artistically over the edge. I dragged myself towards the bench to turn off the gas taps.

"What made you convinced Grey was the murderer?" Lucy asked, perching on a stool to get her breath back. "I know he has a reputation—"

I was about to interrupt indignantly but then thought better of it.

"—but that's quite a leap to murder."

"We investigate," said Bloodshock.

"In particular, we spoke to Skybeam," added Spartan.

I perked up. "We've not found him yet, what did he have to say?"

"I'll show you." A flap opened in the middle of his armour's chest and formed a holographic projection. It showed his three friends talking to Skybeam.

# # #

"Did you notice anything unusual?" Channis asked.

"Servos on left knee broken," Skybeam said, tapping the offending joint.

"Sure, but did you see anything unusual while you were fixing them?" That was Spartan's voice, coming from outside the projection area.

"Broken servo unusual! What Spartan implying?"

Channis put her hands up to placate Skybeam. "I'm sure that's unusual. But was there anything else? Something you might have seen or heard that would help tell us more about the Professor's death."

"Told Croft. Not sure. Took systems off-line to fix knee. Includes helmet microphones, all sound muffled. Maybe heard something though. If not imagine it. Sound like strong wind blowing, then crack. Didn't know what it was. Would have stopped if knew. Liked Professor."

Channis asked, "What time was this? Do you know?"

"Not long after class. Five minutes, maybe? Fixed servos and left. Was not late for next class."

"This sound. Before or after last student leave? Grey, you said?" Bloodshock curled his hand into a fist to show his knuckle spikes.

Skybeam shrugged, no mean feat in power armour. "Not remember. Before, maybe?"

Bloodshock turned towards the camera. "Got him." The projection flickered to an end.

#

"'Got him'?" I said. "Was that all it took?"

Bloodshock folded his arms across his chest. "Know about you, Grey."

"Nice."

Putting aside Bloodshock's bias, the recording was potentially extremely useful. I tried to resist jumping to conclusions, but... the crack could have been the snapping of Veritas's wing bones, maybe.

"A strong wind, followed by a crack," I said. "I didn't hear any sounds like that, so if Skybeam didn't imagine them, they must have happened after I left."

"Sure," Bloodshock drawled.

Channis and Penumbra were coming around. Spartan had propped them up against one of the lab benches. "How are you feeling?" he asked them, before catching them up with why we'd stopped fighting.

"All a big misunderstanding," Lucy reassured them. "Probably means we're due to team-up to defeat the true threat. That's how—"

The door to the lab blasted open, Apogee floated in the corridor beyond, and behind him, I caught a glimpse of David giving Lucy a thumbs-up.

"What's going on in here?" Apogee demanded, eyes blazing with light.

"Just a crossover," said Lucy.

I burst out laughing.

# # #

It took a little more explaining than that, and I tap-danced around the truth a little to put all parties in a good light. Bloodshock gave me a dirty look but didn't contradict me. What would Veritas have said about the ethics of lying by omission?

"These things happen," said Apogee, looking around the mess we'd made of the lab. "But if it's going to happen again, try and do it in one of the practice gyms."

"Yes, sir," we said in unison.

"It would be a shame to waste such an excellent learning experience, however. Technically, I suppose I can't set homework for people who aren't in my class, but I would encourage you all to write up what the takeaway lessons are from this encounter. Feel free to send me a copy to look over. Grey? Penumbra? Since you are both in my class, I'll be expecting your essays by Friday. Let's say, two thousand words? That seems about right to me."

"Yes, sir," Penumbra and I said with slightly less enthusiasm.

"Well then, since that is settled, David, could you hold the bin open please?" Apogee gestured and a wind rose from nowhere. It circled the room, danced about our ankles, picked up the smashed glassware and other equipment that had suffered during our fight. "Careful, some of this is sharp." He gestured again and the wind deposited the trash safely into the bin. David let the lid close again.

I closed my hand over Bloodshock's shoulder, holding him still, I could feel him tensing under my fingers. Wind. Like the sound Skybeam had heard. One sound effect did not a murderer make. But there was no doubt, this was going on the murder board.

Apogee dusted off his hands, even though he hadn't used them. "It's late. I'm sure you're all exhausted from your crossover, I think it would be marvellous if you headed back to your dorms now."

We shuffled out.

David leaned in. "We're not really just going to slink off to our rooms, are we?"

"This time, yes. I have a feeling we've a long way to travel on this case yet and antagonising the teaching staff will only make it harder. We've made a good start today, learned a lot of important things. Let's see what the others have for us, and where we should focus our search tomorrow. Lucy, thank you again, you were amazing."

"Keep us posted on what the others have to report," she said.

"Will do."

I watched them leave together, my stomach feeling unsettled.

#

I stayed dutifully in my room, but Apogee had said nothing about guests. Seventhirtyfour and Pilvi arrived first, said hello and sat quietly waiting for the others. There was no conversation, awkward or otherwise. Pilvi made a point of sitting further away from me. Avrim arrived pale and red-eyed, Gadget Dude followed him in, looking concerned. Dez was last to pitch up; it wasn't always easy to read her reptilian expression, but if I had to guess, I'd say she looked worried.

I cleared my throat. "Okay. So. Um. Let's start. I guess I'll go first. I've not tracked down everybody from the class yet and those that I have spoken to didn't have much to say. But that doesn't mean I have nothing. While it's too early to categorically rule anyone out, I think we can put a tentative line through Bloodshock, as he attacked me thinking I was the murderer. It could be a double-bluff, but, no. I think, pending evidence we can rule him out. We did get some information from Skybeam, via Steel Spartan. Skybeam stopped to make some minor repairs at the stairwell doorway, around the corner from the classroom. He reported hearing something, a strong wind followed by a—" I paused to look at Avrim, then plunged ahead, "—a snap. Given he wasn't late for his next class, that puts it very soon after I left Veritas."

"Did he mention seeing you?" Dez asked.

I thought. "No. He was rather vague on that point."

"Okay."

"It's not much for a day of canvassing, but there's still hope. I have two-thirds of the class to find. As it is, we have a point for a potential time of the assault and this wind noise." I added both points to the murder board. "Avrim, did you learn anything new from Professor Croft today?"

When he spoke, Avrim's voice was flat and ragged, but he didn't stumble or hesitate. "She confirmed what she told us last night. The autopsy refined the details a little, the grapnel cable didn't strangle her so much as snap her neck. It... would have taken considerable force to do that. Croft has begun a DNA catalogue of the scene; she told me that there were no surprises on the list yet, but to run a complete analysis could take days or weeks. It was a public space, used for other classes earlier in the day, that's a lot of DNA to sample and catalogue. Once that is completed, we will have a suspect list."

"Maybe," I said.

Avrim looked at me sharply. "What do you mean?"

"We've talked about the DNA cataloguer in Croft's class. The modern system is incredibly accurate and comprehensive, it's true, but it doesn't mean it can't be fooled. If the murderer was wearing a completely sealed suit, they might not shed DNA to the environment at all. In most mundane cases it's difficult to commit a crime in a space suit without standing out, but enough armoured power suits stomp around campus that people wouldn't think it unusual. And seeing Prof Croft with her sterile field last night, if you had access to one of those you wouldn't need a suit."

"So, the DNA scan is useless?" Avrim's words fell like lead.

"No, no. It will give us a great pool of suspects, it's still most likely that the murderer will be among them. I'm just saying we mustn't forget there are ways around it."

Avrim's feathers bristled and he made a note on his wristpad.

"What else have we learned today? Seventhirtyfour,

Pilvi, where are we on defining the attacker's strength?"

"Here's the full work-up," Seventhirtyfour said and flicked a file from his wristpad to mine. "But the summary is fairly simple. Polifan wings are strong, but a human could break them with a blunt weapon. The strangulation is another matter. The amount of force required for that tips us over into some power or tech required."

"The killer is super strong?" Avrim asked.

Pilvi shook her head. "Not necessarily. They could be telekinetic, super-fast, or they could be able to control metal or—there are probably a dozen ways that strength could be augmented without being traditionally super strong. But definitely beyond 'normal'. Or—well it's just within the physical range of an athletic Germile who got the pull exactly right, but it's not something they would be able to rely on."

"Noted," I said. "As for the Grapnel gun itself, it could have been someone's personal kit, but Gadget Dude says there is one missing from the Academy store, too. Unfortunately, we've no way of knowing when it was taken."

Gadget Dude raised a hand. "Had idea. May not work. Can Grey help tomorrow?"

"Sure thing, anything that might take us forward. And that brings us to Dez. Do you have anything to add?"

Dez's tail twitched and she hopped down from her perch on my desk. "Guys, I think I have something. But I don't think you're going to like it. When I asked around about Veritas and her enemies, one name came up several times."

I was afraid of that. "Look, I know I had a tense relationship with Veritas last year," I began, but Dez gave me a weird look and I trailed off.

"Not you, Grey. Get a grip. You had, what three conversations with Veritas before taking her class? Most people don't know about any of that. Nobody thinks of you as her arch-nemesis."

"Oh. Good."

"No, the name that seemed to come up the most, well now we've heard Skybeam's report, I'm even more worried. The name was Apogee. Professor Gale," Dez said, then paused dramatically.

"Why? Apogee is a hero, the best of the best," Seventhirtyfour said. "There's no way—why would anyone think that?"

"Partly it's timing meets celebrity," Dez admitted, "he's new on campus and suddenly Veritas is attacked? But some of the older students I talked to have another theory. Veritas and Apogee were classmates, graduated together in the first graduating class of the Academy, 22 years ago."

"Really?" asked Avrim, he seemed startled.

"That's true," I said, "Apogee mentioned that to me himself."

"Yeah, but did he mention that there were some difficulties at the Academy in those first years? Some students died in an accident, but nobody talks about it. It almost sank the Academy before it properly began," said Dez. "I did some research, and even the Academy's history books are spotty about it. Supposedly something went wrong in an aerial combat exercise. Two Polifan and a human Tech student were killed, but I couldn't find anything to say exactly how."

"Did you find anything about who else was involved in that exercise?" Pilvi asked.

"No," Dez admitted. "But the student base wasn't that large and Veritas and Apogee both fly. Flew. It's not a huge leap to think they might have been involved in the accident too."

I added it to the murder board. Stared at it for a moment. "It doesn't feel right. For sure, those are both interesting points on the map, but it's too early, and the evidence is far too woolly to be considered even circumstantial. Plus, I'll be honest, I kind of like the guy."

"You can't rule people out just because you like them, Grey," said Avrim.

"I'm not ruling him out. But it's too early to rule him in."

"Whatever. If he killed her, I'm nailing him to the wall myself," said Avrim.

CHAPTER 8
GADGET, P.I.

I don't use the Hall of Justice's lifts much, but Gadget Dude never tired of them. As we ascended, he lay flat on his stomach, face pressed up against the safety field, trying to get a good look at the mechanism under the platform. It was probably for the best that he couldn't reach it. For my part, I leaned against the railing and looked out at the main hall as we gently rose. A large three-storey window let plenty of natural light into the Atrium, and artistically placed cut-outs in the window also let in flying students who couldn't be bothered to use the front door. The bright Atrium was the Academy putting its best foot forward. Visitors would be treated to gleaming white floors, swooping columns, a bronze statue of a group of young heroes, and access to two of the four canteens, the virtual arcade and the gift shop inviting people in. It wasn't technically misrepresenting the place, but the beat-up shabbiness of the rest of the campus, while comfortable and serviceable, was, it has to be said, a little less polished.

As the lift carried us on out of the Atrium, the walls closed in, and the view was distinctly less impressive— not much to be done to make the walls of a lift shaft exciting. Denied his view of the lift mechanism, Gadget Dude rolled over and bounced to his feet. I stepped carefully between him and the lift controls. He wouldn't always try and disassemble them, but better safe than sorry. It was why he wasn't allowed to ride the lifts alone.

We stopped at the eighth floor, about a third of the way up the tower, and headed to the Grapnel store.

Gadget Dude put on a wide toothy smile and pushed open the door, to reveal a small office surrounded by doors to walk-in storage lockers. In the middle of the office, a young Cholbren woman sat behind a desk working at a console. Three grapnels guns lay in pieces next to her.

"Oh no, you don't! Scoot! Out! I'm not letting you in again, I'm still tidying up the mess you left yesterday." The Cholbren rose from behind her desk with a thunderous expression. Her shoulder fur bristled as she pointed back through the door.

"Grey, Loc. Loc, Grey," Gadget Dude said.

"Really, Dude?" I asked.

He shrugged.

I stepped between them. "Pleased to meet you, Loc. My friend and I are here—"

"Investigating the murder? I know, that's what your little devil friend said yesterday. And it's why I've had a parade of amateur sleuths through my stores, disorganising them. None of them was the devil incarnate, though." She stabbed a finger at Gadget Dude. "That was him."

"Gadget Dude, what did you do?"

"Nothing, much. Not touch evidence, left as found. Important. Was other cupboard open. Did help with that."

"Gadget Dude..."

"Fixed them, that all."

"They were *supposed* to be broken," Loc roared. "The point of the class is to get students to repair them."

"Ah."

"And it's not like he just repaired them." She scrabbled around on her desk and picked out one of the disassembled grapnels. She pointed it at Gadget Dude and pulled

80

the trigger. Instead of firing a grapnel, it began playing a rather jaunty tune. "How is that fixed? And what is this bit even for?" She pointed to a small blue cylinder, wired into the mechanism.

Gadget Dude squinted, then beamed. "Wondered where left that!"

Loc held out the gun. "Fix it. Or, rather, break it. Like it was."

I took it from her, adjusting my grip on it until I covered the speaker and deadened the tune. "I can help with that. I did pretty well in the repair class last year. Gadget Dude has something he wanted to try to help with our investigation. I'll help fix these grapnels and keep an eye on him, so he doesn't interfere with any more."

"Not 'interfere'," Gadget Dude muttered under his breath. I kicked his ankle; not hard enough to hurt but enough to get his attention. He smiled at Loc. "Not interfere," he promised.

Loc picked up a small crate of grapnels from behind the desk. "You help me with these, and if you keep a leash on that menace, I'll let you do your test."

The crate must have had two dozen grapnels in it, all of them modified in one way or another. "How many did you do, Dude?"

Gadget Dude held up his hands. "Had free period."

# # #

We kept the door to the grapnel store propped open, and Loc and I set to work on the grapnels, removing Gadget Dude's modifications, then breaking them to Loc's specifications. All the while, Gadget Dude worked in the storeroom, building one of his more complicated devices in the centre of the room. It had a large dish on top and a screen on the front. He popped out from time to time, to collect components we had liberated from the grapnels we were fixing. He added them to his device; he seemed happy at least.

And as the pile of work on her desk decreased, Loc too seemed mollified.

"Have you been working with Tom long?" I asked her. Tom ran the Grapnel classes at the Academy.

She shook her head. "No, I only graduated last year, I'm still looking for a more permanent place to do the hero thing. Tom asked me to stay on for a while and help organise. Not just here on the eighth floor, but across the whole Academy. There's a lot of inventory to manage."

"I bet. Is that your superpower then, your organisational skills?"

"More or less," she said. "I'm a Skills graduate, no power or tech to speak of, but I think I can help people. The Academy isn't just about the flashy end of superheroing, you know."

"Oh, I know, it's what drew me in the first place. What's the line from the advert? 'Somewhere in the galaxy, whatever you can do—'"

"'—whoever you are, is special.' It's true though, the Academy has a great track record, helping match heroes to worlds that need their skills. A friend of mine graduated last year, he's using his skills as a costume designer to create environment suits for colonists on a world out east that has valuable resources but a corrosive atmosphere."

"That's awesome."

"Of course, he's also had to fight off raiders, the Academy does train us for combat, after all. But it's his textiles knowledge that makes him a superhero."

"What's his name?"

"We called him Plaid Lad while he was here, but that was mostly to tease him. I think he's just gone back to using his real name, Alemap."

"Plaid Lad, that's funny."

She snapped the case back on one of the grapnels and dropped it into the Ready pile. She quirked me a smile. "What about you, Grey, there was a lot of talk about you last year. You know your way around a multi-tool there, are you Tech?"

"Me? No, not at all. Skills all the way. I've just dabbled in a lot of different things at one time or another. Don't know that I can point at one thing and say, 'that's what I do better than anyone', like your organisational skills, I just know a little bit about a lot of things and can generally bluff my way through the rest." I extracted a small silver box from the firing mechanism of another grapnel, turned it over in my hand, trying to figure what purpose it was supposed to serve. Defeated, I dropped it into the extraneous components box and set about rewiring the grapnel to fire properly. Or, well, actually not to fire properly; it was supposed to be broken.

"But you did fight off an alien invasion?" Loc asked.

"I didn't do a whole lot of fighting. Probability Kid, Avrim and Dez were on the front line. I... contributed."

"And your little menace?" She waved her multi-tool at Gadget Dude. Oblivious, he tapped his latest creation with a silver hammer.

"We literally would have died without him. He isn't a bad guy, you know. He doesn't have a malicious bone in his body, I'm sure he thought he was helping when he did this." I held up the next grapnel I had to fix, it was wreathed in a web of transparent tubing, through which a viscous purple fluid pulsed. "Well, maybe not this one specifically, but in general. He's young for a Zalex, approaches the world with a wide-eyed don't-think-about-the-consequences enthusiasm, which I'm sometimes kind of jealous of. Seriously, he's a good guy."

"Maybe so," Loc relented. "But if I see him unsupervised in any of my storerooms again—"

"Oh, I get that." I held up my hands to stop her. "He's banned from using the lifts solo, too. And the Virtual Arcade. And the fifth-floor bathrooms, now I think."

She laughed. It's possible she thought I was joking.

"Fine, he's forgiven. What is he doing in there anyway?"

We watched him for a moment. His device seemed completed, and as the sensor dish on top rotated slowly, shadowy figures flickered into being on the screen. Gadget Dude grumbled happily to himself and twisted dials on the device's top and side. As he did, the number and size of the flickering figures changed, but never quite came into focus. Undeterred, Gadget Dude continued playing with the dials.

"He thinks he can use that thing, whatever it is, to pick up information about who took the missing grapnel."

Loc frowned. "If he can create a weird time-space visualiser, why not just use it on the murder scene?"

I opened my mouth to reply, couldn't, and closed it again.

"It's not going to work, is it?" she asked.

"I don't think life is generally that obliging, no."

Loc looked into the box of grapnels still to be repaired; we were down to the last three. "Leave those," she said, "I'll do them. I want to show you something."

"Sure thing."

She led me into a small cubbyhole at the back of her office. It held a table with a kettle and mugs, a sink, and a console. There was hardly enough room for us both.

"We have no security footage of the grapnel store," she said, switching on the console, "but I did install a few cameras further down the corridor. I'm planning to use them to track stores down the line, but I hadn't got the database on-line yet. They have been recording for the last few days though, and there's one clip I think you might be interested in. I've shown it to Professor Croft, of course, but not any of the other would-be-detectives."

"Thanks."

She brought up a file and played it. "We don't know for sure when the grapnel was taken. It might have been weeks ago. So, this may not be connected at all, but—"

A figure, dressed in black with a black face mask, appeared on the screen. Male and human, as far as I could tell. Athletic build. He would be unremarkable (at least by Academy standards) were it not for the fact he was clearly trying to be sneaky. He all-but tip-toed along the corridor, pressing himself against the wall by intervals, looking furtively back and ahead. He wouldn't have been more suspicious if he'd been wearing a badge reading 'I'm definitely not suspicious, honest'. I double-checked; he wasn't.

"Who is that guy?" I asked.

"No idea. And again, he may not even be related to the theft. But if he isn't—"

"—that would be a weird coincidence," I agreed. "Can I take a copy?"

She hesitated, then nodded. She flicked the file to my wristpad.

"Thanks, Loc. I really appreciate it."

"Thank you for helping with the unrepairs."

"It was actually kind of relaxing. We'll get out of your hair though. Gadget Dude," I called, "I think it's time we give Loc her room back."

"But, almost working!" Gadget Dude complained.

I joined him in the grapnel store. "Is it? Really?"

He studied his feet. "No."

"Then, grab the device, let's get out of Loc's way."

"Okay." He reached an arm into the guts of his machine. There was an audible click, and the entire device fell apart into its component pieces. Gadget Dude hurriedly refilled his utility belt, stuffing the larger pieces into his pack.

"Thanks, again, Loc," I said.

She waved, and we beat a hasty retreat.

Back in the lift, Gadget Dude looked up at me. "You get?"

I nodded. "You were right, she had a recording, and I think there may even be something useful on it."

Gadget Dude beamed. "Also right, needed you."

We exchanged a fist bump and rode the elevator back down to the Atrium.

#

By the time the whole team gathered for our evening catch up, I'd scoured Loc's recording for any kind of clue to the sneaking man's identity.

"First thing," I said, "I don't think this guy was in the Ethics class. Nobody matches that body type, except maybe me, and I know it wasn't me. I think it rules him out of being the killer too."

Avrim growled at that.

"No, I know, we want a clue, we all do, but there is no way somebody that bad at sneaking gets into Veritas's classroom, does the deed and gets out without somebody seeing him."

Avrim pointed at the recording, playing in a loop on my console. "That could be some weird bluff."

"I mean, it could be, but we all know it's not." I checked the faces in the room. Everybody, including Avrim, knew I was right.

"So, is the recording no help at all?" asked Seven-thirtyfour.

"Yes and no." This next part was a bit out there, but it felt right. "I think I've seen this guy before. Remember last year, after the explosion in the canteen, Gadget Dude and I spotted someone trying to sneak to the security room to get the footage? I can't be a hundred percent, but I think it's the same person."

"You never worked out who that was either," Dez pointed out.

"True, but we have more to go on now. If I'm right, if it's the same guy, we know more about him. First, he's at least a second-year student. Not only have we seen him in two consecutive years, but he knew where the grapnel store was on the day before term technically started. Second, he's not a Skills student."

"What makes you so sure of that?" Seventhirtyfour asked.

"No second-year Skills student is that bad at sneaking. You can't get through a year of a Skills curriculum without some stealth training. Even if you dodge all of the obvious classes like Building Infiltration and Being One With The Night, there were stealth components in half my classes last year." Dez, Pilvi, Lucy and Gadget Dude all nodded. We'd all been Skills last year.

"This guy is Powers, but without powers that lend themselves to sneaking, or is Tech out of his tech," I concluded.

"That rules out," Pilvi paused to do the maths, "five-ninths of the student body. It still leaves a large suspect pool."

"Don't forget male and human, that brings us to close to a ninth of the student body," I said.

"Assuming he's a student," Pilvi fired back.

"Assuming that," I agreed.

"Is link between last year explosion and Veritas?"

Gadget Dude asked.

"Great question." I wrote it on the murder board.

"Like Dez said, though, we never worked out who tried to blow you up back then," Seventhirtyfour rumbled.

"I've given it some thought, since. We know that Mrs. Gravane had, probably has, representatives at the Academy. I don't think it's much of a stretch to assume Mirabor did as well. I always assumed the attack came from him. Is this guy still an agent of Mirabor? If so, why would Mirabor target Veritas? Or is this guy just an agent for hire? I don't think we know. At this point, I don't think we *can* know. Which brings us back to Seventhirtyfour's question. Is this recording useful? No, not directly. It gives us more points on the map though, and we should keep them in mind, going forwards."

"This is going too slowly," Avrim said, bitterly.

He wasn't wrong. The longer the case went without a break, the less likely it would ever have a solve. The first forty-eight hours were crucial and had given us nothing of substance. "We are only one investigation. Prof Croft will have more to go on, I'm sure. We'll find the murderer. This guy," I jerked a thumb over my shoulder, indicating the infiltrating man, "may be the link we need. We've done well today. Thanks, Gadget Dude."

Gadget Dude's broad smile faltered as he looked across at Avrim's stony expression.

CHAPTER 9
CLUES (VARIOUS)

After the first few days, the pace of the investigation slowed down. I interviewed everybody from the class, even making a point to talk to Skybeam directly, but after those first few hints, nothing new came to light. We had nothing strong enough to build a case on, and no access to the nitty-gritty technical details that Prof Croft was using for her investigation. Which is not to say she didn't talk to us, or Avrim at least, as next of kin.

The DNA sweep was eventually completed, and we had a list of people who had been in the room where the murder happened. Fifty different DNA traces that analysis suggested were fresh enough to be worth considering. The list covered all of Veritas's students and the Super Social Media class that had used the classroom earlier that day. I interviewed all of them too but was unsurprised when they added nothing.

Gadget Dude reported that the security footage had not been tampered with after recording. That meant that the blurring he'd spotted was either a glitch in the data stream or an indication of some power use. Invisibility? Super speed? Some tech influence like Lucy had? Too many possibilities. Superhero crime investigation can be *really* frustrating.

We either had a lot of suspects or none. And it didn't look like we were going to break the case quickly.

Avrim was convinced that it was Professor Gale and would ditch classes just to watch Gale going about campus. I wasn't the only one to talk to Avrim about it. He wasn't helping himself or the case by obsessing over one suspect.

"People are going to forget," Avrim told me. "I see it already, people going to classes as if there weren't a murderer amongst us."

He was right, and I understood his frustration, but what was the alternative? Close the school down? Live in fear? Neither of those felt like the Justice Academy way. Instead, Professor Croft would work the case, and so would we, when we could. Veritas's killer would be found. I had faith in the system.

Not everything was back to normal.

The second weekend of term marked the start of the Power Ball season. I'd hardly seen Seventhirtyfour in that time, and there'd been no talk of getting the team together to join in this year. It would have felt weird, true, but it was also weird not to at least have the conversation.

I made my way to the Dome alone. Apart from for case business, I'd hardly seen any of the gang. Pilvi was still mad at me and was too busy with her new Powers friends. Gadget Dude was looking after Avrim. Dez had her band. Lucy had David.

Me, I sat alone in a crowd of a few thousand screaming spectators and let the match wash over me. I couldn't tell you who played, or what the score line was.

For ten years I'd lived my life flitting from one space station to the next. Never really looking back, never really looking forwards, enjoying the surprise, even when it was rubbish. Then the Academy got its claws into me. I thought I'd found a home. I'd spent my summer holiday looking forwards to something. It was a new experience.

So was being disappointed.

There it was.

It wasn't anybody's fault. I'd tricked myself. Fallen for one of my own lies. The lie that the second year was going to be awesome, and it wasn't. Not because of the murder, though that didn't help, because... of stuff. Other people had stuff too. Go figure.

I sat for the longest time on the bench in the stands. When I finally moved myself to leave, I stalled in the entry hall. I tried to put a foot out into the quad, but I felt the pull of the sky, plucking at my shoulders, trying to pull me from the planet surface. My heart beat loudly, my breathing became difficult and I... I was going nowhere for a while. I retreated to the back of the entry hall and slumped to the floor. I watched other stragglers saunter out into the quad as though nothing was going to happen to them. A fair percentage of them flew away. Bastards.

"Grey?"

I looked up. "Oh hello, Fusillade, I didn't see you there." She was with a group of three other students I didn't know.

"I was hoping to run into you. I wanted to thank you, and what with Ethics being cancelled, wasn't sure I'd get the chance."

I pulled myself to a standing position, dusted myself off. "Thank me, for what?" I asked.

"What you said, about giving the Academy a chance. Two weeks in, I have friends, my studies are going well. I didn't expect it, but you were right, this place does have a way of fitting you in." She laughed. A delighted, carefree sound.

"Well, there you go then," I said. I sounded gruff to my ears, but I think I managed to keep the grump out.

"We were just heading to the Fortress of Epictude for the after-match. Do you want to come with us?"

I looked out into the quad again. Maybe I was ready to face it now. But, "Thanks for the offer, maybe next time," I said.

She smiled, she had a pretty chin, I did wonder what the rest of her face looked like.

"Okay, Grey, bye then." She waved and the four of them headed out into the quad.

"Bye," I called after her.

#

I spent another twenty minutes alone in the Dome's entry hall before I made another attempt at the quad. This time went better. There was still a shake in my hands, but I balled them into fists and that helped.

I took the scenic route back to my dorm, to prove to myself, again, that I could.

The door to the spaceport terminal wasn't locked, I ducked inside and worked my way through without turning the lights on. My footsteps echoed hollowly through the deserted building.

The Academy's fleet wasn't huge. Three smaller passenger shuttles, including *The Metropolitan* which ran back and forth between Meanwhile station. They had a dozen unmanned mail pods, though only one of them was in its cradle now, the others presumably out on their mail collections from nearby star systems. The Academy also had a small space station of its own. Unoccupied most of the year but used from time to time for classes that dealt with space-based superheroing. Not classes I felt I needed. I doubted there was anyone on the whole planet more at home on a space station than me. That was the life.

Larger craft stopped by the Academy two or three times a term. Proper deep-space ships that could go further than the shuttles, which barely made it two or three systems over. Not owned by the Academy but hired by them to bring in supplies and passengers. Curious, I stopped by a console and pulled up a schedule. The first one to stop by would be in a few weeks.

I drummed my fingers on the console.

That was... interesting.

No.

I closed the terminal and power-walked back to my dorm.

#

I needed to be doing something.

I was up to date with schoolwork and didn't feel like reading ahead. Nothing new had broken on Veritas's murder in days, but I got out the murder board and stared at it anyway. There were too many blank spaces on it, things we just didn't know. For all I felt that Professor Gale didn't do it, he was the suspect with the most arrows pointing to him.

Well, his name and mine were tied on that front, but I knew I hadn't done it.

DNA hadn't placed him at the scene, but Seventhirtyfour had pointed out Apogee could create a wind cocoon that would prevent DNA shedding.

This mysterious accident in his first year, where three students had died, that was all we had in place for motive. It was more motive-shaped than motive-fact. How could we find out more about that? I pulled up the student records from that first year. The only names I recognised were Veritas and Apogee. If it came to it, I'd ask Professor Gale directly, but I was hoping I could go into that conversation with a little more knowledge.

How about teaching staff? The list wasn't long, the Academy had been much smaller back then. My search pulled out only ten matches. I paged through each in turn, looking for any familiar faces. The first match was Captain Hawk, a much fresher-faced hero than the one I knew, but the same man. He had been headmaster since the very start of the Academy, so I should have expected to see him on the list. Somehow, it was still a surprise. Could I ask him about the accident? Asking Apogee was more appealing than confronting the headmaster.

The next two pictures came up, a Welatak and a Germile, I didn't recognise either of them, but I thought I'd seen the Germile's hero name, Doc Pluto, somewhere.

The next one was a familiar face, although again a good deal younger. Professor Red Ninja. He taught superhero self-defence, and I was in his Intermediate class this term. Maybe he could give me some information.

I skimmed through the rest, five more strangers. I tapped next and stared at the normal 'No More Matches' message.

Something... wait... I counted on my fingers. I swiped back through the list. It definitely said ten matches, so why was it only showing nine results? There. It skipped past what should have been match two. Captain Hawk was number 1 of 10, then it skipped to number 3 of 10 when it showed the Welatak teacher.

There was something there. Something strange about the Academy's first year. But was it connected to Veritas's death? We couldn't be sure until we pulled on the thread and saw what came loose.

I checked my wristpad for the time. It wasn't late, but it wasn't early either, probably not the time to go chasing off to find Professor Red Ninja. I'd see him in class on Monday, that would likely be soon enough, considering this mystery was already two decades old. The mystery of the missing record though, that was something I could investigate now. Or, well, not me. I needed to talk to Dez.

People sometimes misunderstand our group dynamic and think that Gadget Dude is our go-to for *all* things techy. It's not true. If you need something building or dismantling, he's the dude, for sure, but as I understand, his approach to technology is more an instinctive grasp of how things fit together. He does get the science, but I wouldn't call him a scientist. That's Pilvi's job, particularly when it comes to life sciences. Likewise, Gadget Dude can hack a computer if he needs to, but this job smacked of data retrieval, and for that, when push came to shove, I'd pick ex-librarian Dez every time.

The only problem was, she was a woman in demand.

"Say again, Grey," she shouted over the comm. I could barely hear her over the music in the background.

"There's a missing record in the Academy files, I need you to find it."

"It's no good, I can't hear you. I'm doing a gig at the party on the beach. I'm up next. Can you come to me?"

I did consider it, for a heartbeat. "Don't worry about it, Dez, I'll find you tomorrow."

"Okay!" she signed off.

I bounced to my feet and circled my room twice. Alright then. I'd needed something to distract me earlier, but now I was too pumped to settle. After two weeks of nothing, we suddenly had two new leads. I didn't know if they were leads into the case, or just into a much older mystery, but either way, it felt good. I needed something else to solve.

There was Mrs. Gravane's case, the team that had tried to break out Mirabor. I hadn't thought about it, like at all, since I'd finished up my call with her. But I was on fire. What could we get from these?

I dug the files out and popped them up on my console. Incapacitor, Big Bang and Laugh Riot. The police files on the first two were pretty complete, there wasn't much to be added there. Maybe I knew somebody from my past life who could help track them down... no. I couldn't think of anybody. So that left Laugh Riot. What gaps could I fill in there? I remembered thinking she must be the connection to Mirabor, the other two were just goons. I remembered thinking... well. Hmm. Actually, there was a woman connected to Mirabor who might have powers. He'd even said her transformation had been incredible. Kayda Buchanan. She was a native to Nymanteles and an explorer by trade. Possibly Mirabor's girlfriend? We'd never quite gotten to the bottom of that. I had a photo of her somewhere. It took a few minutes to dig through my files to bring it up. I put her picture next to Incapacitor and Big Bang. Could she be Laugh Riot? We had no idea what her powers were. Or what she did after we caught Doctor Gravestone. Mirabor.

Kayda wasn't on Nymanteles when we'd fought Gravestone, but she had a house there. Surely, she must have been back since? And if she had, and if she was as unsettled by her ascension as Mirabor had been, she must have made her presence felt, somehow. I needed to talk to someone who'd been on Nymanteles recently.

That was a whole long chain of ifs, but they were all logical. I gestured through the control field on my console and pulled up Lucy's comm.

She answered with a mumbled, "Hello." She was wearing a baggy Justice Academy t-shirt. The screen showed it was dark where she was.

I realised she was in bed. *Alone!* Shut up brain. "Oh, I'm sorry, did I wake you?" I checked the clock. When did it get so late? It can't have been more than a few minutes since I'd called Dez, surely?

"Grey? No. Well, yes."

"Sorry. I'll call back in the morning."

She sighed. "It's okay. I recognise that look. You have a bee in your bonnet, don't you?"

"A what in my what?"

She smiled at me in the darkness and tucked her hair behind her ears. "Never change, Grey. What has you so worked up?"

"You were back on Nymanteles over the summer, right?"

"Yes? Oh, mum said to say hello by the way. I forgot to say that before."

"That's nice of her. Um. Right. I'm just wanting to know, were there any reports of seeing Kayda Buchanan over summer?"

"I don't think so."

"Oh." I sagged. I thought I was on to something. And maybe I still was, but I didn't have any evidence. "Did anything strange happen there over the holiday? Superpowered goings-on?"

She considered for a moment. "Oh, in fact, mum mentioned something Chief Gult had told her. There was a rash of burglaries a couple of weeks after the holiday started. Reports were that the thief was a speedster. She didn't stay still long enough for anyone to see her properly though. Mum asked me if I knew of any superspeed villains."

"Interesting. But they saw enough to say she was a woman?"

"No, but some people, those who weren't deafened by sonic booms, some reported hearing—"

"Her laugh," I said.

"How did you know that?"

"Something Mrs. Gravane said about a case she had her people investigating. I've not spoken to her for a couple of weeks, they may have worked this out already, but I think Kayda Buchanan is our speedster and tried to break

Mirabor Gravane out of prison."

"Gosh. Tried? Or—?"

"As far as Mrs. Gravane said, he's still secure and receiving treatment."

"That's good."

"Yes."

"Grey—"

"I should—"

"Don't go, not yet. I wanted to say," she paused, "I'm sorry for not talking to you about David, you know, before. I wanted to tell you, but it never seemed quite the right time."

"It's okay. He seems nice. A bit of a doofus maybe."

"Grey!"

I cut myself with a smile. "I'm happy for you. Honestly."

"Thanks."

"Goodnight, Lucy."

"Goodnight, Grey."

CHAPTER 10
THE PARADOX

I was too wired to sleep, so I set a net search going for Kayda Buchanan. Where had she been, what had she done since we took down Gravestone? I'd talk to Mrs. Gravane in the morning when I had slightly less of a manic vibe going on, let her know my theory about who Laugh Riot was. If I could also give Mrs. Gravane a theory about where to find Buchanan, so much the better. It wouldn't hurt if I could find some evidence of precisely what her powers were. "Speedster" is one of those catch-all categories that could cover everything from simply running fast up to speed phasing, speed tornadoes and speed healing.

The sun was already coming up when I had the search parameters defined, and I finally let myself fall into bed. It would take a few days to run a full search. Should I tell Mrs. Gravane my suspicions now, or wait until the...

Somehow, I dozed off mid speculation.

#

It was early afternoon before I crawled back out of my bunk. As I stumbled out of the shower, I realised how much my room smelled of somebody sitting and stewing over a problem for too many hours. I bundled up my bed linen, stuffed it in a bag, added some clothes and headed to the laundry room.

I dumped everything into the machine and programmed a good long zap. With ten minutes to kill, I commed Dez again.

"Hey, Grey," she croaked, not turning on the camera at her end.

"You sound rough. Bad night?"

"Freaking awesome night. One encore too many though, and not just for the set. I'm heading out to get a traditional folksy cure in a bit."

"What's the cure? I may need it someday too."

She paused to cough away from the mic, but the sound carried. "Okay, sure, what you do," she said when she got back to me, "is take a liter of vanilla ice cream."

"Okay."

"And then you eat it. The cold is good for the throat, the sugar helps with the energy levels. You can add chocolate sauce if you prefer."

"I'd thought there was going to be more to it, but sure, it sounds like a plan."

She coughed again. "What were you calling about last night?"

"I need you to look into the Academy database and work out why it's behaving oddly. I was looking at a list of teachers for the year that accident happened. It says there were ten, but only shows me details on nine of them."

"Weird."

"Yeah. I thought with your—" I lowered my voice, "—librarian skills—" and raised it again, "—you might be able to retrieve the missing data."

"It's okay, Grey, I'm not keeping the librarian thing secret anymore. I figure I've proved my action hero credentials by fighting off an alien invasion. Now I want people to know I have layers."

"So many layers," I agreed.

"Although, if you were to see any others of my species knocking about..."

100

"Say no more."

"Okay, Grey. I'll have a poke around and report back. Oh, hey, Grey?"

"Yes, Dez?"

"You and Lucy? Is that a thing still?"

"No. I mean, no. She's with David. He seems... she's with him, so, why do you ask?"

She croaked a laugh. "Dude. That's what I thought. This girl was asking about you last night at the gig. I couldn't quite work out if she was into you or investigating you in the Veritas case. She did seem super interested in whether you had a girlfriend either way."

"No. No girlfriend." I said, definitively.

"Okay, okay. Wish I'd told her that. I'm not much of a judge of human women, but I think she may have been kind of cute. Oh well, I'll know for next time."

"Gee, thanks, Dez."

"Gotta go, Grey, I hear the ice cream calling."

The laundry beeped and I stuffed the clean sheets and clothes into my bag again, muttering about Dez all the way.

# # #

Look, I know I come across as this super cool guy with my life together and all, but between you, me and Säde, Dez had kind of hit on a weak spot there. Relationships.

Growing up, particularly by the time I'd reached the age of being interested in the whole, you know, thing, I'd tended to move around a lot. Most places I didn't stay more than a few weeks. Some places, not more than a few hours. Never really time to make a connection.

There had been moments. And girls. And, but, look. All I know about relationships comes from sitcoms and movies. And one of the main things I learned from them is that relationships are complicated, and relationships that start with lying are doomed to be even more complicated. Since my life from age eight was nothing but lies, I guess I just never met the girl to make the complications worth it. The complications or the truth. It just never seemed fair to them, so, no, no girlfriend.

I...

You didn't want to hear any of that, did you? Why am I asking you? You can't answer.

Right, sorry, Säde. Yes, I know, this isn't therapy. Where was I?

# # #

I didn't get a chance to talk to Professor Red Ninja the next day. He had us practising blocks under the supervision of his TA; I didn't notice the Professor slip away. I'd catch him later in the week, I was sure.

It did mean I found myself heading towards Prof Gale's class still with a question mark over whether he had a part in all this.

"Most of you have been at the Academy long enough now to realise that the reality of superheroing is different from the fiction," Gale said. "That doesn't mean there can't be parallels. Let's start with some fiction and see how we could apply it to our real lives. I want you to think of your favourite fictional superhero crossover. It can be from a book, a movie, a comic, wherever. Think about the story structure. Take a moment to write out the beats of how that story goes. Don't stress about details too much, just generally, what happens in it?"

There was a susurration of students as they followed the instruction. I doodled something on my minipad; don't tell Seventhirtyfour, but I still hadn't read any fictionalised superhero stories. I don't need anyone else to make up stories for me. I'm quite capable of doing that for myself.

My reading around superheroics was strictly confined to textbooks, for homework.

"Everybody got something?" Gale asked. "Good. Let me tell you how the story goes. Hero A is on the trail of a villain. Maybe she's tracking him. Maybe she even finds and fights him, but if she does, she loses. In the course of the investigation, she encounters Hero B. We all know this bit, right? Sing it with me."

"There is a misunderstanding, and they fight, before inevitably teaming up to defeat the real villain." We made a good effort at chanting along with him. Although it did fall apart into laughter by the end.

Gale held up a hand "Okay, I may have said that before. But here is the thing. This is where the Crossover Paradox principle comes into play. We know that hero A cannot defeat the villain alone. That's why there's a crossover, right, that's the purpose of the team-up. Have a look at what you wrote. Who ultimately defeats the villain? There's likely teamwork involved, but who delivers the knockout blow? Hands up anyone who wrote down that it was whoever Hero B was."

I looked around. Hardly anyone had put their hands up.

"A few," said Gale. "I think you may want to go reread your comic book. This is the Crossover Paradox in a nutshell. The story tells us that Hero A cannot possibly defeat the villain, yet at the end of the day, it is Hero A that wins."

There was a general murmuring at that.

"We'll come back to how 'realistic' that is in just a moment. But before that, let's look at the story from Hero B's perspective. They were also on the villain's trail, that's why they crossed paths with Hero A after all. They also suffer a misunderstanding which causes them to fight before inevitably teaming up to defeat the real villain.

Their story is the same as Hero A's. So why don't they get the victory?"

Someone near the front of the class answered. I didn't hear what they said from way at the back, but Gale repeated it.

"Precisely. It's not their story. So, what am I saying? If the Crossover Paradox has any real-world application, one of the most fundamental things you need to understand if you find yourself teaming up with another hero... is this your story? Or theirs?"

# # #

I waited at the end of class. I wasn't alone, several others had questions about coursework or some of the topics covered in the lesson. I had something else on my mind. I couldn't put off talking to Gale about the accident any longer. No matter how much I enjoyed his lectures, if he had something to do with Veritas's death, we had to know. I didn't want to confront him in front of a lot of the class though. If he was innocent, I didn't want my questioning him to get out.

The last student out before me, a Cholbren, stopped at the door. I didn't know him, but he must have heard something about me, because, "You want me to stay, Professor?" he asked.

Gale gave me an appraising look. "I'll be fine, thank you."

The Cholbren shrugged and left us to it.

"So, what can I do for you, Grey?" Gale asked.

"I was hoping you might be able to give me some insight into the Veritas case," I said.

He stole a glance at his wristpad. "I have a few minutes." He gestured towards the front row of the lecture theatre seats. "Let's chat."

"Thanks." I sat, close, but not next to him. "You and Veritas both joined the Academy in its first year, you said?"

"That's right."

"Were you close? Were you friends?"

"The Academy was a lot smaller back then. A couple of hundred students and maybe a dozen teachers. Everybody knew everybody. I wouldn't say we were close, but we got on fine. Veritas got along with everyone once they got past her power. Some adjusted faster than others, but yes, I think I'd say we were friends."

"She got along with everyone? So, no enemies at all?"

"Did you know, the original Academy building was underground? The terraforming was still a little ragged and new back then, all our dorm rooms were built into the side of a canyon, sealed with a forcefield at the top to keep the local bugs and beasties out. It wasn't the paradise the place is now. A lot has changed in a couple of decades."

"The entire place had a roof back then? Sounds nice. But, Veritas..."

"Mmm? Yes. No, no enemies that I know of, but as I say we weren't that close." Gale checked his wristpad again.

"Do you know who she was close with? Any students she hung around with? Any teachers who she got along with well?"

Gale blew out a long breath. "Now you're asking. This was a long time ago, Grey. Twenty years. I think she used to go around with one of the other Polifan. Sparrow Girl? Something like that. That was before..." He trailed off, frowning.

"Before the accident?" I said.

He looked up sharply. "I think that's about all the time I have now. If you have more questions, send me a message, I'll try to get to them."

"What happened in that accident, Professor?"

He stood. "And I would appreciate it if you could intervene with your friend Avrim. It is quite distracting having him always in the corner of my eye."

"The accident, Professor? What happened?"

"Apogee."

His costume formed around him, the winds buffeting me away as it did.

He flew out of the lecture hall without another word.

# # #

I jogged back down the stairs, head buzzing. Something about that accident had Gale rattled, but I had nothing to link it to the murder. Gale had seemed pretty relaxed about talking about Veritas before the accident came up. Was that because he was innocent, but the accident was upsetting even now? Or was he fine talking about Veritas's death until he realised, I knew about the accident?

"I miss tricking people," I muttered.

"What?" asked the purple Zalex coming up the stairs.

"Sorry, talking to myself."

And when I asked him about what had happened at the accident, had he said Apogee to suit up, or because Apogee was what happened at the accident. Both questions were going on the murder board when I got back to my room.

My breakthroughs of the weekend were trickling to a halt again. They had sustained me and the case for a couple of days, but I saw another brick wall coming. My only hope was that Dez could unlock something when she looked at the database. Or that my search would turn up something about Kayda Buchanan to offer up to Mrs. Gravane.

For now, though, I still had enough to keep my mind occupied as I assayed the quad. Even if Avrim swooping down from the sky was a bit much.

My Polifan friend did not look himself. Over a fortnight of stressing about the case without any chance to relax had taken its toll. There were dark circles around bloodshot eyes, and, never heavy-framed, he'd visibly lost weight, making his face hollow and his cheeks sharp.

"Did you confront Apogee yet?" he asked.

"I spoke to him, just an initial chat. He didn't say anything incriminating. Nothing to point a finger."

"Tell me exactly what he said."

When I did, Avrim looked triumphant. "When you asked him what happened at the accident, he said 'Apogee'? Apogee happened at the accident?"

"I think he was just saying his magic word to summon his costume," I hedged.

"No, man. He slipped up. He let the truth out. He caused that accident, and my aunt knew it. When she confronted him about it, he killed her. I knew it."

I put a hand on his shoulder. "Avrim, we don't have enough. I'm not saying you're necessarily wrong. But we don't have enough to make a case."

He shook my hand away. "I don't need to make a case, Grey." He beat his wings, almost knocking me from my feet. "I've heard everything I need." He was airborne again, and as he rose, my stomach sank.

I stabbed the comm on my wristpad, calling everyone. "Guys, I need eyes on Avrim, I think he's about to do something catastrophically stupid. We need to stop him from confronting Gale."

CHAPTER 11
MAN DOWN

I vaulted over the guard rail of the Hall's entry ramp and pelted after Avrim. "He's heading for the sixth-floor balcony," I shouted at my wristpad, though with my arms pumping as I ran, god knows how it sounded. I rounded the corner, dared a look upwards, and there was Avrim, stepping onto the edge of the balcony, steadying himself with his wings.

A slash of white light painted the windows above Avrim.

"I have him," said Pilvi over the comm.

She struck like a lightning bolt; a flare of light so bright I had to shield my eyes. Then the two of them plummeted, spinning groundward, light blazing from Pilvi's eyes as Avrim punched her repeatedly in the side.

"Pull up," I shouted.

Avrim got the upper hand, he snapped his wings wide, using them more as a parachute than to provide lift. Their spin stopped; their descent slowed... but they still crashed into the quad with a sickening impact. Avrim pulled himself upright, and Pilvi followed, but I could see from the way she favoured her left side that she was hurt.

I tried to move to intercept, but the burst of adrenaline that had gotten me out of the Hall had fled, and now something in my back brain was shouting at me that I was outside. My feet refused to move; my knees buckled.

I fell to all fours, not able to reach them, lungs heaving in my chest. I reached for my grapnel gun, but my hand was shaking so much I couldn't even unclip it.

By now, other students in the quad had noticed something was going on. Several of them stepped forwards to intervene, but I waved them back, with one unsteady hand. "No. Stay back," I gasped at them. The situation was too complicated, they could only make it worse.

Pilvi launched herself at Avrim, double fists striking down as she passed over him, aiming at the Polifan's wing, striking towards the same point where Veritas's wing broke. Pilvi's blow landed, but without enough force to break bones. Avrim's eyes widened as he, too, realised what Pilvi had tried to do. He grabbed at her ankle as she flew by, snagged it, planted his feet and pivoted. Pilvi swung around wildly, her momentum twisted but not halted. She smashed face-first into the unforgiving quad. The light in her hair faded to almost nothing.

No. If Avrim got airborne again, there'd be no stopping him. I pushed down the voice in my head and staggered forwards, I just needed to get to Avrim and hold him down. There was no art to my attack, my phobia had its hooks in me, it was all I could manage to move, but move I did, arms outstretched to grab him.

Avrim delivered a textbook elbow strike to the back of my shoulders and put me down on the ground again.

"Stay out of this, Grey," Avrim said. He beat his wings ready to launch, but before he could, a gout of flame washed above Avrim's head. He ducked to avoid a singeing.

"Now, Triple Threat," a Brontom shouted, though I couldn't see which one. What I did see were three green arms stretching out across the quad, grabbing for Avrim.

The Polifan blocked one, batting it down and stepping

on the wrist, but the other two hands plucked at him, one trying to crawl around his torso to surround him. Avrim looked back along the arms to where the Brontom squad stood a few meters away. He jumped at them, keeping low to avoid Sergeant Nine's flames, but beating his wings to drive forwards.

"Watch out, Twin Strike, he's going to—" Seventhirtyfour shouted, but too late.

Avrim, out from under Nine's flame, swung upwards, snapping out a kick that caught Twin Strike in the face. He rose, beyond Triple Threat's stretched reach. He hovered above us all.

"Why are you trying to stop me?" he cried out, his voice ragged, his wingspan framed by the Hall of Justice behind him. "You know you'd all do this too. If someone you cared for, one of your family, had been murdered, you know you'd confront their killer. I just want justice."

"We would," I admitted. "But we don't know we have the right man." Even now I was unwilling to say Apogee's name. If he were innocent, I didn't want to shout a public accusation.

"Let him prove himself innocent. If he does, we will look again."

"That's not how this works, Avrim. I know you're hurt but look at what you've done here. Pilvi is unconscious. I think you broke one of Triple Threat's wrists. I'm bleeding," I said. I was too, a minor face abrasion, but blood was seeping down my cheek. Avrim took a breath to respond, but I barrelled on. "This has to stop. Let's talk to Prof Croft. Or Captain Hawk if you want. We can present what we've found out, see what they have to say about it. We can take this one step at a time; we don't have to jump to a thousand. If you have the wrong man, what does that do to him? What does it do to you? That you've done all this and damned the consequences? This isn't you. This isn't right. It's not what Veritas would have wanted." I trailed to a halt, out of breath, out of words.

Avrim's expression changed. He still looked angry, but also confused. "Grey, what did you do?" he said.

"Avrim, please." It was Gadget Dude. He and Dez had joined us, just breaking through the edge of the crowd gathering around us. He was holding something that looked like a megaphone in his hands but wasn't using it to call up to Avrim.

"Gadget Dude, not you too?"

"Come down. Talk. Don't make me." Tears stood in Gadget Dudes wide eyes.

"I'm sorry," Avrim said. For the first time, there was a note of uncertainty in his voice. Still, he beat his wings and began to rise.

"Sorry, too," Gadget Dude said and held up the megaphone for Dez.

Dez sang a single pure note, held it.

My stomach flipped. Worse than any vertigo I'd ever felt, up was down was up was down. I felt cold all over and my muscles cramped. At any moment, the world would fling me from its surface and there was nothing I could do to stop it.

Darkness descended.

# # #

"He's waking up!"

I was on a bed. The unmistakable smell of antiseptic filled the air. I prised my eyes open and was rewarded with the comforting yellowy-brown of the Academy med centre. "Ow," I said.

"Such a relief to see you back with us, bud," said Dez. "Gadget Dude said that there might be some leakage to the sound wave, but most people just had an upset stomach and wobbly legs for a bit. We didn't know it would affect you so badly. Sorry about that, but at the end of the day you should let your teammates know your vulnerabilities, so I think we can probably all agree that it was essentially your fault, and we forgive you and we can all move on."

"I'll cop to that if you agree to talk quieter. And less. I have," I squeezed my eyes closed as my brain stabbed me in the head, "a killer headache."

"Give Grey some space, Dez," Pilvi said.

She limped into view; her face taped up with antiseptic gel pads. She looked down at her leg. "Just a sprain. If I stay off it, it'll be fine in a few days. Fortunately, staying off it shouldn't be a problem." Light pulsed from her eyes and she floated up off the floor. She wobbled a bit though and landed back on her good leg. "Well, maybe I won't do too much of that quite yet either."

Gingerly, I shuffled myself upright. There was a gel pad on my forehead too, I could feel it, but otherwise, I seemed to be in fair shape. At the far end of the med centre, Triple Strike sat in another bed, three of her four arms still stretched to several meters long, supported at regular intervals by slings suspended from the ceiling. She gave me an embarrassed look which was so familiar from Seventhirtyfour, it broke my heart a little.

"What's wrong with Triple Threat?" I whispered.

"Avrim broke one of her wrists in the fight. The med-techs are worried that if she... destretches?... before the bones heal, she could do permanent damage. And apparently, she can stretch three arms or none, so she's kind of stuck like that for a few days until the osteostims do their work," Dez explained.

Triple Threat gave an embarrassed shrug.

"And what about Avrim? Where is he?" I asked.

"Close by," said Pilvi. "They're looking after his injuries, but for now he's secured in an isolation room with Professor Red Ninja outside the door."

"Is he badly hurt?"

"Not very. A few burns from my sunbolts, a few bruises from his fall. Nothing vital hurt."

"Good. What did your megaphone thing do?" I asked Dez.

"Don't ask me for the science," said Dez, "but it was something to do with affecting your balance. If you were standing on the ground, it wouldn't—shouldn't—do much more than make you feel dizzy, maybe a little nauseous. But if you're flying under your own power it will bring you down, hard."

"Sure." That made sense. It had been a perfect storm with my already heightened state. I wondered if something like that would be a problem for me if I were indoors at the time. I resolved not to find out if I could avoid it.

The door to the med centre swung open and the Avenging Spider popped his head around it. "Ah! You're awake. Good show. You lot, me, the med centre, it all feels awfully familiar."

"Hi, Tom. What can I say, I needed to get my loyalty card stamped."

"The Captain wants to see you all as soon as you're fit. Are you fit?"

"After a fashion."

"Good. We'll take the lift, I think."

"I'd appreciate it."

Dez, Pilvi and I followed him out, leaving Triple Threat hanging alone.

# # #

It was quite the gathering in Captain Hawk's office.

The headmaster sat behind his desk, with Professors Croft and Gale flanking him. On our side of the desk, me, Dez, Pilvi and Gadget Dude sat together. Sergeant Nine sat a little apart. Tom sat by the door, not quite in the meeting, but not formally asked to leave either.

"Well, this is a mess," Captain Hawk began.

"Captain, I think—" I started, but then my brain stabbed me again and I stumbled to a halt.

"I think I will take my chance to talk, if it's all the same to you, Mr. Grey," he said.

I sank into my chair, and Hawk carried on.

"We have tolerated Avrim's actions to a point because we understood he was grieving. Your investigation was permitted because it seemed a positive response to the tragedy."

"And there was a chance you'd turn something up," said Prof Croft. "Oh, don't give me that look, headmaster, Grey is one of my best students, he really could have found something." She didn't meet my gaze, but my heart swelled a little all the same.

"Be that as it may," Captain Hawk continued, "now that your investigation has led to the stalking of a teacher and brawling around the Academy grounds, it is time to put an end to it. I am withdrawing our sanction of this and must warn all of you in the strongest terms that continuing to pursue it could well lead to your expulsion. No matter how generous an individual patron you might have." That was a dig at me and Mrs. Gravane, I supposed, but Sergeant Nine shifted uncomfortably too.

"What about finding Veritas's killer?" I asked.

"The official investigation will continue, of course. Veritas was a well-loved member of the faculty and her death hurt us as well. Rest assured that we want to find her killer just as much as you do."

"And if you're not sure about the word of the headmaster, and you should be," said Croft, "I know you will believe mine. I will not rest until we find out who was behind this." Now she did meet my gaze and held it. I looked away first.

Dez mumbled something behind me. Captain Hawk must have heard it too.

"There is a question?"

"Sorry, headmaster, but, what about the accident? The one in the first year?" Dez asked.

"That is a private matter with no relevance to the current circumstances," Hawk said.

Gale cleared his throat. "Captain? Perhaps I might...?"

Captain Hawk nodded, then sat back in his chair, watching us like... well, you get it.

"I have spoken with Professor Croft at length about the... the incident in the first year that you seem so fascinated by. I have satisfied her that it cannot be connected to the current tragedy." He paused, long enough for Prof Croft to nod in agreement. She also shot me a look, that I couldn't quite read.

"While it involves certain confidences that must still be kept," Gale continued, "I promise you there was no ill will between Veritas and me over the incident. As I have told Grey, Veritas and I were never close, but I remain grateful to her for—"

Captain Hawk shifted in his chair, placed his hands on the desk, and Gale stopped, rephrased what he was about to say.

What was going on here?

"I will always be grateful to Veritas for what she did during the incident. I hold her no ill will. And she had none towards me." The phrasing was awkward, Gale's presentation was not as smooth as I expected, but... I didn't hear a lie in it.

"And that must be an end to the matter," Hawk said, his words ringing like steel. "I see your frustration and disappointment. I understand it. But I am telling you to drop it. You are amongst the finest students we have at the Academy, and I do not relish the prospect of losing any of you. Please, respect my wishes and continue your studies with us, but leave the investigation to the authorities. This is a place of learning. Use it as such."

"We can learn by working the case," Pilvi said, chin raised defiantly.

"Ms. Rissanen—"

"Säde."

"Säde. You know the mantra of the Academy as well as anybody. We will help you find the place where what you can do is special. Is needed. For now, for this, that place is not here."

He let his words sit for a moment. "Good. Now that is settled, we can move on. Disruptive though some of your recent activities have been, I have spoken this through with Professors Gale and Croft, and we agree that the best thing for everybody is to get back to normal as quickly as possible. To that end we will, on this occasion, overlook your various campus brawls. I believe, we believe, the lessons have been learned and we may move on." He took a moment to look at each of us in turn. "Let me reiterate, *this* is your second chance. If I hear that you are continuing to investigate against my express wishes, then I will have no choice but to remove you from the Academy. Am I understood?"

I nodded, the others did too.

His expression softened. "I am grateful, and impressed, that you were able to bring both incidents to a close without serious injury."

Sergeant Nine frowned at that but kept quiet.

Captain Hawk clapped to bring the subject to a close. "Well then, that's settled. Dismissed."

"What about Avrim?" asked Gadget Dude. "What happen to Avrim?"

"Ah. Yes. Avrim is, for the moment, suspended. We have contacted his family on Artamantis, and they will come to collect him. To be clear, Avrim is not expelled. We appreciate he has gone through a lot, but we feel he can best heal away from here. When he is ready to return, we will welcome him back."

"Is not fair."

"No, no it's not. Very little about any of this is fair. But it is the best we can do for him. He needs time and support."

#

I caught up to Sergeant Nine as he stomped out of Hawk's office. "Sergeant, I just wanted to say thank you. If you and your squad hadn't intervened, we couldn't have stopped Avrim, and who knows what might have happened."

Nine looked down at me, his face stony. Seeing such a familiar face, the same face as Seventhirtyfour, jaw set, brow furrowed, it was a strange disconnect, like getting signals crossed and having the audio of one transmission play over the video of another. "I told Four we couldn't get involved. He hired the squad. Spent every last credit he had earned to hire four Brontom warriors to stop that Polifan. We did our job."

I blinked. "He managed that quickly."

"We are efficient in all we do, including contract negotiations."

"Well, all the same. Thank you. And thank Seventhirtyfour for me. Hopefully, campus life will settle down now and I can see more of him anyway."

Sergeant Nine's frown deepened. "No."

"What?"

"Brontom seek to be an effective efficient fighting force. We are only as strong as the weakest amongst us. Four has always had a reputation as an outsider. I tried not to prejudge him, but I have seen it for myself. We can help him with that. Help him back to peak efficiency. To do so, he must be isolated from all bad influences." Nine gave me a hard stare.

"Now look, that's not—"

"With you and your group, he has twice jeopardised his education by taking extended off-world jaunts. He has lied to me, his superior, on multiple occasions. Disrupted assigned duties for himself and other members of the squad. And now he has involved us all in matters beyond the scope of our primary mission here. All because of you and your little schemes. Part of the contract he negotiated to bring down the Polifan with minimal injuries was that he would agree to stay away from you if I ordered it. I have so ordered."

"No."

"If you have any respect for Four and his education, you will also respect that order." He turned to leave.

"No, wait, you need to listen," I said. Nine actually paused. But I couldn't think of anything to say that would persuade him. Not a single word.

Sergeant Nine marched away.

# # #

Dazed, confused, head and heart aching, I stumbled away from Hawk's office, down a level, then collapsed into the first unoccupied breakout space I found. Pilvi, Dez and Gadget Dude found me soon after.

"We aren't really going to stop investigating, are we?"

asked Dez.

"How would we continue?" Pilvi said. "No, listen, I agree. I want to keep going, just as much as you, but how? Croft's not going to give us any of the technical evidence now, and if we keep going on interviewing people, all it would take is one person telling Hawk and we would be out. I—I don't know that I can risk that."

"Spy drones?" Gadget Dude suggested.

"Physical evidence of us continuing the investigation? That's riskier than talking to people."

Gadget Dude shrugged.

"What do you say, Grey?" Dez asked. "I can hit the databases some more, there must be more to be found there. And we still haven't seen what that missing record holds. I'm working on it. It's proving tough though."

I shook my head. "I think we stop."

"We can't give up now!" Dez protested.

"This case started with us losing Veritas. Now we've lost Avrim. And Seventhirtyfour. The cost of continuing could be losing any one of us, and I don't know, I don't think I can take much more loss right now."

"Seventhirtyfour?" asked Pilvi.

I explained what Nine had said.

"We could break Seventhirtyfour out," said Dez, "this is just the situation we took Rescueology last year for."

"Seventhirtyfour made this deal. He thought it was worth it. And maybe Nine's right. Maybe I am a bad influence. Seventhirtyfour has the right to the education he wants, and I've done nothing but distract him from it."

"He paid a price to save Avrim," said Pilvi. "I know Seventhirtyfour is hurting over this deal too."

"Yeah. Maybe. Sure." I held up my hands in surrender. "Look, I'm sorry, guys. It's over."

I pulled myself up off the sofa. "I'm out."

CHAPTER 12
FLYING FREE

My name is subject to change and I'm a professional grifter.

My time as Grey had been a lot of fun. I met a lot of interesting types, learned a lot of new things, and I'd be walking away from my time as him with a tidy profit. Make no mistake though, it was time to walk away. One thing a life of drifting around the galaxy from one space station to another taught me, when it stops being fun it's time to move on. I'd taken everything I could from the experience. I wasn't here to get a degree. If I ever needed a degree for anything in the future, I was confident I could have one, so really, what was the point? Besides, I'd stopped an alien invasion. What more could the Academy teach me?

It was also abundantly clear that nobody at the Academy needed me.

I had a bit under three weeks until the passenger ship stopped by the Academy, and I was going to be on it when it left. No need to plot an escape in secret. I went on the net and booked a ticket. I used the name on my ID, but that was just a convenience, I wasn't trying to hide that I was leaving.

Three weeks left. It was tempting just to coast through. But I was still technically Grey until I left, and Grey would go to class. The art of a good con is going method, and if my character would do something, I'd do it. Right up until the moment to strike.

Most lessons were timetabled twice a week, so I had six more sessions of each of my classes. I dug in and squeezed each of them for everything I could get.

I picked up some fresh bruises from Professor Red Ninja's class, but there were some interesting techniques I could use for the future. Sitting in Gale's class was a little weird. The subject of when and how to switch up opponents during crossover fights was not something I'd have much call for but had some subtleties that weren't obvious. It was at least intriguing. Most of the rest of my classes were kind of niche, probably not relevant to my life to come, but learning is never wasted, you never know when one scheme or another might hinge on knowing the best way to bond latex to make a costume. I filed it away.

Then there was Professor Croft's Criminology class. It's astonishing how much you can learn about doing crime by learning how to solve it. I wasn't going to miss a minute of that learning, for sure. Plus playing with chemicals could be fun, and we were right in the middle of a block of lab time, looking at different ways to detect and recognise blood in a crime scene. Chemicals reacted differently for different species' blood, there were pages of reaction formulae to understand and, between you and me, it was a whole lot of fun.

Three days until it was time to leave. My last Criminology class at the Academy.

I added a single drop of the reagent to the last four test tubes. Gave each tube, in turn, a gentle shake. Held the second tube up to the daylight. The solution was changing colour to a distinct orange tint. The 'victim' was a Zalex. All simulated, of course, we didn't bleed one of Gadget

Dude's relatives dry just so thirty students could play with test tubes. Unless that was in the advanced class.

Croft looked up from behind the console on her desk. "That's time, class. Everybody tidy up what you're doing and join me at the front."

There were still 15 minutes left in the lesson. Weird to be finishing lab time early, but we did as we were told. Tidying away reagents and samples, treating everything as though it were real, dealing with the fake biohazards with respect. Even if most of what we used in the practice lab was fake, there were safety protocols to commit to muscle memory for when they might not be.

"We have finished a little early today," said Croft, "because I thought it was high time we had a pop quiz."

There were predictable groans from the group, but Croft just smiled and gestured at her console. The back wall lit up with an image of a room.

A private office by the looks of it. Planetside, I reckoned, and not just because there were trees outside the window, that could be a hologram easily enough. There were too many objects sitting lose on surfaces for this to be a ship or a station. This was a room where the occupant didn't even consider the possibility of gravity failing. He didn't seem like he would be considering much of anything now. He was dead in his chair, body limp in the kind of a way only a dead body could be, at least until rigor set in.

"Everybody taken a good hard look?" Croft asked. "Our victim was murdered less than an hour ago. You are first on the scene and have secured it against interference. Let us say that this is a crime committed by a super. And that you have a suspect in mind. What signs would you look for to confirm that the perpetrator wore power armour? Let's have... Infernus, what would you look for?"

Infernus, a fire-based Cholbren hero, pressed his lips together in thought. "I don't see any scorch marks in the image, so the perp probably didn't jet his way across the room. So, I'd start by looking at the carpet. No obvious footprints there, but power armour is heavy. Some of the carpet fibres are bound to be super crushed. Swing in a microvisualiser and take a look at the carpet."

Croft nodded, made a note on her minipad. "Thanks, Infernus. Okay, different scenario. Your suspect can phase through solid matter. Rare, but not unheard of. Let's say, hmm, maybe Green Blade? What traces do phasers leave?"

Green Blade didn't miss a beat. "Phasing is harder through denser material, so I'd start with the more dispersed areas. I'd check on the make of glass in the window. If it's not especially hardened, our perp is most likely to have phased through there. If they did, there are three ways you can check it. Residual radiation would be the most reliable if you know the energy signature of your suspect. If not, glass is essentially a fluid and phasing through a fluid can affect its properties. See if the glass is softer, more malleable than normal. Alternatively—"

"That's a thorough answer, thank you Green Blade," Croft said, making a lengthy note on her minipad. "Good. Okay. Time for one more. Let's imagine our suspect was a speedster. Why don't we have Grey tackle this one?"

She caught me off guard, I'd been trying to work out what the third thing Green Blade would have tested the window for. I opened my mouth to answer, but nothing came out. I closed it again. Gave the picture another look. The victim's desk was disorganised, I'd taken that as a clue to the scene being planetside, but "I'd start by taking a closer look at that desk. Speedsters are notoriously difficult to quantify because they don't all work the same way. Some generate energy fields as they run, like Kid

Jetstream's lightning, some step a little out of phase with the world to reduce the impact of their passage, some, well there are lots of variations. But the one consistent thing is the amount of kinetic energy, and if they decelerate or even change direction, some of that energy has to go somewhere. I suspect that desk looks like a mess because a whole lot of loose items got blown across it as the speedster powered through."

"Or the victim could just have a messy desk," said Croft. "I think you need to spend a little more time thinking about that one Grey. I'll ask you again next session, let's see what you can come up with. Okay, good work today everyone, class dismissed."

# # #

That was weird.

It was my last session before I left, though Croft didn't know it, so I didn't need to spend more time thinking on the puzzle, but as I ambled back down the stairwell towards my dorm, I couldn't help it.

I'd spent more than a year in Croft's classes, and she'd never once stopped early for a pop quiz. Not that she'd never quizzed us, but that only happened when that was the point of the lesson for the day. So why change the pattern now? Changes of behaviour were important, I'd learned that long before coming to the Academy, but it was also something Croft had taught us. So, for her to be exhibiting a change, it had to be significant.

Could she be trying to tell me about the case? Surely not. Veritas's killer was a speedster? That was one of the power sets we had on our list. Had Croft just confirmed—

"Hello, Grey."

I shook my head to bring myself back to the moment. My field of vision was filled by a golden circle with the letters 'P(k)' in it. I was nose to chest with Seventhirtyfour.

"I thought I'd find you here," he rumbled.

"Hello, Four," I said. I backed up a step so I could see his face.

"You don't need to call me that. When Brontom gather in groups we instinctively call each other by our smallest unique number. Sergeant Nine calls me Four. I always liked Seventhirtyfour better."

"Nine has made it clear I'm a bad influence, maybe if I'm a bit more Brontom about things, he could change his mind."

Seventhirtyfour looked hurt. "Grey, please. I'm worried about you."

"You're worried about me? I got you into all sorts of trouble with your boss. Worry about you, Four, worry about you."

"I've been having premonitions. I can't seem to shake them. I think you're facing a choice, soon. One path leads you away, one keeps you here. One leads you to prison. One leads to… worse. I can't see which is which."

"Sounds like I'm screwed either way. Thanks a bunch."

"Grey!"

Why couldn't he see he was better off without me? "There's only one path ahead of me, Four, and it leads where it leads." I stepped around him and continued down the stairs.

"Just, don't rush into anything, Grey," Seventhirtyfour called after me. I could hear the hurt in his voice.

Three days until I left the Academy.

"Goodbye, Four."

#

I managed to dodge any more goodbyes. That was the plan, a clean break. Everybody could get on with their

126

lives.

Live light, travel light, that's been my philosophy. Wristpad, grapnel gun, toothbrush and a couple of changes of clothes. The bag was chunkier than I remembered from the last time, maybe I should leave one of those sets of clothes behind. I could always get what I needed topside. Heck with it, I could drop anything I didn't need too. I slung the bag over my shoulder and sauntered out through the kitchen. Two of my housemates were in there having coffee. We nodded at each other as I passed through. I still hadn't learned any of their names. Too late now.

The quad was almost deserted as I walked across it. Most of the Academy was in the Dome watching the weekend's Power Ball matches. The ship was already down and docked, I could see its bulk over the back of the terminal building. There was a bounce in my step as I considered getting back into my natural habitat. No more planets for me. If I never set foot on dirt again, it would be too soon.

A handful of passengers from the transport came out from the terminal building as I was heading in. I let them pass instead of trying to go against the flow. Neglected instincts ground into dusty disused action as I assessed each as they passed me. Two of them had the look of salesmen. Likely here to meet with Hawk and try and sell him some new doodad or other. I'd need to watch them a bit before making a play for their valuables. Sales and grifting are too close, some salespeople make excellent targets as they travel with plenty of flash, but some are just a little too wise to the grifting art to make it worth taking them on.

Another delegation, I suspected they were scientists, a little shabbier than the business types, they were probably here to meet with one of the Academy research departments. Easy to con for the most part, but rarely had enough to be worth taking. Not the best choice of marks.

Next through the door was a lone Welatak. He had a hood up on his saline suit, so there wasn't much to go on. He looked a bit rough to be a suit or a scientist. Maybe a student's relative? I caught a glimpse of some tech under his hood, something cybernetic. Why did that ring a bell?

"Excuse me, please?"

"Yes?" I turned to see a young woman, about my age, round-faced with dark hair. She looked nervous, perhaps a little overwhelmed.

"Your name, it wouldn't be Grey would it?" she asked.

"No. Well, I mean, yes. Actually, yes, I'm Grey."

"I thought so, you look like your pictures. Pilvi has told me all about you."

"You know Pilvi, then?"

She laughed a nervous laugh. "Oh, sorry, yes, my name is Kaarina. I am—I was—am Pilvi's girlfriend. You don't know where I can find her, do you?"

"I haven't seen her for a couple of days, but, at a guess, she's probably watching the match, over in the Dome." I pointed, though given that the Dome is an actual dome seven storeys tall in the centre, she could probably have worked that out for herself.

"Oh, I see," Kaarina said, looking a little daunted.

I checked my wristpad. I had time before the ship was due to take off again. "Come on, I'll show you," I said.

"Thank you, Grey."

# # #

The teams to play in any given Power Ball match are determined randomly; whoever was playing when Kaarina and I entered the dome must have been popular, or the match was a close one. Either way, the spectators were out of their seats and roaring in excitement.

Entering at ground level, we passed empty concession booths, while the grandstands rose above us. The building shook with the sound of thousands of rhythmically stomping feet. Everybody in the Dome was either staring at the match or were in it.

The volume rose in pitch, then crashed back down, as, at a guess, someone tried a shot on goal and missed.

"We're never going to find Pilvi in this lot, sorry," I shouted at Kaarina, but she can't have understood, over the din.

She shouted something back to me, but I didn't hear a word. If they ever make a movie of my life, I'm assuming the actress playing Kaarina would be shouting, "We're never going to find Pilvi in this lot," for comic effect. Likely we'll never know.

Instead, the Dome lights changed to red spotlights as the announcer declared, "Power Play: Circuit Breakers."

Somehow the noise doubled in volume, a rising thunder of hope and dread, then the building erupted again, half of the spectators roaring in triumph, the other half wailing in despair.

As the final whistle blew, the wall of noise faded a little, though it was still punctuated by the sound of one team's supporters singing their lungs out.

Almost immediately, people began flooding past us. I pulled Kaarina off to the side. "Keep an eye out for Pilvi, I will too," I said, ears still ringing. "Sorry, it's not always this hectic."

Kaarina said, "That was... Marwick is an agri world, I don't think we have this many people on our entire planet. I've certainly never seen so many people in one room before!"

I was jostled by a Germile student I didn't recognise as the crowd streamed past us. I shot him a dirty look, but he was long vanished in the throng. "From the way Pilvi spoke about her home, I'd assumed it would be fully settled." I still had to raise my voice, but conversation was now possible.

"Oh, it is. But if your economy is based on producing food for export, you minimise the number of people eating it locally. The farms are vast, mostly worked by drones. Pilvi's family were my neighbours growing up; they lived 300km away."

"That's quite a neighbourhood."

"She was always worth the trip." Kaarina smiled, shyly.

"Does she know you're coming to visit?"

"No. I'm worried that I'm kind of ambushing her. But— we left things so strangely. I need to know what's going on with her."

"Strange, how?"

"Just, distant. And not just from me. She came home for summer and didn't come to visit me at all. That was... tough, but I dealt with it. We always knew there was a risk with a long-distance relationship, that we'd grow apart. That's just... but I was strong. Message received."

This conversation was rapidly heading in a direction I didn't feel equipped to handle. "Sure," I said, trying to sound sympathetic while frantically scanning the crowd for Pilvi's glowing hair.

"But I got talking to Vesa, Pilvi's younger brother? She had hardly stayed with them either. Pilvi visited their farm for one evening before going on a camping trip, alone, that lasted most of the holiday. Pilvi loves her family, and they love her. Why would she—she has powers now, I hear. Did they change her?"

I opened my mouth to say of course not, but Pilvi had been distant with us too. Not camping in the wilds for weeks distant, but "I don't know," was the only answer I could give.

"I see her! Pilvi! Pilvi!"

Light flared, and Pilvi was there, hugging Kaarina.

I stood awkwardly to one side for long enough to realise this wasn't a 'me' moment, then faded back into the crowd and left them to it.

I spent a few minutes, letting the crowd wash around me, working up the energy to make a break across the quad. Three times I checked my wristpad for the time, three times I was cutting it finer. Eventually, a pair of tall battlesuits walked out together, and taking a deep breath, I ducked into their shadow. They weren't a real roof, but they'd do to get me moving. Still time to make my flight, but I'd have to hustle, so hustle I did.

I checked in with my 'real' ID and boarded the ship.

Time to put the Academy behind me.

CHAPTER 13
SHAGGY DOGS

The antigrav covered most of it, but there were still enough Gs to push me back into my seat. I did, I confess, look back as the Academy fell away behind me, rapidly vanishing to become a dot on the coast of planet C23580's jungle. In no time at all, we were free and in the black. We were still accelerating, but now the antigrav could keep up and the warning lights blinked off.

This was not a well-travelled route. The passenger cabin could accommodate a hundred passengers, but there were only twenty of us dotted around the cabin. Two had boarded with me, the rest were on a long haul and for them, the Academy had been no more than another stop on their journeys.

I guess that was me, too, now.

This was the correct choice. Definitely. The Academy had been good for me, no question, but all good things must etc., and now was time for etc.. And if there was a pang as I heard the jump engines wind up, well, that's just part of growing up, right? Moving on?

How long before anyone noticed I'd gone? Nobody saw me leave, and the identity I'd used to book passage was not one that was widely known. Would people look for me around campus? Would anyone care enough to look? Ugh. No, I'm not into woe is me self-pity, life's too short. Some people would notice and look. Seventhirtyfour if nobody else, assuming Nine let him.

Once I was safely away, I'd send messages back. Mrs. Gravane at least should know to stop paying my tuition. I felt a little guilty that she would never get her return on her investment, but I was hardly the first person to disappoint someone by dropping out of college.

#

Two days later, we docked at Plenitude station. I'd booked to travel further, but my feet were itching, so I disembarked anyway. I immediately headed to the Plenitude market—they had everything—and I came out the other side with a completely new look. I lifted a loud-print shirt from one stall, a cheap but bulky camera from another, a satchel and a cap from two more, and finally a stack of travel brochures to stuff in the satchel. I could have afforded them all (the brochures were free) but I had to test my reflexes, and I kept things simple.

The best disguises are the ones that let you move around unnoticed. Subtle, nondescript street clothes to make you forgettable, or a uniform to blend into the background. The most *fun* disguises are the ones where people will remember the wrong things about you. The shirt was a fashion disaster, that clashed with my cap, I took photos of everything and showed my brochures to anyone careless enough to stand too close to me. Waxing lyrical about all the amazing sights I was planning to see or had seen. Mega Tourist. Not a recommended approach for covert agents, but super entertaining. I pitched my laugh to loud and braying and went about the station making a nuisance of myself. When I got bored with that game, I booked passage on another ship travelling in a random direction.

At the next station, I switched flights and persona

again. Now I clutched a battered briefcase to my crumpled suit jacket while wearing a worried expression and starting at every unexpected noise. This character was a nervous flyer and spent most of the next leg of my wander dabbing his brow and worrying out loud about the quarterly financials.

I travelled like that for a week, switching between one broad character and another with each change of ship. None of these disguises, and they weren't disguises in the traditional sense, would have fooled anyone for a long period, but each was fun to do for a day or two, and I was working out the kinks, remembering techniques I'd not used for a year or more. Once I felt ready, I stopped, looked around, and found out where I was.

Tamban Station. Further towards galactic north than I'd expected to be but arriving at unexpected places was always part of the fun. I'd never been here before because it had never sounded like the kind of place that people visited. I mean, plenty of people did, that's why there was a station here at all, but it wasn't really on the way anywhere interesting, or even on the junction between routes to interesting places. It was something of a jump drive blind alley. People only came here if they had a reason to come *here*.

And after an hour or two wandering the corridors, I was hard-pressed to think why people would want that. The station was dour, utilitarian and even its market was unimaginative. Below us, Tamban the planet was inhabited, but it was an unremarkable industrial world, rich in materials that were useful but dull. A workhorse of a station over a workhorse of a world. No doubt people lived, loved and prospered here, but there wasn't much to recommend it to a galactic wanderer as well-travelled as I was.

Perfect.

I needed a place to run a scam or two, just to get the imagination firing again, and this was just the sort of place I'd find a target. A few hushed conversations and I found the names of a couple of local loan sharks; the sort of people that were most often described as "if you are desperate, you could try them, but I'd stay clear if I were you." And the name of a dive bar with a reputation for ripping off tourists. It sounded like the perfect cocktail for an old classic.

I went through the clothes I'd accrued over the last week and picked out the perfect ensemble: crumpled suit jacket over the loud shirt, faded jeans and a pair of chunky work boots that had seen better days. I looked like a guy with no budget or taste trying to dress to impress. I dumped the rest of my disguises into the recycler; I'd get more when I needed them. Suitably attired, I headed to the bar.

It was dimly lit, and quiet. I'd picked my time of day carefully, for this one I didn't want to get lost in the crowd. Instead, I hiked myself up onto a barstool with a sigh, and put my minipad on the counter, tapping it in a way that looked like a nervous tic.

The barman shuffled over; he was a scruffy looking human, wearing station overalls that hadn't been cleaned in a while. "What can I get you?" he drawled.

I clattered three old credit sticks on the counter. "A whisky?" I said hopefully.

He pushed them around with a finger, looking dubious, but he picked them up all the same to check their balances. He drained two of them, took the remainder of the cost off a third and handed it back. "Sure. Coming right up." I knew what had been on those sticks, I'd just paid a heavy mark-up.

"Just need a bit of courage," I said, as he poured my drink.

"Yeah?"

"Yeah. I've got an appointment with a bank. To apply for a business loan."

To his credit, he paused before giving me my drink. "You sure you want whisky on your breath, son?"

I nodded. "It's not really a bank. It's more... have you heard of the Q'doc brothers?"

He winced but handed me my drink. "That's quite a meeting to be heading to."

I tapped my minipad again. "I've got no choice. The investment money ran out months ago, and I owe so many people. I need to get on top of it. I just need a bit more time to sell this."

"You want to sell your pad?"

"The algorithm on it, yes. I used to have a server room, and a dozen consoles running it, but I sold them all off, one by one, and now, I have one cruddy minipad left. This is it. This is the last copy. If I can just make someone see, it could change everything!" I let myself sound a little manic and downed my drink. Thankfully, it was so watered down it barely hit me. "But nobody has. Not yet. I just need a bit more time. As it is, I'm down to my last..." I looked at the balance on my credit stick and made a face.

"What's your algorithm do?"

I opened my mouth to tell him, but let my teeth click shut again. "Sorry, it's proprietary."

"Sure."

I put a nervous expression on. "These Q'doc brothers. I know they're a bit... they wouldn't just take this off me, would they?"

He shrugged. "Don't know them. You hear talk. It ain't pretty."

I checked my wristpad. "It's time. Listen. Can I... leave this minipad with you? I'll pick it up again after my meeting. I'm just... suddenly I'm not sure I want to take it into the lion's den."

"I could put it behind the bar, I guess."

"You're a life-saver. I'll put your name in the acknowledgements when I sell the algorithm."

"Sure." He took my minipad and propped it up next to the menus. "Good luck with your meeting."

"Thanks."

I ducked out of the bar, looking harried. Once out of sight, I ambled to the market. I tried browsing for twenty minutes, but nothing leapt out at me, so I installed myself in a cafe. As I sipped my third-rate coffee, I logged into my Gravane corporate mail account on my wristpad. It wasn't an account I used much, but they'd set me one up when Mrs. Gravane started paying my tuition. It looked super official, which was nice. I sent my regular mail account a quick message. My wristpad beeped as the message arrived, but I was careful not to open it. Instead, I sampled a slice of second-rate cake and finished my coffee.

The me that walked into the bar an hour later looked utterly defeated. Shoulders slumped, shirt untucked, hair mussed. I'd clearly been roughed up a bit, though no bruises showed up yet. I winced as I craned myself up onto the barstool.

The barman came over to me, was he stepping a little more eagerly? "How did it go?" he asked, setting down another whisky for me without asking.

"Not well," I sighed. I waved away the drink. "Thanks, but I shouldn't be spending my last credits on alcohol."

He tutted. "It's on the house. They didn't give you the loan?"

I shook my head. "They weren't interested. Thought

I was a lost cause. Did have their goons punch me a bit, so I didn't feel completely neglected." I tried a laugh, but it turned into a wince. "When the local legbreakers think you're a bad investment—maybe it's time to give up."

"That's a shame, man." He passed back my minipad from behind the bar.

"Thanks. Is this really how it all ends? I was so sure. So certain I could make it big. Now, I don't even know how I'm going to make rent next week."

"Serious?"

"Like a pulse bomb," I said.

He drummed his fingers on the countertop. "Listen, you seem a nice guy. Hate to see you this way. How much is your rent?"

"Three hundred, why?"

"I've been meaning to buy a new minipad. What say, I buy this off you?" He picked my minipad back up off the counter. "It seems in good nick. What say I give you three-fifty for it? That's not a bad offer for second hand. And if you're not using it anymore?"

Got him.

I opened my mouth to accept, but instead, I took the minipad back off him. *No.* "Look, I get that you know nothing about software development," I said. I slipped the minipad into my satchel and tucked my shirt in. Straightened my jacket and my spine. "That's understandable, no reason you would, but really, this is a dumb scam. You saw I was wearing a wristpad too, right? Surely it must have occurred to you that the message you read on the minipad might have come to me too?"

"What message?"

I tapped the minipad screen to show the alert. "'From Grey at the Gravane Corporation, subject, Algorithm sale, I am pleased to offer 20,000 credits for exclusive'... well the rest is cut off, but you got the idea, I'm sure."

The barman's faced reddened, and his brows dipped. "Are you accusing me? I try to help a guy out—"

"Oh, please. You thought if you owned the only copy of my 'algorithm' you could turn your 350 into 20,000 overnight. I don't mind being hustled, but I object to being stupided. What were you going to do about the password on the pad? How would you know what to hand over to the Gravanes? Never mind the intellectual property rights and my digital fingerprints all over my 'code'. Really, that was idiotic. You weren't trying to help me out, you were taking advantage of someone at the end of their rope."

"Get out. You're barred."

"Yeah, yeah."

I downed my free weak whisky and stalked out of the bar, the barman shouting at my back. I was shaking with rage. That was not how that was supposed to go. It had all gone flawlessly. Three fifty would have been enough to replace my minipad and still come out ahead. Not a huge profit, but I'd never in my life chased after the big fish. Exactly who was I angry at? Him? Me? The Academy?

The Academy. For nudging my sense of right and wrong, so that this... it still felt fun, but it also felt... dammit. Well, this would put a crimp in my grifting if I didn't get a handle on it quickly. Time to get off Tamban, find somewhere new to work a different con that wouldn't tweak my sense of fair play so much.

When did I even acquire a sense of fair play?

Perhaps my mistake had been in leaving the Academy as a passenger. It made life too comfortable, too easy. For the next jump, I should probably work my passage. A bit of good hard honest graft would set me straight. At the very least it should remind me what a chore honest work could be.

I had no contacts here, no one to give me a reference except the barkeep, and I doubted he'd be nice. If I couldn't call in a favour to get a job, I'd need to join the recruitment scramble. A pain, but I'd never waited in the scramble too long. It was step one in getting my mojo back, so I took a moment to get my bearings then headed to the docking ring.

It was the wrong time of day for the big recruitment rush. That happened first thing in the working morning when anyone looking for work would huddle around the dockmaster's office. The dockmaster or ships' agents would call out what they needed, and whoever matched the criteria could shout up. I was rather good at the shouting out part, whether I matched the criteria or not.

Despite the time of day, there were still a few transients lounging around the hallway outside the office. I leaned on the wall by the lifts and studied them before approaching. They were generally the beefier types, there looking to pick up short-term loading work. I'd stick out like a sore thumb amongst them, but if the right job came up that would work in my favour. Odds were nothing would turn up today, but it was never too early to start being a known face around the scramble.

I bounced off the wall and took a step. Paused. Two Galactic Patrol officers approached the scramble from the far end of the hall.

What are they doing here?

They were in full uniform, dark blue accented with shining copper. The male Frantium officer scanned the transients in the scramble, while his partner, a human female, checked data on her wristpad. No doubt they were here on business. They didn't linger on any of the people outside the dockmasters, dismissed them all quickly. Whoever they were looking for, their description didn't match the would-be stevedores.

My fingertips tingled. I didn't look like a stevedore.

Station Security were one thing, you'd see them all over the place, but the Galactic Patrol were another matter entirely. They were generally the ones to swoop in after the fact and scoop up the baddest of the bad. The actual criminal types. I'd tangled with Station Security on countless occasions but never tussled with GP. If they were here actively working an investigation, something weird was going on. I didn't like it.

Backtracking into the lifts was appealing, but if they spotted me and were after me (why would they be after me, what had I done?) trapping myself in a lift would be doing their work for them.

Instead, I ducked into a side corridor. Offices, break room, storage. Nothing interesting, but there was a hatch at the far end, and I fancied putting that between me and the coppers.

If they weren't after me, then all the detour would cost me would be a little time, I had an endless supply of that. If they were after me... But why? What had I done? I'd stolen a few odds and ends and almost conned a barman. That was hardly enough to raise Station Security's blood pressure, no way they'd sic the GP on me for that. So why was every instinct I had screaming at me to run? I mean, other than that being the way my luck ran?

The hatch led onto a service corridor that ran around the docking ring, allowing station personnel access to the machinery of working docking bays. Most of the side rooms off it would require a security pass to gain entry. I had an old cloning tool on my wristpad but hadn't had a reason to copy anyone's pass so far this trip. The data pass that I *did* have installed on my wristpad was nearly two years out of date and for a different part of the galaxy. I was stuck on this circle until I found another unsecured hatch. It still gave me more manoeuvring room than being trapped in a lift.

I wasn't alone. This was a working area, and while it was far from crowded, people in station overalls passed me in both directions. I got a few curious looks, but none of them stopped me to ask me what I was doing there. None of them lingered long enough for me to clone the security pass on their wristpads either, alas.

I followed the curve of the corridor around for five minutes, covering maybe a third of the circumference. Up ahead, I caught a flash of blue and copper. I stepped back, flattened myself against the wall. More Galactic Patrol. What was going on?

She was talking to a dockworker. I strained to listen over the steady background hum of a space station. I lost most of it thanks to the burst of engine noise from a nearby departing ship, but the copper seemed to be on her comm.

"...doing down here?" the dockworker asked.

"—looking for... *Justice Academy*—" was all I caught of the GP's response.

Damn. My instinct was on the money, they were here for me. Why did two plus two always have to equal four? Also, I didn't appreciate her putting air quotes around Justice Academy. Did she think it was a joke?

I looked back over my shoulder. Retracing my steps felt futile, but I wasn't confident I could slip by that GP unseen, not in this narrow corridor. What I wouldn't give for a passing carnival to hide in. I needed another option.

The problem was, I'd already been looking for other ways out, and so far, the closest option was not great. I backtracked ten meters to a grate in the floor. If the station was as standard as it seemed, the panel should lead to an access tube that ran parallel to the corridor. There in case maintenance needed to get to the pipes, cables and conduits that ran underfoot. Or, rather, it gave access for repair drones. For reasons I won't go into, I had discovered that it was possible to squeeze myself into the duct if the need arose. And right now, things looked to be arose-ing. It was a tight fit, narrower than the corridor itself, not even space to crawl, I'd have to pull myself along it. Hard to be subtle, but it would carry me directly under the GP's feet. If she realised I was there, I had absolutely no way to escape.

Well then, I just had to make sure she didn't realise I was there.

I lowered myself into the duct, pushing my feet back down the tube. I lay flat on my back and lowered the panel back into place above me, taking pains to do it as quietly as possible.

It wasn't quite pitch black. Tiny pinpricks of light blinked on a few of the devices in the tube, but all they did was emphasise the blackness around me. It was a tighter fit than I remembered from the last time I'd had cause to use a route like this. I had to pull my shoulders in, the walls pressed in on me. The smooth, cold metal of the floor on my back rumbled faintly to the note of the station's background hum. The ceiling was so close that when I breathed out, I felt my own exhalations on my face, reflected back at me. Breathing in was worse. As my chest rose, it brushed against the ceiling.

Still better than there being a sky above my head.

I wriggled. Feet, palms, the motion of my whole body driving me along the tube, centimeter by centimeter. It was tough and slow work. These access tubes weren't designed to be easy to traverse. If a chase ensued down here, it would not be a quick one.

Occasional footsteps echoed above me. The sound surrounded me like a drumbeat, and my imagination conjured images of the metal flexing above me, pressing in at the sound of a particularly heavy tread. I dismissed the thought and pushed on.

My spatial awareness has always been good. I was confident that my wriggling had gotten me past the one copper, but getting past was not enough, I had to get enough around the curve to be out of sight. Perhaps further even than that, there was no guarantee she'd stay in one place. I pushed on.

Why were Galactic Patrol after me? That's what I didn't get. Thinking about it, they wouldn't be called in for anything I'd done here. The only reason I'd ever heard of them getting involved in an active investigation was when the suspect left the system where the crime had been committed. I just hadn't done anything to put myself on their radar. Not recently, anyway. And if they were looking for Grey from the Justice Academy, then it had to be about something recent.

I took a moment to catch my breath. Wriggling was hard work and used muscles that didn't usually get much of a workout. I relaxed as much as I could inside my metal tube and tried to think of something, anything, that would get them breathing down my neck. If I couldn't work that out, I had no way of knowing how serious they would be about it. If I didn't know how serious they were, it made the calculus of what risks to take that much harder.

This couldn't be about Veritas's murder? Could it? I thought that was all settled. But maybe... maybe me leaving the Academy had made me look guilty? They still couldn't have any evidence though, because, simply, I hadn't done it. And surely, they would need some hard physical evidence to convince the Galactic Police to get involved. No, it couldn't be about Veritas—I just couldn't think what else it could be.

I wouldn't solve it trapped in a duct; I wriggled on.

CHAPTER 14
REMAINING SILENT

Eventually, I could wriggle no more. If I went too far, I'd just end up back where I started. By my reckoning, I'd made it another third of the way around the ring, and it was time to surface again, while I still had the strength to move at all. My whole body was complaining at the abuse. Muscles I didn't remember having felt like they were on fire. At the next access panel above me, I paused, waited for the echo of footsteps to fade, then gently pushed the panel open. For the moment, the corridor was empty. I slid up and out, replacing the panel in one swift action. It made a soft thunk as it settled back into place, not loud enough to carry far.

I stood, arm and leg muscles protesting. I couldn't linger, but I needed to get the blood flowing again. I took a moment to stretch, braced against the corridor wall. Willing a cramp in my left leg to quietude.

Right. Out of here.

The third hatch I tried opened without a pass. It let into another short corridor, lined with offices. I ran along it, turning my face away from the security camera by instinct. No doubt that was how they'd tracked me to this area of the station. I hadn't been taking precautions before now, I hadn't known anyone had a reason to find me. It really put a crimp in my ability to get around. It definitely ruled out the two easiest ways to get off station. There would be

147

a camera at every departure desk, and certainly, the area around the dock master's would be covered. I wouldn't be joining the scramble this time.

I needed on to a ship, and it would have to be... unconventionally. Fortunately, that was very much on brand.

There were routes into some of the docking bays from below or above. Above would be harder, but probably safer. On balance, most people trying to cover the sneaky ways into places tend to look down. Everybody has heard of escape tunnels, right? In my experience, only Cholbren and Polifan thought about *up* as a secret route. Which made it my safest bet, if still far from certain.

I took a ladder rather than a lift, climbing two levels despite my legs' protest. I needed to get behind one of the departures areas, and I'd need an up-to-date pass on my wristpad.

I slipped back into the market area, scooped up a new hat and shirt from stalls with distracted owners. The key to an effective disguise in a populated area like the market was not changing your appearance so much as it was changing your profile. People scanning a crowd for a guy with dark hair will tend to dismiss blond people. A light-coloured cap was almost as good as dying your hair in the right circumstances, and a baggy shirt could add a few kilos, particularly when worn on top of your other clothes. I wasn't trying to look like someone else, just less like me. It wouldn't hold up under any scrutiny, but in a crowd, it was hard to be scrutinised. Facial recognition would still be a problem though, so I kept a careful eye on camera positions and angles.

I spotted a crewman taking a break in a cafe, I slotted myself into a seat at the table behind him. A few taps on my wristpad and I set it to trying to clone his pass. It would have been easier if I still had my Ripper. I'd given that up when I'd tried to turn a new page after joining the Academy though. A few seconds later, my wristpad gave me a frowny face icon. I hadn't updated the infiltration software in a long time. I changed a few settings and tried again. If I couldn't get his pass... would I be stuck here? I could try other station staff, but their countermeasure software would be at least as good as this guy's.

Another frowny face.

No. I needed this pass—

The air conditioning above my head kicked in. It tickled my hair. It must be working overtime to counter all these people in the market. I looked up; there was no vent there. Where was the breeze coming from?

Unexpected airflow in a space station is never good. I was halfway to my feet before I'd even thought; I didn't have to think about where the nearest emergency hatch was, I always knew. Ten years living in pressurised boxes hanging in a vacuum will do that for you.

I was still too slow.

Not fully out of my seat, I caught a blast of air in the chest. It picked me up off my feet and slammed me into the nearest bulkhead.

People around me shrieked in alarm and scattered.

I gasped a lungful of air and held it, heart racing. If the whole market depressurised, well, I'd let the air out slowly to compensate for the pressure differential if I had to, but I'd rather over-oxygenate first. Even as I did so, something odd struck me. The people around me, after the initial shock, had stopped to gape. This was no air leak; it was impossibly localised. There was no sign of panic you'd expect from a catastrophic accident. The wind just kept blowing, kept the pressure on me, pinning me to the wall.

I let myself breathe again. Though the wind did snatch at my breaths, I didn't seem to be in danger of suffocating.

That established, and it only took a frantic few seconds to do so, having ruled out what this wasn't, working out what it was took priority. I looked in the direction the wind was coming from, blinking against the air pressure. A figure clad in crimson and gold hovered next to a nearby stall, one hand raised, pointing at me.

Apogee.

The air flowed around him, pushing at me, then presumably swirling back towards him. Behind him, a squad of four Galactic Patrol officers fanned out, stun bolters primed and ready.

"Grey, you are under arrest," Apogee said.

"You have the wrong person," I gasped, shouting to be heard over the torrent of air. "My name is Adrian Painton," I lied.

Pinned against the wall, fight against it as I might, I couldn't even pull an arm away from it. Maybe I could move along it. I inched my hand down towards my grapnel gun. If I could reach it, maybe I could grapnel out of the air blast.

"He's going for a gun!" one of the Galactic Patrol officers shouted.

Spots of red and orange burst across my vision, and everything went dark.

# # #

Oh. Right. Galactic Patrol stun pistols. So, *that's* what they felt like.

I blinked twice, forced my eyes to stay open, stared up at the blank steel ceiling. The bench I lay on was cold and hard. A distinct tang of disinfectant hung in the air, but not enough of the typical ambient sounds of a hospital.

It wasn't the first time I'd woken up in the station brig. It *was* the first time I'd merited my own cell. The normal routine involved waking up with a motley crew of undesirables, occasionally one or more of them would be going through my pockets looking for contraband Security might have missed. Waking up alone in a cramped single cell was quite a different experience. Muffled voices echoed off the walls, but the solid plate door between me and the outside world was unyielding.

I swung up into a sitting position and took a moment to check my own pockets for over-looked contraband. My wristpad was gone. Ditto, my grapnel gun. They'd taken everything except some contraband lint. I couldn't immediately see how that would help me escape, but you never know.

Stretching my arms wide, I could touch both side walls of the cell. The facilities were basic and unappealing, still splashed with drops of what I hoped was the disinfectant I could smell. There was a small drain in the centre of the floor, a small air vent up near the ceiling. No hidden access panels or hatches to conduits. Designers of cells could be most unobliging in that regard. I was going nowhere until the Galactic Patrol came to open the cell door.

I'd save my energy. The narrow dimensions of the cell made sleeping difficult, but I propped myself up against the wall, stretched my legs out along the bench and closed my eyes.

# # #

I dozed for about an hour. I woke to the sound of the small hatch in the cell door being slid open. A copper stared in at me.

"You're awake," she said.

"That much I knew," I confessed. "It's the rest I'm a little hazy on. Nobody has read me my rights, or even told me why I'm locked up here."

She closed the hatch without comment.

Five minutes later, at a guess, the door opened, and Apogee stepped inside. Two GP officers, dressed in their blues and copper stood behind him to, presumably, stop me making a break for it. Redundant, as with that many bodies in my tiny cell there was nowhere for me to go.

"What's going on, Professor," I asked. "What am I doing in this cell? What are you doing here at all? Don't you have classes to teach?"

"The officers will deal with the protocols in a moment, I wanted to speak to you alone first," Apogee said.

I nodded at his guards. "But they wouldn't let you at a prisoner alone, I see."

"Please, Grey, this is serious."

"Then tell me what this is about because right now I'm finding it all a bit ridiculous."

Apogee folded his arms across his chest and stared down at me in what was, I suspect, intended to be an intimidating manner.

"Sorry," I said, intimidated.

"You have been arrested under the authority of the Justice Academy's agreement with the Galactic Patrol and are to be returned to the jurisdiction where your alleged crimes were committed."

"You're marching me back to the Academy? Why? What am I supposed to have done?"

"You have been arrested under suspicion of the murder of Professor Anress 'Veritas' Delorn, and the attempted murder of the first-year student David Forsythe."

The Veritas accusation seemed kind of inevitable, but "Who is David Forsythe?" I asked.

One of the coppers in the doorway coughed. "Excuse me, sir, there are protocols to be observed."

Apogee studied me for a long moment, before turning

on his heel and leaving the cell without another word.

The coppers formally charged me and read me my rights. When they got to the bit about lawyers, I interrupted.

"I need to call my lawyer," I said.

They continued their protocol but did summon a comm drone when they finished. I didn't have a lawyer, hadn't needed one before now. I could usually talk my way out of whatever, but I'd never been accused of murder before. This time I'd need some heavy-duty legal support, and while I didn't have any, I knew someone who did. I didn't relish the call though, I hadn't quite gotten around to telling Mrs. Gravane that I was dropping out, despite her generous scholarship. I wasn't sure how she'd take the news when I was already in a station brig, lightyears from where she expected me to be.

"Mr. Grey," she said. Her image stuttered above the comm drone. It was night wherever she was, and she was dressed for a fancy gathering of some sort. An opera, maybe. That's what rich people go to, right? It was the least 'business' I'd ever seen her, but the outfit was no less severe.

"Hi, Mrs. Gravane, um."

"You have left the Academy," she said.

"I... yes. How did you know?"

"Your friend the Brontom contacted me when you went missing. I informed him I did not know your whereabouts."

"Right. I've wanted to call to let you know, myself, but circumstances kind of got away from me."

"That does fit your established pattern."

I had hoped to be able to gauge her reaction to the news myself before I asked for a favour. But she'd already gotten through her reaction and was getting down to some serious terseness.

She looked away. "Yes, I shall be right there," she said to someone I couldn't see. She turned back to me, her face set in stony disappointment. "Now, if there's nothing else?"

"I've been arrested," I blurted. "I'm accused of a murder and an attempted murder at the Academy."

She could have told me to deal with it myself. I'd have deserved it, for snubbing her generosity at the least. She could have asked me if I was guilty. That didn't seem to even occur to her. Instead, she just asked, "Where are you?"

"Tamban Station."

"I shall make some calls. Do not do anything stupid," she said and cut the comm.

# # #

Within fifteen minutes the reactions began. First, they moved me to a new room. Still a cell, with locks and guards and all the rest, but a much more comfortable place with a bed rather than a steel bench, a desk, a chair, and en suite bathroom facilities rather than a disinfectant-drenched chemical toilet in the corner of the room. There was even a food dispenser, and if the choices were limited, they were better than normal brig-fare.

Nobody came to pester me for an hour. I spent the time stretched out on the bed looking for potential escape routes. Not to escape, not yet, I was very aware of Mrs. Gravane's instruction not to try anything stupid, but I wanted options in case of extreme circumstances. There was no handy Grey-sized service duct entrance, but three panels looked to be more recent additions, suggesting they were covering something. Maybe something useful. It wasn't the moment to start disassembling the walls, but

I felt better knowing I had at least potential options.

I amused myself with planned restructuring, until the hatch opened. Apogee stepped inside, or, rather, Professor Gale as he was in his tweeds, not his uniform. He took the seat, uninvited. I stayed on the bed, didn't bother to sit up.

"You have a surprising political reach, Grey," he said.

"I just called someone who might know a lawyer I could talk to."

"Hmm. You still don't seem to be taking this very seriously."

"That might be because it's still ridiculous. I didn't murder Veritas. I *liked* Veritas. I was busy trying to find out who *did* murder her until you and Captain Hawk told me to stop. And as for this attempted murder..."

He said nothing, just took off his glasses to polish them.

"Ah, but you can't talk to me about this, can you? Not until my counsel is present. You're just here in case I volunteer something unprompted, right?"

He put his glasses back on. "No. This time I am here in my role as your teacher. I have a responsibility not just to see justice done, but to see that my students are treated fairly. Your political play has extended your stay here. I intended to take you straight back to the Academy, but now we must both await the arrival of your counsel. She has sought an injunction that we cannot question you until she arrives in person. A request that people who have never heard of you, or the Academy, have chosen to grant. Tamban is too far off the beaten track. It will be at least a week before she arrives."

"So, I'm stuck in this room for a week?"

"At least. I had hoped to have you back at the Academy and a hearing scheduled in that time, but now the whole thing is going to be drawn out. And if my alter ego is on hand to make sure you don't escape, I am here to make sure you're treated well. The two responsibilities are not contradictory."

"Sure."

"So, is there anything you need?" He held up a hand to forestall my answer. "Please, fight the urge to flippancy."

I shut my mouth and took a moment to carefully consider his question. "No, thank you, Professor."

He nodded and stood. "The guards will be able to find me if you do need anything."

"I did have one question, I'm not sure if you can answer it."

He paused at the doorway. "Ask."

"How did you even find me? I had no idea I was coming here, how did you?"

"You are not the only person with access to precognitives. I got here before you. Technically, you found me."

"Go me."

He left me contemplating the nature of free will in a galaxy where precognitives existed.

# # #

I stewed in my comfortable cell for ten days. Apogee, coppers and Station Security checked in on me from time to time, but otherwise, I sat alone. Sat, by then, in a rather unflattering prison uniform. On the third day I asked Apogee for some net access, he didn't grant it but did bring me a pad loaded with Academy textbooks. I spotted a few legal textbooks among them too. It wasn't much, but it was that or spiral around the whys whats whos and hows of my arrest. I chose the textbooks.

When the hatch opened on the eleventh day and a forty-something woman I'd never seen before strode in, I knew things were moving again.

She took the chair, so I perched on the edge of my bed

and gave her a smile. She looked familiar, but I couldn't place where I'd seen her before.

"You're my lawyer?" I asked.

She folded her hands in her lap. The mannerism was so familiar, it sparked the connection. I'd seen her mother do the same thing many times.

"You're a Gravane," I said.

"My name is Serrenessa Gravane, I believe you know my brother, Mirabor."

I ran through what I knew about the Gravane clan. Mirabor said he was the youngest of six. Mrs. Gravane had spoken of her family often. "Serrenessa. You're the one who went into politics, right?"

She gave a thin-lipped grimace. "I did indeed 'go into' politics. However, before being elected to the Galactic Senate, I ran a prestigious law firm. My credentials remain valid, so mother asked me to represent you in this matter."

"You're a senator? And you've come to the back end of nowhere to defend someone you've never met?"

"First, I am Gravane," she said, and that seemed like all the answer I was getting, but then she added, "The Galaxy is a large place, the affairs of the Senate are often conducted remotely. My presence here will not prevent me from attending to my wider duties."

"Oh. Good."

"You have impressed mother, that much is clear. I, however, reserve the right to make my judgement. I have questions and it is in your absolute best interest that you answer me truthfully at all times. You need not fear eavesdroppers. Even should the Patrol officers attempt to breach attorney-client privilege by listening in, my senatorial privacy field would stymie the attempt." She tapped her wristpad.

"Sure. Ask away."

"First, to the best of your knowledge, were your actions responsible for the death of Professor Delorn?" She checked her wristpad. "Also known as Veritas?"

"I didn't kill her, no."

"That is not what I asked. Please refrain from editorialising. In the interview which is to follow, you must answer only what is asked, no more."

"And no less, got it," I said.

"The 'less' rather depends on the question," she said, primly. "So, I ask again, to the best of your knowledge, were your actions responsible for the death of Professor Delorn?"

"To the best of my knowledge, no."

"Better. Did you assault the student David Forsythe?"

"I did not." It wasn't a lie. I still didn't know who Forsythe was, but since I'd not assaulted anyone, I was still confident I was being truthful.

"Now, tell me a lie," she said.

"I never lie," I said.

She tapped a few commands on her wristpad.

"Well then, defending an innocent man. How refreshing."

"Innocent of these crimes, definitely," I said with a wry smile.

"Do not editorialise," she said, sharply.

"Sorry."

"The facts of this case are simple. If they are set on a trial, I am confident we can win. My intent is to avoid that eventuality, but this end can only be achieved if you follow my instructions during the interrogation. Answer factually. Answer concisely. Do not offer information that is not asked for. Avoid flippancy. If I tell you to shut up, shut up. Is that understood?"

"Yes, ma'am. If I want to avoid a trial, I keep quiet. I can do that."

I suspect we both knew that was a lie.

# # #

Two Patrol officers escorted me to the interview suite. They sat me in one seat beside the table, Serrenessa moved the other from my side into the corner, and sat there, working on her wristpad. "The Government won't wait on you, Grey," she told me.

Apogee joined us a few minutes later, he was in uniform, though without his mask. A Patrol officer walked beside him, carrying an evidence box and a couple of datapads. They took the seats opposite me, Apogee cast a glance over at the Senator, but said nothing to her.

He gestured through a control field on the desk. "Begin recording," Apogee said. "Apply date and time stamp. Present are Professor Simon Gale, Detective Sergeant Worrel Krade. I am here representing the authorities of the jurisdiction in which the alleged crimes took place. DS Krade is here as the appointed representative of the Galactic Patrol." He paused, and I had to bite my tongue to stop saying something to fill the gap.

"Also present, Senator Serrenessa Gravane, representing..." he gestured to me.

"Grey," I said.

"Please state your full name for the record," Apogee said.

I opened my mouth, but Serrenessa interrupted. "My client chooses to be identified as Grey. It is the name he has identified as throughout the period relevant to this investigation." She never looked up from her wristpad.

"Grey," I repeated, for the record.

Apogee and Krade exchanged looks but chose not to make an issue of it.

"Let us start with the more serious charge, the murder of Veritas. Full name Professor Anress Delorn," Apogee began. "Tell me about the argument you and Veritas had on the day she was murdered."

"There was no argument. She was introducing—"

Serrenessa coughed, and I stopped talking.

DS Krade leaned forward. "For my benefit, please describe the discussion that took place between yourself and the deceased at the start of her class on the day of her death. The discussion which other witnesses character-ised as an argument."

I glanced at Serrenessa; she was engrossed with what-ever was on her wristpad, but she waved me on.

"She was introducing a discussion on the ethics of lying. Given my history, she made a joke at my expense, a mild joke, I might add. I was a good sport enough to play along, and that was it for us. One of the other students, Bloodshock, made a more pointed jibe later, but even that didn't bother me."

Krade rolled his eyes at the name Bloodshock, but really, who could blame him?

"What did Bloodshock say that was so pointed?" Apogee asked.

"I think Fusillade had asked something about my fight with Doctor Gravestone," I looked over my shoulder at Serrenessa, I hadn't realised this would get close to what happened to her brother. She had stopped working on her wristpad but showed no other signs of distress, so I con-tinued. "Bloodshock said something like 'Grey always lies, he's not a hero.' Except, you know, Zalex-y."

"And that annoyed you," Apogee said, flatly. He made a note on his pad.

"Nope. He's entitled to think what he wants about me, I'm comfortable in my own skin."

Still, thinking about it again, there was something weird about that conversation. Not Bloodshock, he could think whatever he thought, but it suddenly occurred to me that Fusillade was surprisingly well informed about what happened on Nymanteles. Particularly when she claimed to be so new to the Academy and the world of superheroes generally. That was... odd.

"Grey?" Apogee said, an edge to his voice.

"Sorry, Professor Gale, I was light-years away. What did you ask?"

"I said, if you were so blasé about events in the class, why did you stay behind?"

I shrugged. "It was just a spur of the moment thing. I just... I joined Veritas's class to re-examine my choices, and that talk about my fight with Gravestone, it got me thinking. I wanted to ask Veritas for her thoughts."

"Your relationship with Veritas. You would describe her as a mentor, then?" Apogee asked.

"I'd describe her as a teacher who I had one class with, and the aunt of a good friend of mine."

"And your relationship was always amicable? Even in your first year?"

I ran a hand through my hair, frustrated. "Your 'gotcha' questions all seem focussed on things which are basically common knowledge. Everybody knows I spent my first year avoiding Veritas because I was lying about who I was. But that's ancient history. You know that."

"My client is not here to answer for his general behaviour, but for the specifics relating to this case," Serrenessa said.

"Agreed," said Apogee. "Let us return to those events. This conversation after class makes you last to see Veritas alive."

"Apart from whoever killed her, sure. Why are you lay-ing all this on me now? We talked at length about Veritas's murder with Captain Hawk. Nobody seemed to have a problem with me then. What new thing have you got that puts me in the spotlight?"

Apogee was unphased, relentless. "Let us turn our attention to the murder weapon."

"A PS 10N grapnel gun, the same model I use, yes. Me and a couple of hundred other students. We even established one was missing from the repair supplies. Talk to Tom. Or Loc. Talk to Gadget Dude. *We* told *you* that. It's not new."

"Grey," Serrenessa said, and I shut up, I was editorialising, and I knew it.

Krade pulled my grapnel out of their evidence box and looked it over. "It seems rather cumbersome," he said.

I kept quiet. That wasn't a question. Don't offer up extra information.

Krade turned the grapnel over in his hand. "How would you even kill someone with one of these things?"

"The cable was wrapped around the victim's neck. It was pulled until the neck snapped," Apogee said.

"He doesn't look strong enough to do that." Krade put my grapnel back in the box.

"Hmm. I'd like to ask you about the events on Nymanteles," Apogee said.

Wait, what? "Wait, what?"

"I fail to see the relevance," Serrenessa said.

"Then let me explain," said Apogee. "I have been looking at the reports of the death of Sunbolt. Another member of the faculty you seemed to have an abrasive relationship with."

"Grey," Serrenessa warned.

I wasn't having that, though. "This has nothing to do with that. Sunbolt was a friend. Sort of. He died saving my life. And Pilvi, and Seventhirtyfour. He died a hero."

"So the reports have it. In the ensuing explosion, Säde... Pilvi inherited some of Sunbolt's abilities, correct?"

Where was he going with this? "Don't ask me how, but, yes, that's what it looked like to me."

"And consulting with Sergeant Nine of the Brontom, it seems that Probability Kid's powers were increased as a result of his exposure to this explosion."

"Really?" That was news to me, but I suppose it made a kind of sense. Seventhirtyfour's powers kept growing as he became more familiar with them. They might have been augmented when the Ascension Machine exploded. If they were, he'd never mentioned it to me.

"You were also present at the time of the explosion, correct?"

"Yes."

"So, to be clear. Sunbolt died, Säde gained powers, Probability Kid's powers increased and you... walked away unaffected?"

"I was injured. I wouldn't say unaffected. I'd barely say walked."

"But you were the only one in that explosion not to manifest an increase in powers, afterwards?"

I gaped. "Are you trying to suggest that I did gain powers, and somehow hid them, only to use them to murder... do you know how ridiculous that sounds?"

"Sit down, Grey," Serrenessa snapped behind me.

I hadn't noticed I'd stood up. "Apogee, this is all insane. You must see it. You've built a case on... on coincidence and conspiracy theories. If this is what you have if this is everything? Let me out of here now," I gave Krade an imploring look. He certainly looked dubious at Apogee's case.

Apogee remained unflustered. "Sit down, Grey. If you

want hard evidence, let us look at the assault on David Forsythe."

I sat. "Okay, tell me how and why you think I attacked someone I've never heard of."

"Never heard of? I have seen you in his company. He came to fetch me when you had your scuffle with Bloodshock's group."

"Wait, *that* David? Lucy's David?" I had a sinking pit in my stomach. I could see exactly where this conversation was about to go, and I wasn't here for it.

"That would be Lucy McKenzie, yes? The victim's girlfriend?"

"Yes."

"How would you characterise your relationship with Miss McKenzie?"

"We're friends. We both fought in the Battle of Nymanteles."

"Friends. Hmm. I've spoken to several students who—"

"You don't have to say it. I hate to shatter the jealous love triangle you're so clearly working up to, but it wasn't like that. Maybe if she hadn't met David over the summer, something might have happened between Lucy and me, but maybe it wouldn't have. We'll never know because she *did* meet David, she's happy with him, and I am happy for her. Would I choose to socialise with David? No. But I don't know him, maybe if we spent some more time together, I'd see what a great guy he is. But as it is, I got on a spaceship and left the Academy having only had two conversations with the guy."

I stumbled to a halt. I couldn't look at Serrenessa, I could feel her glare burning a hole in my back. A wordy answer like that was exactly what she told me not to do. I could see her point. I probably hadn't helped my case, but really, I had nothing against him.

164

"David was attacked in the corridor outside a seventh-floor classroom by a human male of about your build," Apogee said, "he was dressed in a black bodysuit and mask. David was unable to identify his attacker, only noted that he had a grapnel gun. Fortunately, the attack was caught on camera, and I can also add the model of the gun. Care to guess what it was?"

I made a face. "A PS 10N."

"Correct."

"Again, it's a common model."

"Do you recall the last time you were on the seventh floor of the Hall of Justice?"

"No. None of my classes were on the seventh. Not for a while. Maybe back when I was doing my investigation of Veritas's murder. Why? When did the attack happen?"

"About ten minutes before you arrived out of breath to check-in for your flight to leave the Academy. And from the scene of the crime."

"Before I arrived there, I was in the Dome, helping Pilvi's girlfriend find her."

"Did anyone see you?"

"Pilvi and Kaarina. Plus a few thousand other people I expect, but only as a face in a crowd."

"We have spoken to Pilvi and Kaarina. There are several minutes unaccounted for between you leaving them and your check-in for the flight."

"I have problems sometimes with open areas. It took me a while to work up to leaving the Dome and entering the quad."

"That's certainly one story. Or maybe you realised this was your last chance to strike at David and, having worked out where he would be, you attacked him knowing that you would be able to make your escape before anyone could realise it was you."

"No."

"Time was tight though, tighter than you realised, and you botched your attack on David. You left him alive but injured. You had to hope your disguise was enough, and you ran to the spaceport to leave the Academy."

"No."

"Well, you were lucky, David couldn't identify you. But you were also unlucky. We swept the area and found just enough DNA to match his assailant. Your DNA. And if you hadn't been in that corridor in weeks, how else would it be there?"

"It was planted. Or something was wrong with the scan. I don't know. I wasn't there. I didn't attack David."

"You did attack David, you tried to kill him. You punched a hole in a wall in the process and left enough skin cells behind."

"No."

"And then you fled the Academy, thinking you'd gotten away, scot-free."

"No."

"Motive we always had. Realising you have Powers gives us the method, and we both know you are smart enough to buy the timing for the opportunity. The DNA has you."

CHAPTER 15
THE DESCENT

They escorted me back to my room, Serrenessa stalking behind me. She wasn't on her wristpad now, just followed along, jaw set, face like thunder.

She didn't sit. Instead, as the room door whooshed closed, she pointed me to the chair.

"I have come an exceptionally long way to help you," she said, "because you helped my brother and because you earned mother's respect. From what I saw today, I have no idea how. I told you what to do, you ignored me. I told you to stop talking in the interview, I don't think you even heard me. For someone who apparently cut his teeth on scams and snow jobs, you spent the entire interview playing on their terms. After mother's description of you, I expected you to run rings around them. They had you on the back foot from the time you stepped into the interview room."

"I—"

She held up a finger. "I'm not done yet. They are playing for real, making decisions that will affect your life to the point of destruction, and you are still playing the offended sulky child. That's not my mother's impression of who you are. It's too much to expect you to be Gravane. At the very least you could try being yourself."

Shame burned in my stomach. She was right. I not only didn't play the interview well, I hadn't played it at all. If ever there had been a time for me to be on form that was it. I'd blown it.

"So, what happens now?" I asked.

"You managed to avoid confessing, which is some small victory." She held up a hand as I protested. "Yes, I know you're not guilty. I believe you. It's not me you have to convince. It means there will be further interviews. They will no doubt apply to get you moved back to Academy jurisdiction. I will fight it, but based on today's performance—"

"No," I said. "Don't fight that. If they want me back on Academy world, I'll go."

"Not the best play, Grey. Here at least you have the impartiality of the Galactic Patrol on your side. They haven't made up their mind about you. The Academy has invested a lot of time and energy in your guilt."

"The Academy's identity is founded on truth and justice. They may have gotten this wrong, for now, but if we put the truth before them, I know they will live up to their name." Besides, I'd feel better knowing I was in the same system as Seventhirtyfour, Pilvi and the rest.

"I hadn't pegged you as a naive idealist," she said.

"I'm doing an elective in Upstanding Citizenship," I said.

"They are railroading you, kid. I've looked at the Academy fiscals, they are living barely within their means. Word is already spreading about a murder and an attempted murder on campus. It's making investors shy, and it's going to repress their student intake next year. They can stop the cash haemorrhage if they close the case quickly. They need this conviction."

"Then I need to offer up the real murderer."

"Do you know the real murderer?"

That was the stumbling block of course.

Her wristpad chimed. "I need to get back to senate

business," she said.

"I understand. Thanks for coming. Trying to help. Sorry I screwed this up."

"I'm not withdrawing from the case, Grey. I am Gravane. We see things through. That means seeing to my senate duties *and* your case. I'm going to need time. To review the case, to review the Academy judicial code. If that's really where you want this case heard?"

I nodded.

"Fine. Then I will counter-petition them to get a judge I trust to treat this case fairly. It could take a month or two to get you on their docket, though. Can you hang in that long? Resist confessing that long?"

I gave a hollow chuckle. "I can. Consider me kicked into gear. They won't get me like that again."

"Hmm." She turned to leave, then paused. "This Lucy McKenzie person, I think she's a blind spot of yours. Tread carefully when they start asking you about her."

I shrugged. "Sure, not a problem."

She shook her head. "Teenagers. I will be in touch. Probably not for a few weeks, but I'm on the case, don't worry. We'll beat it. Stay strong. Be Gravane."

"You too?" I wasn't sure how to respond to that.

The door closed behind her, leaving me alone with my thoughts.

# # #

Two days later, they moved me from my cell to a Galactic Patrol ship, ready for my return journey to Academy world.

The trip itself took four days; much quicker than the random walk I'd taken to reach Tamban Station. Apart from sporadic unremarkable interviews with Apogee and Krade, I had a lot of time to think.

Solving Veritas's murder, and the attack on David, that still seemed my best way to prove my innocence. I wasn't going to conjure new evidence sitting in a cell in a Patrol cruiser, so I needed to look at what I did know in a different way.

Ah. I did have something new to consider, in fact. Something that hadn't happened the last time I'd worried at this case. The attack on David. How did that factor into the picture? It seemed impossible that it wasn't a part of the larger whole. Too big a coincidence. Apogee hadn't told me much about it, and wouldn't. He'd keep that close for interrogation purposes, but what he had told me was... intriguing.

Questions: Why attack David? Why frame me for it? How did my DNA end up there? Was the timing significant? Was the attacker the same person who killed Veritas? Why didn't I have a console to build a crime board in my cell?

There was a lot.

First principles, then. Method, motive, opportunity.

I couldn't do much with opportunity. As far as I could tell, David was attacked in a corridor in front of witnesses. His assailant appeared human and male, though both of those could be faked. Who had the opportunity? Hundreds of students. Put a pin in that.

Motive was interesting. On one level, if this assault was unconnected to everything else going on, if it was just directed at David because of something he'd done, I had no way into it. If it was connected though..., what could I tell about the motive based on what it achieved? What had it achieved? Short term: scaring and hurting David. It's what pointed to me if you assumed I was jealous of his relationship with Lucy. Which was ridiculous. Obviously. Ahem.

What else had it achieved? It had gotten me arrested.

That wasn't me being... that was just a fact. You could pull off a random attack on a student and not leave evidence if you really wanted to. But evidence had been left. DNA. Either my DNA, harvested and deliberately planted on the scene, or possibly someone else's DNA and the scans had been tampered with. As Prof Croft had drilled into us many times, when you're investigating a crime and super-powers are involved, you have to broaden the possibilities.

Method. The attacker punched a hole in a wall, Apogee said. So, super strength and toughness. Or, well, there were so many alternatives to that it was hardly worth thinking about. Telekinetics. Energy manipulation. Tech augmentation. Superspeed. The list went on. The limiting factor might be the method used to fake my DNA at the scene. If it was my DNA... I didn't *remember* being harvested. Of course, that could have been achieved without me knowing, even something as low-tech as breaking into my dorm and stealing a comb. Had I lost any combs recently? Interfering with the scan though. Creating a false positive for my DNA. That screamed Tech student.

Or...

Thinking back to that day, the day I left the Academy and David was attacked. I had seen a Welatak at the spaceport, just before I'd met Kaarina. He'd had some kind of cybernetic implants. Why did that ring a bell?

I bounced up off the couch in my cell, started pacing. Oh, oh, oh. That Welatak. The phrase 'cybernetic Welatak' reminded me of the conversation I'd had with Mrs. Gravane, right at the start of term. There had been a cybernetic Welatak involved in the attempt to break out Mirabor. Incapacitor? That was the name. Could the Welatak from the spaceport be Incapacitor?

Why would he suddenly turn up at the Academy? He

wasn't part of the Veritas investigation. The attempt to break out Mirabor Gravane had happened way across the other side of the galaxy.

But what if it had been Incapacitor? Were any of the others who arrived with him Laugh Riot or Big Bang? I hadn't been paying much attention to be sure, but I didn't think so. None of them had been Germile, anyway, which ruled out Big Bang. But if my guess about Laugh Riot and Kayda Buchanan being one and the same, we had evidence to suggest she was a speedster. Maybe she'd passed me so quickly I hadn't seen her.

Or maybe she'd been at the Academy much longer.

Wait. What?

Croft had all but told me that the person who murdered Veritas was a speedster. I mean, she hadn't told me, but... could the murderer have been Kayda? On-campus since the first day of term?

Why would she want to kill Veritas? No, scratch that, if she was here secretly, maybe she just wanted to stop Veritas from finding her out. Veritas's truth field could really put a crimp in assuming a false identity. I stopped my pacing so suddenly, I almost tripped over my own feet. If Kayda was here under false pretences, she was doing exactly what I had the year before. That felt... What was going on here?

More interestingly (sorry, Veritas) why would Kayda even come to the Academy? As far as I knew, the only thing she wanted was...

Oh.

Ohhhhh.

Now my arrest made sense. Now I could see why they'd plant my DNA. Kayda must have been annoyed to find I'd left town already. Well good news, Ms. Buchanan. I'm coming home.

# # #

When we landed, we didn't arrive at the Academy spaceport. Instead, we touched down on a smaller landing platform outside of the main Academy campus. There, the Galactic Patrol officially handed their prisoner over to Captain Hawk.

A small party formed up around me, and Hawk led us wordlessly through the jungle.

I heard the hum of a forcefield before we broke through the foliage.

And there, looming above me, was the gate to Tartarus.

I'd steered clear of the place throughout my time at the Academy, particularly during my first year, when I was convinced that I was one failed lie away from being thrown in. I hadn't worried about that possibility for a long time, but now, here I was.

Universe gonna irony, I guess.

It was surprisingly mundane. A plain steel slab set into a heavy concrete wall. Not even a sign to tell you what the building was, but I suppose that wasn't necessary. Even the students who weren't criminals knew this place and what it was for. In my worst imagining of this, I'd pictured a thunderstorm overhead, blackening the sky and punctuating the proceedings with jagged knives of lightning. Instead, I could make out the far-off sounds of an Academy beach party in progress. At least it was dusk. That lent a modicum of drama to the proceedings.

Our party was small. I was flanked by two of Professor Red Ninja's TAs, there to stop me if I decided to run. To where? A little further back Captain Hawk and Professors Croft and Gale stood, watching. Nobody looked like they wanted to be here any more than I did. Though I suspect if push came to shove, I wanted it less.

I wondered where Seventhirtyfour, Pilvi and the rest

were. Did they even know I was back on the planet? Would they try and stop this if they did?

Captain Hawk stepped forwards. "Grey. You are to be confined within Tartarus's suppression field. There seems to be some question as to whether you have powers. In either case, within these walls, you will not. As an established flight risk, you are being detained until a trial date can be set, and an Arbiter from the Galactic Judicial Service is available to hear your case. This period is not to exceed six standard months. If for any reason a trial date cannot be set within that time, a review board will be convened to determine whether there exists sufficient evidence to detain you longer. Do you understand the limits of your confinement?"

"Yes." I should, it was the third time they'd been explained to me. Serrenessa had mentioned it too, but she was working to get a judge to hear my case much sooner than that. "Again, I'm innocent."

Hawk nodded and pressed a control on his wristpad. The shimmering forcefield which covered Tartarus twinkled out, and the giant steel door juddered into motion.

The guard on my right unlocked my handcuffs.

"You may proceed inside," said Hawk.

"You aren't coming with me?"

Hawk just gestured me towards the steel door, now open wide enough for one person to step through. I cast a glance over at Gale and Croft. Their expressions were stone.

I wanted to tell them that the real murderers were still out there, that locking me up didn't make anybody safer. I wanted to tell them this was unfair. That I would never do the things I'd been accused of. That—

My guards gave me a gentle nudge and I stumbled the first step forwards onto the ramp up to Tartarus.

The space beyond the door was dark, no clues about what to expect once I was through. I fought the urge to look back. I'd said everything I could. They'd listened, to be sure, but I hadn't changed their minds. They thought this was the right choice. I couldn't blame them for being cautious, just that they had the wrong guy.

I was halfway up the ramp. Nobody coming with me. Did that mean drone guards to keep me in line once inside? Was I being sent into solitary, with only drones to keep me company? For six months? That seemed needlessly cruel. No, not six months, Serrenessa had promised. Surely, they could find an Arbiter before that, and if they thought their case was so strong that they'd be willing to do this to me, then—but their case couldn't be that airtight, because I was innocent.

My mouth was dry.

Four more steps and I'd be through the gate. The area beyond was a little clearer now, but all I could see of it was an empty room. Maybe another, smaller, door on the other side? It looked like it had a roof. That was something.

"Okay, here goes." Two more steps.

Something in the door mechanism gave a loud bang, and a twist of smoke rose from one of the door's motors. The ramp exploded in a wave, the force knocked me from my feet, but there was no great heat to it just some sort of loud pressure wave.

Captain Hawk swooped towards me, standing between me and the explosion. "Are you okay, son?" he asked.

I nodded, ears still ringing. Something had... it wasn't just... had somebody pushed me?

"Kate, what happened?" Hawk shouted.

Professor Croft shook her head, stabbing at controls on her wristpad. "It looks like one of the gate motors blew out. It must have shorted out some underground cabling."

She didn't sound very convinced. "Otherwise, everything checks out as normal."

"I don't like it, the timing seems very suspicious," said Apogee; somehow, he'd found time to suit up since the explosion.

"We don't use these motors often," Croft pointed out, "if it were to blow, it would make sense to happen when we strained it. But yes, I agree. This stinks. Something is wrong."

Hawk nodded. "Agreed. Mr. Grey, I think we must delay—"

"No." My mind was racing.

"I'm sorry, young man?"

That had to be it. It had to. It explained so much. "I'm done with being messed around. Either throw me in Tartarus now or let me go," I said, picking myself up off the floor.

"That's not on the table, Grey, I'm sorry," Captain Hawk said, not unkindly.

"Then lock me up. Professor Croft, is there anything wrong now? Will the door still close behind me?"

She looked at me, back at her wristpad, then up at me again. It was plain she didn't trust either me or her pad. "The door has three motors. Even with one blown, we can still seal you in, yes."

"Fine, then do it."

"Grey," Croft began. I cut her off.

"I've just had enough; I want to get this over with. I was ready, am ready, to go now. I don't want to go through all this build-up again. Please, headmaster. You know you're going to put me in there eventually. It was just a blown motor. Don't put me through all this again."

Captain Hawk crossed his arms. "You are the one in custody, you don't get to make these calls."

"Fine," I said and sprinted into Tartarus before anyone could stop me.

CHAPTER 16
OLD FRIENDS

I was curious if anybody would follow me in, to drag me out of the place they'd been trying to throw me moments before. They must have debated for a long minute or two, but eventually, the door rolled into motion again, closing, if haltingly, running on only two-thirds of its motors.

It wasn't quite closed, the indicator on the inner door still showed red, when I turned around to see if my suspicions were correct.

They were.

Standing in the corner, out of sight from the outside were a human woman and a Welatak with cybernetic components grafted to his face and saline suit.

I nodded to them, and the woman covered her mouth to stifle a laugh.

"Should I call you Kayda? Or Laugh Riot? Or Fusillade?" I asked. She wasn't wearing her helmet, but her uniform was unmistakable.

"Laugh Riot?" she said and laughed. "Is that what people are calling me? I love it. Let's go with that."

I leaned back against the inner door, just in time for its indicator to turn green.

"Are you planning to stop us going in?" asked Laugh Riot.

I shrugged. "I mean, maybe. You aren't fast in here, are you? And I've no tech for Incapacitor to affect. I think I can give it a go at least."

"You've worked it all out, have you?" she asked.

"I think so. You shouldn't have pushed me on the way in. That was the last piece. That's when it all came together."

"Then let's find out if you can take us both," said Incapacitor, and took a step towards me.

Laugh Riot put a hand on his arm to stop him. "He does look so like my Mirabor, I'm not sure I want to spoil his face."

"Then I won't hit his face," Incapacitor growled.

I fell into a combat stance. "So Mirabor is here, then?"

"The one place in the galaxy where they have the technology to keep his powers suppressed? Yes. My poor Mirabor. We were too late to rescue him before, but we chased him here."

"Where you found Tartarus was too tough a nut to crack? You needed to persuade Captain Hawk to open the door."

She bobbed her head in a bow. "It took longer than I expected, but it's all worked out well in the end. I'm surprised you didn't simply tell the authorities if you had it all worked out."

I shook my head. "I'm good, but even assuming I could have persuaded them of this crazy story, you would have had too much time to get this door open and get to Mirabor. This way, I can stop you, and then persuade them."

Laugh Riot lunged at me, hands like claws reaching for my throat. I was relieved that the suppression field Hawk had mentioned affected her powers. She was fast, but not superhumanly so. I ducked below her grasp, then sprang up, putting all my weight behind a punch to her gut.

As she staggered back, gasping for air, Incapacitor clubbed me over the back of the shoulders, a double-fisted strike that lacked finesse but still landed heavily. I staggered under the blow but caught him in the knees with a kick as I stumbled.

Okay, time to concentrate. I needed to put Incapacitor down quickly if I could. Before Laugh Riot could fully recover. No time to let up, Welatak are strong and tough-hided, I couldn't afford to be subtle about this. Fortunately, I had two advantages, firstly he was more of a hacker than a brawler, secondly, while strong, Welatak are optimised for life underwater. I couldn't risk breaching his saline suit, I wanted to put him down, not risk his life, but that still left me with options.

I pressed my attack, jabbed at his neck, shoulders, face. He blocked most, his style slow and sloppy, but he had some training it seemed. It didn't matter, none of those strikes would affect him much even if they landed. I just needed to keep him off balance, not thinking. Keep his focus on defending his upper body, while I bided my time, waited for his balance to tip. One awkward half-step left his legs slightly overlapping; I dropped to the floor and swept his ankles. Incapacitor tumbled over. I pounced, landing an elbow strike to his stomach, before grabbing the sides of his head and smashing it into the ground. Not as vicious as it sounds, Welatak are thick-skulled, and often attack with their heads in ramming manoeuvres underwater. It wouldn't hurt him but left him dazed, on top of everything else.

I looked up. Laugh Riot had recovered sooner than I expected. She'd scrambled to her feet, but instead of helping Incapacitor, she'd skirted the fight and was reaching for the door.

"Oh no you don't," I said. I hopped over the fallen Welatak and grabbed for Laugh Riot, but as I did, Incapacitor must have caught my heel. I stumbled, came up short.

Laugh Riot shot me a look of triumph, then slipped through the inner door to Tartarus proper.

I got my feet under me again and scrabbled after her.

I staggered to a halt. I hadn't given a moment's thought to what Tartarus looked like on the inside, but whatever I'd assumed, I hadn't expected this. I was on a balcony that circled the entire circumference of the above-ground Tartarus, a balcony that overlooked a vast pit that descended into the ground, circled by more balconies beneath me. Five? Ten levels? It was too dark to see the bottom. There were doors off every level. Dozens, hundreds of rooms.

What was this place?

And then I remembered. A conversation with Professor Gale that felt like a lifetime ago. The original Academy facilities had been underground, and now I'd found them.

I shook my head. Where had Laugh Riot gone? There. She was running down a flight of stairs to the next level down, laughing as she took the stairs two at a time. Somewhere in these hundreds of rooms was Mirabor Gravane. I had to get to him before she could.

"Welcome, new guest, designate: Grey," said a robotic voice behind me. "Please follow me to your assigned room."

It was a flying drone, heavy, armoured, and if the tubes on the side were what I thought, armed. The whine of the antigrav keeping it aloft was quiet but distinct.

Still, it didn't sound hostile. "Hello, drone, am I allowed to ask questions?"

"Of course, guest: Grey. I am here to facilitate your stay and make it as comfortable as possible." Orange lights on the front panel danced cheerfully as it spoke.

"Great. Are there any other guests currently in residence?"

"There are one... two... one... two... one other residents. Guest: Mirabor has been allocated accommodation on the third level." Some of the orange lights blinked green. What was that? And why had it stumbled over the number of other prisoners?

Incapacitor stood in the doorway to the room I'd just left. He'd slipped my mind entirely.

"Whatever it is that dampens Powers in here doesn't affect tech," he said. "I guess the designers expected all tech to be removed from the prisoners here." He pressed a button on one of the myriad pieces of cybernetics on his suit.

"Guest: Grey identified as hostile. Subdue and detain," said the drone; all of its light shone green.

"Oops," said Incapacitor.

I didn't stop to look, I just ran, followed by the sound of the drone's guns spinning up.

Its first shot missed me, its second clipped my arm. Non-lethal munitions, thankfully, but the impact stung, and that was only from a graze. A direct hit could deaden a limb and put me down on the ground in no time. I couldn't risk that. But its aim was too good. I ducked left, then right, but the shots followed. A second blow on the back of my calf had me staggering, instead of running. I had to find cover, but I couldn't afford to get caught in a room, so I couldn't risk ducking into a doorway. The stairs were too far, but there was more than one way off the balcony.

I planted a hand on the balcony railing, flipped, held, dropped.

I had just enough time to spot and plan my landing. I hit the next balcony down on the balls of my feet, absorbed what I could of my momentum with my knees and sucked up the shock of the rest. Nothing broken, but I stumbled the landing thanks to my numbed leg, and I'd be aching over it tomorrow. One level didn't feel enough though, the sentry drone could hover, might well be able to follow me. I didn't stop to find out. I pushed off out of my crouch propelling myself towards the edge of this balcony. This time I gave myself a moment to judge and plan my fall. No more than a couple of heartbeats, but it made my next drop notably smoother. As I fell to the next level, Laugh Riot's laughter faded above me. I'd gotten ahead of her.

This was the third level. Assuming they counted from the top. This was where Mirabor's room was. Not sure what I'd do if I found him, but the only way I could think to have any control in this situation was to control the prize, and for now, that was Mirabor.

I spotted another security drone, its face lights still a chilled-out orange. Did that mean that it was unhacked? Or just that it hadn't spotted me? If the former, it could direct me to Mirabor's cell, give me more of an edge. It was worth a go. I approached from behind cover, a row of benches that were presumably a hold-over from before Tartarus was a prison. I was ready to duck and cover but said, "Hey Drone, can you direct me to Mirabor Gravane's location?"

The Drone swivelled to look at me, perforce bringing its guns around as it did. "Guest: Grey, welcome to level three. We do not track individual guests but Mirabor Gravane's suite is number 328. Follow the balcony in a clockwise direction."

"Thanks."

"You are most welcome. Have a nice day."

I jogged on, the stinging numbness in my leg fading into sharp pins and needles as I did.

The door to suite 328 was closed when I reached it. Should I knock? It was an odd stray thought to have when approaching the lair of your arch-nemesis, or even his cell.

But Tartarus was not the hell hole I'd imagined. It was... quite pleasant. It felt like the hotel section of a mid-tier station, and suddenly it felt weird to just go barging in.

Laughter echoed around walls. It was hard to judge, but it sounded closer again. No time to second guess myself. I put a hand on the door handle and pushed it open.

# # #

The room was empty.

I mean, of course it was. With the whole of Tartarus to roam around why would you stay in one place? Any advantage I had by getting here first was lost. Laugh Riot could still get to Gravane before me.

The apartment was comfortable, if bland, the kind of place that mid-range chain hotels offered, or, well, the student rooms in the Academy proper. The main living area had a cooking unit against one wall, two doors in the back led, presumably, to the bedroom and bathroom. The décor's style came from before I was born, but it looked to be in good repair, and the general yellowy-brown colour scheme was rather soothing. Not the kind of jail cell a name like 'Tartarus' conjured up, particularly when there was no lock on the door.

There were signs of recent habitation—a coffee cup left on the side still had dregs in the bottom, but no sign of mould. The room smelled lived-in, but not stale. I checked the bedroom: the bed was unmade and looked like it had been slept in. He had been here recently. Probably no more than a few hours ago.

Should I wait for him to come back? Or go out looking for him?

If I stayed, Gravane could encounter Laugh Riot before he even got here, no chance for me to control the meeting that way. Or Laugh Riot could find this place before

Gravane got back and find me trapped in this one apartment. If I left, I'd be freer to move and escape, but the first person I ran into outside could be Laugh Riot or Incapacitor as easily as Gravane. The clock was ticking.

Mid-dither, the door to the living area crashed open and Mirabor Gravane barrelled in. He caught me flat-footed in the middle of his living room. His eyes went wide, and his knees buckled, his forward momentum faceplanted him into the carpet.

"When I heard the gunfire, I wondered if it was you," he said. He rolled into a sitting position, propped against the wall, panting. "Go on then, get it over with. I will not beg for my life. I will die that much a Gravane at least."

"What? Why on earth would I be here to kill you?"

He searched my face, and I returned the favour. It was like looking into a warped mirror. When we'd first met, I hadn't thought the resemblance was that strong, but life had treated him a little harder since then, burned away the softness to his face. My life had been perhaps a little easier, maybe it had dulled some of my edges. We had the same dark eyes, a similar jumble of ethnicities in our skin tone and bone structure. His hair, always longer than mine, was down by his shoulders now. I saw no sign of the wild energy he had as Doctor Gravestone. Not that that let him off the hook, he'd done plenty of awful things before he Ascended.

"You're not, are you? Not here to kill me?" He shook his head. "I murdered your friend, tried to kill you. I thought for sure... the power from the Ascension Machine, has it not changed you at all?"

I didn't have the heart to tell him I'd lied about the Ascension Machine giving me powers. That and it still might be useful for him to think it had. Sorry, Bloodshock. I let the lie stand.

"Laugh Riot... Kayda Buchanan, she's here to break you out. I plan to stop her," I said.

"Good," said Gravane. He popped to his feet. "In that case, let me return to my original strategy." He grabbed a small backpack that was leaning against the wall, slung it around his shoulders. "We can't stay here, but I know a few places to hide. Come with me."

Somehow this was the opposite of how I'd seen this going down, but I shrugged and fell in behind.

We left the apartment and cut across the public area outside, keeping low and quiet. As we ran, Tartarus echoed with manic laughter.

"Laugh Riot," I whispered. "She's getting closer."

"Kayda. I used to love her laugh, but this?" He shuddered. "Keep moving. There's an access panel up ahead."

We passed three likely candidates as we ran, but Gravane ignored them all, instead, he took a right down a gap between two student apartments, then ducked under an industrial unit—heating or air at a guess—before hauling himself up to an access panel behind it. A good choice, nobody would stumble across this place without knowing about it, or without weeks to search.

An easy tic tac; I bounced off the wall to get up to join him.

He pushed his pack to me. "Hold this." He opened it and pulled out a multitool and set to opening the panel.

Curious, I peeked inside the pack. A minipad, a couple of bottles of water, a few energy bars, heavy gloves, some other tools, and a change of clothes. An emergency pack he clearly had ready for exactly this sort of situation. There was something else in the pack too, it took me a moment to recognise them; the power damper cuffs Gadget Dude had built when we'd captured Gravane on Nymanteles.

Gravane put the multitool back and snatched the pack

from my hands. "Get in," he said, nodding towards the now open vent.

I got. Gravane followed me and pulled the panel closed behind us. He didn't seal it tightly, but there was a catch he threw to keep it lightly shut. The catch looked new, not part of the original infrastructure.

I pointed. "You installed that just in case?" I kept my voice low, but it still tended to echo off the vent's walls as they sloped gently down behind us.

"Yes. After the attempt at the last facility, I knew there was a risk they'd try again. I've spent my time here preparing."

"Why? Don't you want to get out of prison?"

"Of course, I do. But I can't, not yet. It's taken me months of therapy to come to terms with what I did as Gravestone, and before. I'm not proud of any of it. And if they take me somewhere my powers aren't suppressed... it all starts over again. Gravestone comes back. I lose me. I won't let that happen, not again."

"Hence the power dampening cuffs."

He nodded. "Tartarus has let me move around without them. Whatever is keeping my powers suppressed here is keeping me, me. But if something goes wrong with that, or they drag me out of here, I need a backup."

"I can't imagine Laugh Riot letting you keep them on."

"No. Kayda and I... we were close. Not a relationship I'd want to put labels to, but... close. Gravestone and... what did you call her? Laugh Riot, right. Gravestone and Laugh Riot, their relationship was different. Scary. Thrilling. A kind of feedback loop, pushing each other to extremes." He paused, cocked an ear to listen, then frowned. "We were worse together. And better."

I heard it too, now. Two voices, getting closer. I put my finger to my lips. Gravane nodded.

"It's somewhere around here," Incapacitor said, his voice unmistakable despite being muffled by the panel.

"Let me try something," said Laugh Riot with a giggle. Then she sang out, "Mirabor! My Mirabor! Where aaaaaaare you?"

I checked Gravane's expression, he didn't seem inclined to respond.

"That Grey must have him captive. My Mirabor would come to me, I just know it. Can't you get a fix on their location?"

"I've narrowed the signal down to within a few meters. The only tech that's been mobile in the last few minutes, except the drones. It must be them. I'm not magic though, there's enough tech and metal in these walls, it is futzing the signal. I can't get a closer fix. They could be inside one of those rooms, or even on the floor above or below. I can't be sure, but they're close."

I had no tech on me. Incapacitor must be tracking Gravane's pack, and the minipad inside it. I tried to take the pack from Gravane. He resisted, for a moment, holding it tight. But I met his eye, and he relented, releasing his grip, spreading his fingers to let it go. I put the pack on the floor of the vent and gave it a push, letting it slide down the incline away from us. It picked up speed and vanished into the dark.

"Wait!" Incapacitor shouted excitedly. "It's on the move again. Below us. That way."

"To the stairs!" Laugh Riot shouted gleefully. Her footsteps retreated, followed by Incapacitor's heavier tread.

"I can't see my pack," said Gravane. "Quickly, we need my cuffs. We need to follow it down."

"That's exactly where they are heading. Is the access on the next level down as well hidden as this one?"

"No."

"Then, for now, we'll have to forget the pack and the cuffs. You don't need them in here anyway. Let's concentrate on keeping you here, right? That means keeping you away from the dubious duo."

"I'd feel safer with the cuffs."

"We'll get them back. Later. Okay?"

Gravane looked away from me, I couldn't see his expression. "Okay."

# # #

We hustled back towards the balcony.

"The pack isn't going to distract them long," I said. "And then they're probably going to search the vents or realise it was a ruse and come back up here. We have to get off this level."

"Are you sure? This is the area of Tartarus I know best. I have a few more hiding places on this level, good spots. They can't track us anymore; they would never find us."

We paused before crossing the gap at the top of the stairs down, I checked for signs of an ambush. When the coast seemed clear, we pushed on again.

"I don't think we can rely on them not tracking us. They can't follow us using your minipad, but Incapacitor is a Tech Hero... Villain, rather. They can pull the strangest things out of their pockets sometimes. Maybe they circle back to your apartment, find a pair of your old socks and build some kind of scent tracker to follow us." That was... uncomfortably plausible. "We need to put more of Tartarus in play, make them work for finding us. What can you tell me about the layout of this place?"

We ducked behind some benches to let one of the guard drones pass. Its tell-tales didn't look like Incapacitor had hacked it, but better safe than sorry. Once it was far enough away, we pushed on. We were making for a different stairwell. I wanted to go down, two or three levels if possible.

"There are nine levels all told," Gravane said. "Plus, I think, a tenth level for machinery and prison support tech. Floors eight and nine have been converted to more traditional prison cells, all empty now, of course. There is something rather peculiar about the ninth floor. I don't like spending time there."

"How so?"

"I don't know, it's difficult to articulate. I feel light-headed, weak, when I'm on that floor. Initially, I worried that it was a radiation leak, but I found a rad scanner, and it was no hotter there than anywhere else."

"Huh. Okay, let's remember that, it could be useful. For now, though, duly noted, we stay off the ninth."

"Agreed."

We paced carefully down the stairs to level four. I took the lead, straining to hear anything which might indicate Laugh Riot or Incapacitor were waiting for us below.

"So, we concentrate on looking for a hidey-hole on floors five through seven." I paused. Had I heard... no, it was just my imagination. "Any suggestions?" Definitely, just my imagination.

"There are some saltwater habitats on level seven. I had thought that their infrastructure would make adequate camouflage, but with one of our pursuers being a Welatak, perhaps not."

"Let's keep dry, yeah. Anything else? Hold that thought, coast's clear. Get us to the stairwell down, the sooner we're off level four the better."

If they were still looking for Gravane's pack, they should be way across the other side of the level, but I didn't want to take any chances. We sprinted. Our footsteps echoed throughout Tartarus, but that couldn't be helped, and shouldn't help them too much.

Halfway down the stairwell, Gravane tripped, tumbling over his own feet. I snatched at his jacket to slow his fall but let go before he could pull me down with him. He rolled over, thumping hard on three successive steps, before sliding to a halt against the bannister.

I knelt beside him. "Gravane? You okay?"

"A little winded. A little bruised. I'm fine." He tried to pull himself up, holding on to the bannister. He wobbled, and sat down hard, with a thump. "Actually, I feel quite dizzy," he admitted.

"Turn around, let me see your face."

He turned. There was blood seeping from a wound on his forehead. Not a big cut, not a lot of blood, but I know enough first aid to worry about any head injury.

"Gravane, how many fingers am I holding up?"

He took a moment to count, staring owlishly and blinking. "Three."

He was right, but I didn't like the amount of effort it had taken him. "Okay, buddy, I think we can forget about any grand adventures on lower levels. Can you think of a hiding place near here?"

"Can you imagine if that bump on my head had turned me into Doctor Gravestone again? I bet on a cartoon that would have happened." He got his feet under him and pushed himself upright, swaying slightly, despite holding the bannister for balance.

"Careful, Gravane. I'm glad we don't live in a cartoon. But think, is there somewhere to hide near here?"

"Apologies. Yes, you are correct." He shook his head to try and clear it, but went pale, and tightened his grip on the handrail. "I think I may have a concussion."

"Maybe so. The hiding place?"

"Of course. That way." He pointed with an unsteady

hand.

"Great." We set off again, much slower now, and much less time ducking to avoid discovery. I hoped he was leading us somewhere nearby. And useful.

"I believe I may need to vomit," Gravane noted.

"Hold it, if you can, can't help but think a bio spill would help them track us."

"Point taken." He was looking very green though.

He stopped at the door to a student apartment. "In here."

"I'm not sure it'll be enough to just hide in an apartment," I said.

"Wait. You'll see."

We entered, and Gravane pointed over towards a cabinet against the far wall. I went over to investigate. Closer, I could see a slight discolouration of the wall. A rotten smell tickled my nostrils. The wall behind the cabinet had gotten wet; a burst pipe in the last twenty years, presumably. The wall had all but disintegrated behind the cabinet, revealing a dark recess. If we got in and pulled the cabinet back behind us...

I dragged the cabinet away from the wall. Lighter than it looked, and I was glad it was empty. "In you go, Gravane."

I opened the cabinet, pulled out one of the interior shelves, and grabbed the bin. I followed Gravane into the recess, awkwardly pulling the cabinet behind us to conceal our hiding place.

I handed the bin to Gravane. "If you need to be sick. But cover it after with this board."

He took them both gratefully and retreated as far back as the recess allowed. The smell of rot and mould would not be helping.

I could barely make out Gravane's shape in the dark. "How are you doing?"

"I'm okay. Or rather, as well as can be expected. All things considered."

"Right."

"Grey?"

"Yeah?"

"Thank you. For coming in to stop them. For sticking with me. I've not... I have done many things I regret, and more than a few affected you. I'm sorry. And grateful that you are still willing to help me."

"I think that's the concussion talking."

"Perhaps so." His chuckle turned into some noises it's better not to dwell on. The smell, once the retching stopped, didn't help my stomach either.

"What do we do now?" he asked once he could talk again.

"We wait. I don't know if there's anything else we can do. I did consider spending time rigging booby traps to try and catch them, but they would take time out scavenging and time to build. I think we're safer sticking here. It's a good spot."

"Sure."

The truth was, we were only delaying the inevitable. I had no endgame in sight. Laugh Riot and Incapacitor might spend a little time looking for us, but sooner or later, Incapacitor would lash together some kind of tracker or sensor, or maybe the drones could already locate us, and Incapacitor would just have to tell them to lead him to us. Delay is a great tactic if you have an end to the sentence 'We just have to delay until...' but I didn't have an end to that sentence. And right now, I couldn't think how to find one.

CHAPTER 17
TITAN RISING

We waited in the dark, and the smell. Me trying to think of anything like a winning gambit, Gravane, from the sounds of things, trying not to turn himself inside out with his retching.

It was hard to judge the passage of time. An hour passed. Two? No sign of our hunters, but it left me nothing much to do except sit and stew. What other options did we have?

We were two on two, but even before Gravane's injury, I didn't like our odds. Incapacitor had proved tougher than I'd expected, and Gravane without his powers wasn't much of a fighter. With his powers...

With nothing more useful to think about, I spent a little time thinking about the power suppression effect in the prison. It only blocked biological powers, not technology. That was weird. Was that weird? It seemed weird to me. Or did it only block powers given by the Ascension Machine? I had only seen it block Gravestone and Laugh Riot, so maybe, but that would be a heck of a coincidence. No, that didn't seem likely.

If there was one thing I'd learned about superheroes, they liked to give things names that were a bit on the nose. I didn't know much about the name Tartarus. It was some mythical prison for gods, that was about it.

"Gravane?"

"Yes?" he put a good deal of wretchedness into the one word.

"What do you know about the legendary Tartarus?"

"Is this really the time?"

"Humour me. It'll be good to think about something else."

"Fine. Tartarus was a god in Ancient Greece, but also a part of the underworld. It was where the monsters and truly monstrous criminals were sent when they died."

"Great."

"The underworld was ruled over by Pluto... no, that was the Roman version... Hades. But as with all myths, there was some incon... incon... inconsistency, sorry, hard to focus. Some inconsistency around whether Tartarus was a part of the regular underworld or something different, separate. In one telling, I think it went that Tartarus was as far from Hades as Hades was from Earth."

"I thought Hades was a god?"

"Also, a place. Look it's really hard to think about anything right now, don't confuse the issue."

"Sorry. What kind of monsters got locked up in Tartarus?"

"It was a bit of a mess. I think the Titans locked up the Cyclopes. But Zeus let them out and then locked up the Titans in there? Sisyphus. The guy with the rock? He was there."

That didn't seem to help. "What about escapes? Did anyone escape Tartarus?"

"I can't think of anyone. I mean, again it depends on whether we're using Tartarus to be the whole of the underworld or just part of it. But Tartarus proper? I can't think of anyone. But I'm not an expert in the classics."

A prison for monsters and the monstrous that nobody ever escaped from. It was a good name. Not an encouraging one, given our circumstances, but a good one, right enough.

Why did I feel like I was on the edge of solving a mystery I didn't know existed? There was something here. Something about this place. Something that my subconscious was shouting at me, but I couldn't quite see it. Connections. Links. Did any of the mythology help me?

Wait. "Did you say, Pluto?"

"Pluto, he was the Roman analogue to the Greek god Hades, yes."

Doc Pluto had been one of the ten first teachers at the Academy. His name had come up when we'd been investigating the accident that Veritas and Apogee had been involved with. An accident that we didn't think was an accident.

I bounced to my feet. Our hiding place wasn't big enough for pacing, but I gave it a go, all the same. "This is maddening. There's something important right on the tip of my brain. I feel it. Is there anything else you can think of?"

"About Tartarus? Real or mythical?"

"I'll take either at this point."

"Here's something that struck me as peculiar about this place, when they brought me in, they had to lower the forcefield."

"Sure, they had to do the same for me," I said.

"Yes, but the place was empty before they brought me in. Why go to the expense of running a forcefield to protect an empty building?"

I felt a chill. It all fell into place, there and then. It all made a terrible sense.

"Gravane, I'm going to have to leave you here by yourself, for a bit. Will you be okay?"

"I'll be fine, I'm sure. But why do you need to go out?"

"Because I've made a horrible mistake. I just hope there's still time to fix it."

# # #

I ran.

I ran because Gravane was right. Because I'd spent most of the year before wondering where the Academy spent its money. Because on the very first day I'd been at the Academy, I'd noticed the forcefield surrounding Tartarus. I ran because the drone seemed confused about how many prisoners there were.

We weren't alone in Tartarus.

Something happened back at the start of the Academy. Something nobody talked about. Something terrible. Whatever it was made Doc Pluto convert the entire Academy's living space into a prison to hold something, someone, monstrous. A dark secret at the heart of the Academy, something they had kept locked up here for more than two decades.

Probably the hidden faculty member that Dez was working to identify. Probably the cause of the 'accident' that had left two students dead. Whoever it was, they'd been dropped into this hole twenty years ago and everybody had done their best to pretend they'd never existed. What sort of terror makes generally sensible, caring people do that?

The kind of terror that was in here with us.

The kind of terror that had been left in here, their powers suppressed, helpless, alone, forgotten. If they weren't insane when they were thrown in here, they would be now.

And Laugh Riot and Incapacitor were blindly roaming around the prison, poking in every corner, trying to find us. What would happen if they found the other prisoner first? Incapacitor might leave well enough alone, but Laugh Riot, I had no faith that she wouldn't just see some more chaos to let free. I could see her turning off the suppression field just to see what happens. And to get her speed back. Heck, she would probably want that even if they didn't find the prisoner. Either way, it was only a matter of time before the suppression field dropped.

And I'd thrown Gravane's cuffs down an air vent.

Whatever terror waited at the bottom of Tartarus, and every instinct I had told me it was bad, it could only be made worse by adding Doctor Gravestone into the mix.

I ran. Back the way we had come. Much faster than before because speed was more important than stealth now. The sound of the echoes of my beating feet resounded throughout Tartarus but did not summon Laugh Riot or Incapacitor. They must be a long way down, down near the prisoner, near the suppression field. I dug in, found a little more pace.

I didn't even break stride for the tic tac up to the access panel, just swarmed up the wall, and dove into the vent.

I rattled down the ventilation shaft, picking up bruises as I fought to control my descent. The floor dropped away beneath me, and that finally stopped my forward momentum, though now I had a downward component to worry about. I plummeted to the level below. My landing was hard, but I stopped.

Everything hurt, but I hadn't broken my neck. I stretched as much as the ventilation shaft allowed, and everything seemed to be working. "Result."

I hadn't anticipated how dark it would be in the vents. I could just about make out the general shape of the space; the gap above me I'd fallen through, vent tunnels leading off in three directions on this level. A glimmer of light from one direction suggested that might be the way out, but it was too early to head that way.

If I had ended up here in my fall, chances were the pack had fallen here too. Blindly, I felt around on the floor, sliding my fingertips over the cold metallic surface. Nothing. Nothing. Ah. Something. A broken bit of something, jagged edges to a smoother surface. I investigated more in that direction, towards the glimmer of light. A few more fragments, I still couldn't tell from what, until my fingers finally found a bigger chunk. Gravane's minipad. Looks like Laugh Riot or Incapacitor had taken their disappointment out on it.

I shuffled in that direction arms stretched to cover the whole width of the tunnel. If the minipad was here, was the pack, too? I found it a little further along, the rest of its contents dumped out on the floor. I grabbed the pack and dropped a water bottle in, followed by a couple of the energy bars. If we needed to hide out for a while, we'd be grateful of them. Finally, my hand closed around one of Gravane's cuffs. I scrambled my fingers across its surface. I couldn't feel any damage. I dumped it in the pack and resumed my search for its mate.

Seconds passed. As each one ticked, I became more convinced that Incapacitor was down on level nine, pushing buttons, getting closer to the one that switched off the suppression field. Even if I found the second cuff that instant, could I already be too late? The idea of being trapped in here with Doctor Gravestone, Laugh Riot, Incapacitor and whatever terror Captain Hawk locked away here? I was starting to sweat.

There! Yes! The second cuff. Laugh Riot can't have known what they were, or I'm sure she would have smashed them. As it was, this one seemed to be intact as well. That went into the pack and I shuffled as quickly as I could towards the glimmer of light.

I burst out into the wide balcony of level four. I needed to get down to level five, and all the way across to the other side of Tartarus. I looped the pack's straps over my shoulder, took a moment to double-check it was secure. Time to run again.

# # #

Each of the levels, or at least the five levels I'd seen so far, were laid out in the same way. The apartments were all built into the walls of the bowl, with a balcony stretching away from them, with plenty of space for, in happier times, small cafes, library stations, gardens, meeting spaces, or sports fields. Most of the infrastructure for all that was missing, all that remained were empty spaces, shapes in the floor where terminals or cabins once stood. The main thing which broke up the vast open space? Rows of benches, scattered around the place, some of them looking out over the balcony edge, some looking inwards, perhaps to what would have been a basketball court.

It didn't give much scope for hiding, so it was a relief that as I ran, I saw no sign of Incapacitor or Laugh Riot.

I hurdled benches, rather than going around them, every second counted, a fact only reinforced by a strange new sound welling up from the pit of Tartarus. A kind of groaning, rumbling noise, punctuated by sharp snapping twangs. I couldn't tell what it was, but it didn't sound good.

Step, step, jump.

Step, step, jump.

I kept laser focus on the top of the stairs.

Step, step, j—

I almost missed the whine of the drone's antigrav.

I twisted, mid-air, as it fired, and its stun bolt only grazed the small of my back, right below the backpack.

It was enough, my legs were deadened as I landed, and

folded under me as I tumbled to the hard concrete floor. I slapped the ground with my palms and forearms to take as much of the sting of the fall as I could, saving my skull from taking the punishment. Hurt like hell, and I kept sliding, fetching up against the leg of the last bench before the stairs.

The drone whirred as it repositioned for the next shot. I pulled frantically at the leg of the bench, dragged myself under cover. A splatter of stun bolts struck the ground, I caught enough of a flash of the nimbus to set my whole left side tingling, but not enough to numb it.

"Missed me!" I knew better than to taunt the drone, but I can't help it, when I'm nervous, I talk.

It interrupted that train of thought with another salvo. I kept my head down and assessed the situation. No point looking back, even if I could get out that way, I couldn't afford to play hide and seek with the drone for an hour, not when I needed to get to Gravane while the suppression field remained active. I had to make it to the stairs. The good news there is that if I could make it, there was enough cover, and enough options to be creative about how I descended, I could probably get some distance from the drone. Enough to make it to Gravane? I couldn't be sure, but I'd be willing to gamble it. The bad news? Between my bench and the stairwell, twenty paces of open terrain. Bad enough at the best of times, but right now, with my legs feeling like slabs of meat...

Why was it always my legs?

Already, my toes were beginning to tingle. That was a good sign. I punched my right thigh to try and speed up the recovery. Couldn't afford to be lurching my way across to the stairs, that would ruin most of my parkour escape options, even if somehow the drone didn't just shoot me in the head.

In the meantime, I needed some way to at least distract the drone. I ran a quick inventory; did I have anything more practical or effective than the possibility of punching it? I missed my grapnel gun. A water bottle? I'd imagine the drone was watertight, so dousing it wouldn't achieve much. As a projectile... I hefted it in my hand... it had some weight to it, but the drone looked solid, I'd have to get a lucky shot to do any real damage, and only one bottle, meant only one chance. I—

The drone's antigrav gave a more tortured whine as it lowered itself to the floor level beside me.

—hadn't realised it could do that.

Without thinking, I jammed the water bottle into the drone's weapon barrel. The cap end fit snugly. I rolled away, pulling at the back leg of the bench to drag myself away. My feet weren't cooperating, I was trying to get them under me when the drone fired.

A burst of light, an explosion of water, the drone's gun barrel ripped apart.

I scrambled. The drone could well have a secondary weapon system, almost certainly could call for backup. Part shamble, part stagger, I made for the stairs, chased by an ominous whirring clicking noise from the drone and that echoing rumble from deep within Tartarus.

As I crossed the apartment towards the hidden recess, the noise from below simply stopped.

I paused, holding my breath, straining to hear what might follow, but heard only silence. No, not silence, but the gentle familiar background hum of any tech environment. I licked my lips, swallowed. I'd never felt something so familiar suddenly be so ominous.

What was happening down there?

I heaved the cabinet to one side. "Gravane," I whispered. "It's me. You still here?"

"I'm here."

He huddled against the back wall of the recess, facing away from me. In the little light seeping in from the apartment, I could still see that he was shaking, head twitching back and forth.

"Gravane?" I said.

"I'm still here."

"I see that. I went to go get your power cuffs," I told him.

"I thought that might be what you were doing. Grey. I've been thinking..."

My hand went to my belt, but there was no grapnel gun there. "What have you been thinking, Gravane?"

"I wasn't totally honest with you earlier. I've been to the bottom of Tartarus. I've seen what's down there."

The recess was not as dark as it should have been. A faint reddish light speckled the back wall, illuminating the damp and the mould. The light shifted in time to the jerking of Gravane's head.

"That's okay, you can tell me all about it, but maybe put the cuffs on first?" I said. I pulled the cuffs from the pack and held them out towards his back.

"It's a man. There's a man at the bottom of Tartarus. He's wrapped in these massive chains. Wired into a machine. But he's alive. Awake. He said he could smell my power. Taste it. He said that if I could set him free, he would set me free."

I ducked into the recess, stepped cautiously towards Gravane. "That's good to know. We should talk more about him, but maybe I'll just slip this cuff on first."

Gravane snatched his hand away and turned to face me at last. His eyes sparked with the blood-red light of

Doctor Gravestone. "He frightened me, Grey. As Doctor Gravestone, I have power. But that man, that man *was* power. He radiated it. Even bound in chains. Immobile. Suppressed. He was terrifying."

"How long have your powers been back, Gravane?"

He shook his head. "You're not listening. It doesn't matter."

"How long?"

"Not long. Just before you got back."

"Right." Well, this was all shades of bad.

"If Kayda sets him free? You can't face them both, not alone. You need me. You need Gravestone."

"We both know what those powers did to you, Gravane. Mirabor. I appreciate the offer, I do. But these powers cost you your mind, Mirabor. Your sanity. You said yourself, you don't want to go back to that."

The light in his eyes flashed brighter. "I'm not a fool, Grey, I know the cost. I've no desire to pay it. But it is not a light switch. It took months of using my powers to put me on the edge before. Surely a day cannot hurt, a few hours? To save both of our lives?"

"Listen to yourself. That's Gravestone talking, not you, Mirabor. Please. It's good that you've told me about this man, but we can find another way to deal with him."

"You cannot understand the power we are facing. I have seen it. Without my power to protect us, if we stand against him, we will die."

"Then we don't stand against him. You trusted me before, Mirabor. To be able to get out of a situation you couldn't see a way out of for yourself. That's why you picked me when we first met. You trusted me then. Trust me now. I can keep us alive. I can keep us safe. This guy, he's been held here for years, he's not going to waste time hunting us down. Once he's free, he's leaving Tartarus.

And then he's in for a shock, there's a whole college full of superheroes out there."

The light in Gravane's eyes dimmed. One of his hands reached out towards me. "I don't know, Grey..."

"I do. Captain Hawk's out there, Apogee, a whole host of powerful heroes. They put this guy in Tartarus once, they can do it again. There's more of them this time, it'll be a snap. All we need to do is keep our heads down, not draw attention. We can do that. We've been doing that. With my skills, and your knowledge of Tartarus, there's no way he'll find us."

The red light fluttered out in Gravane's eyes. "You're right," he said, sighing heavily. "We can't fight him. Hiding is a better strategy." He offered up his wrists to me, and I clamped first one cuff in place, then the second.

"There we go. Much better," I said.

"Thank you, Grey. Again. The power is... Never mind. So, what do we do now? Stay in here?"

I considered for a moment. "No. This was a great hiding spot if we just had to hide from Laugh Riot and Incapacitor. But if they set this guy free—I worry he could do a lot of damage on his way out. I'd rather be near the top of the prison. If he brings this whole place down around our ears, up is the closest we have to out. Do you know any-where to hide on the top floor?"

"That makes sense, yes. I have a few options."

"Great."

Gravane followed me back through the apartment, towards the stairs.

"Oh, if you see any drones, give me a warning, they seem to have a mad on for me, courtesy of Incapacitor."

"As if we didn't have enough to worry about," Gravane said.

"Never a dull moment." I paused at the top of the stairs,

listening. I could hear...

"It's amazing how much easier it is to think with these cuffs on," Gravane said. "Without them, it's like my power is constantly whispering in my brain to do more, to be more, to fight..."

I held up a hand. "Do you hear that, Gravane? Was that an explosion? Another one there?"

Gravane cocked his head, frowning. "Yes, I hear... wait, I know that sound."

A rush of wind. A staccato beat of tiny explosions. By the time my brain had processed that it was Laugh Riot—

"Found you!" she cackled with glee. She leapt at Gravane and wrapped him in a hug. "Oh, I've missed you so much. My Mirabor."

"Kayda," Gravane said, his voice full of emotion. Whether that emotion was shock, fear or delight, I couldn't tell you. He put his arms up to return the embrace.

Wait. Where, were the cuffs?

"Looking for this?" Laugh Riot's voice came muffled, her face buried in Gravane's shoulder. She snaked one arm out of the hug, to show me one of the power cuffs. Her hand blurred. A tiny sonic boom cracked the air. The cuff shattered into fragments. "Oops."

"This isn't what Gravane wanted," I said, backing away from the stairs.

"I think I know what my Mirabor really wants." She unfolded herself out of the hug, one arm still possessively around Gravane's waist. She held the second cuff in her free hand. Another burst of speed, that too shattered. "Isn't that better, love?"

"Yes," said Gravane. But I saw no sign of Gravestone behind his eyes. Gravane looked terrified.

I stopped shuffling backwards.

"Kayda," I said. "Listen to me. These powers you have.

They affect you. Just like they affected Mirabor."

Her eyes widened, clearly wanting to respond, but I ploughed on, and to my surprise, she let me. "You weren't using your powers at the Academy? Not much anyway, I bet. The woman I met there was friendly, thoughtful and clever. She made friends, didn't she? I saw you that night at the Dome, you were having fun. No little voice calling you to violence, just you and your friends out enjoying each other's company." She stared at me, wide-eyed as I paced back down the stairs, closing the gap between us. I kept talking as I walked, hoping she wouldn't notice that Gravane had slipped out of her arms and was backpedalling away from her. "Don't you want that? You don't need to hurt people, you don't need to use these powers. You can be... better."

I stumbled to a halt, out of words. I didn't know her well enough, had never known her before her powers to call to her better self. Over her shoulder, Gravane had made it to the corner of an apartment block. He cast a glance back at us, and I gave him a nod. If I could hold Kayda up a little longer...

"Oh, you are a tricky one, aren't you, Grey? I never would have guessed." She threw her head back and laughed, a bitter, brittle sound. Behind her, Gravane made good his escape. "You hypocrite," Laugh Riot snarled, then punched me.

The blow was so fast, I had no chance to block or avoid it, barely enough time to roll with it. Spots flashed across my vision as I floundered away from her. She sauntered after me, walking slowly, though her fists were a blur as she punched me again. The crack of her sonic boom rattled around my skull, and I stumbled over my own feet. I fell flat on my back, my parkour instincts saving me from cracking my head on the floor.

Laugh Riot stood over me. "I thought it would be difficult to hit someone who looked so much like my Mirabor. Turns out it's kind of fun. That's interesting, wouldn't you say? Mirabor? My Mirabor? I have a fun new game we can play!"

As she looked around for Gravane, I kicked out, trying to crush her ankle with my heel. I connected, but she spun away from the blow.

"Still some fight left in you? Good. I hate when the fights are over too quickly. And they are always over too quickly." She moved so fast. One moment she was there, and eye blink later, she was gone. Had she gone to find Gravane or—

She kicked me in the side of the head. Not at full speed, I assume, because I survived it, but the world went dark. I tasted blood.

I staggered to my feet, world swimming around me. She let me stand up. She could have finished the fight, and my life, at any moment. I blinked, trying to clear my double vision. It didn't work. I pulled my hands up to a guard position, my form was sloppy, but it was the best I could manage. The more time I could keep her focussed on me, the longer Gravane had to find a hiding place.

"You want to know something funny, Laugh Riot?" I said.

"Surprise me," she said.

I opened my mouth to say something devastating and pithy, but I was drowned out by the sound of a klaxon, urgently blaring from every speaker in Tartarus. And then a rumble, the ground shook, I stumbled, and so did Laugh Riot.

"Aw, I was having such a good time, too. Sorry, Grey, going to have to leave you beaten but breathing after all," Laugh Riot said.

"What is it? What's that alarm?"

"He calls himself Titan. You're going to meet him real soon. Bye now!"

"Wait!"

She laughed. "No." And then she walked away from me.

I couldn't follow, it was all I could do to keep standing. I staggered to the foot of the stairs, leaning on the bannister, fighting a wave of nausea. Why was everything so loud but muted? Like thunder heard through cushions. Even my similes were suffering.

And then there he was, out across the vast expanse of the empty bowl of Tartarus. A man. A large man, rising slowly through the air. His uniform was black, with a white T emblem on his chest. Two chunky shoulder pads and one of his boots didn't seem to be part of his uniform, instead, they looked to be the remains of whatever machine had held him here. They trailed wires, had jagged edges where they had been ripped from his cell. In his left hand, he held Incapacitor by the throat. Alive or dead, I couldn't tell.

He paused, hovering, looking directly at me. Then, without a word, he turned away from me and began to ascend once more, picking up speed as he rose, aiming himself directly at the ceiling which covered the prison.

After twenty years bound in Tartarus, Titan was breaking out.

CHAPTER 18
SILVER LINING

The concrete ceiling might as well have been paper, for all the good it did. Titan crashed through it without pausing, sending boulder-sized fragments into the inky pit below. A burst of energy followed moments later. It seemed the forcefield hadn't proved any better barrier.

I... felt better. Not well, my head was still ringing, but the moment Titan vanished from sight, my nausea, weakness and unsteadiness disappeared, like turning off a light. Had he been the cause? Or did he have some kind of super-healing wake? Both sounded unlikely, but also, equally possible.

A series of cracking sounds drew my attention up again. The damage to the ceiling hadn't ended with Titan's escape. Fractures spread in an irregular staccato. Fragments large and small rained down. The damage was structural, and I needed to get undercover before the whole thing fell on my head.

"Don't worry, I've got you." Gravane swooped down to me, surrounded in an aura of black-red energy. "Let's get out of here, Grey."

"Gravane, no. You can't use your powers."

"You're right, but the alternative right now is us both getting crushed or trapped down here. Shut up and let me save you." He grabbed me and threw me over his left shoulder. "Here goes." He launched us out over the balcony.

"Ah! Ow!" I said as Gravane's energy field stung my skin.

"Sorry about that, I can't turn that off when I'm flying. I'll try to make this—" he paused to blast a ceiling fragment from our path. "—quick!"

I had no control over our escape. No view of it, really, all I could do was watch the depths of Tartarus fall away behind us, over my view of Gravane's ass. Even that view was difficult to focus on as Gravane dodged and blasted falling debris. All I know is, it worked, and the worst I received were a few stinging pebble-sized fragments that got past Gravane to hit me.

As we accelerated through the rapidly expanding break in Tartarus's ceiling my view suddenly changed, no longer the pit of Tartarus, instead, I could see the crumbling ruin of the prison's roof. It was shattered beyond repair, moments away from total collapse and I—

—realised my situation, as that strange reverse vertigo I get from being outside combined with very real vertigo from being up so high.

"Down!" I shouted at Gravane. "Down, down, down."

Perhaps the edge of panic in my voice convinced him we were under immediate threat, but either way, I bumped on his shoulder as he swerved, angling his trajectory back down towards the jungle that surrounded Tartarus and the Academy. The moment I judged us close enough to the ground, I struggled out of Gravane's grip and let myself fall. It was a hard impact, but I rolled out of it with no further serious injury.

I hugged the ground, curling fingers into the undergrowth for security, face buried in loam, blocking out the starlit sky overhead.

"And *you* captured *me*," muttered Gravane, still floating a little of the ground, I judged from his voice.

"I don't want to talk about it," I said.

"So, what happens next? We report to this Academy of yours? I get thrown into another jail cell, fitted for new suppression cuffs?"

"One thing at a time. We still have Laugh Riot to worry about. And Titan's still out there with Incapacitor."

Gravane didn't respond for a long moment. Long enough that I had to chance a look up from the safety of the earth. Gravane was still there, floating just above me, surrounded by his flickering black-red energy field. His attention was not on me though, he was staring at the ground a short distance away. "Grey," he said. "I think you need to see this. We won't need to worry about Incapacitor. Ever again."

Despite my instinct to keep a firm grip on the ground, I levered myself into a standing position. A little wobbly, perhaps, and with an urgent need to find cover, I nevertheless stood and walked, very calmly I felt, in the direction Gravane was looking.

The tangle of Incapacitor's remains lay twisted on the jungle floor, one leg, clearly broken, positioned awkwardly around a moss-covered rock. A macabre sight, only made more so illuminated by Gravane's blood-red aura.

"I think I'm going to be sick again," Gravane said and floated a little distance away.

"Feet on the ground," I chided him, edging closer to the body.

It was hard to make out details in the dark, but the state of the body was... peculiar. I crouched down beside it, careful not to disturb anything. Welatak skin tended towards a blue-grey sheen, but Incapacitor was more white-grey now, dry, almost powdery. His saline suit hung loosely on a frame that had properly filled it the last time I'd seen him. He hadn't just dried out, he seemed almost desiccated. As if every drop of moisture had been pulled from him. But no, that wasn't quite it. What was I looking at?

I could almost feel Professor Croft looking over my shoulder, telling me to catalogue the evidence before I drew my conclusions.

Right.

I suspected some of the damage was post-mortem. The broken leg came from hitting that rock at some speed, for example. But without stripping him out of his saline suit I couldn't determine how much. A closer inspection of what I could see... most of the physical injuries seemed to have happened after Titan dropped him. After he was dead? There was one exception, one injury clearly from before his fall.

His neck was bruised, I could make out Titan's grip pattern in the discolouration. Bruising a Welatak's tough hide would require a good deal of force. Titan was strong. That wasn't new information, not really, not when I'd seen Titan hold Incapacitor up in one hand. What else? Incapacitor's eyes were open, staring in two different directions, black, featureless orbs I'd always found a little off-putting. His eyes, while now sightless, still looked wet. "Not all moisture then," I muttered to myself. "Or... not moisture at all?"

I had none of my forensic kit with me, of course, not even a pair of gloves and a mask, and I knew better than to go touching a corpse that exhibits strange properties. There was a whole galaxy of pathogens and weird abilities that could leave lingering effects that I did not want to get involved with. Even crouching this close might be a bad idea, but what choice did I have? I needed data. Putting my hands on him would still be a bad idea.

I stood, cast about for a prodding instrument. Fortunately, the jungle provided. In this case a stout stick as thick as my wrist and a little longer than my forearm. A little clumsy to hold but did the job.

Gravane still floated close by, hanging a little off the ground, radiating that sickly energy field of his. "Gravane? Mirabor? You okay?"

"Fine," he said, still facing away from me, and Incapacitor's corpse.

"Okay. But you should land. You know the more you use your power, the greater the risk—"

"—that I become a raving psychopath. Yeah, I know."

"So, land, then?"

"Fine," he said again. He drifted to the ground, his back still facing me. The jungle floor crunched beneath his feet.

I shook my head. Nothing more I could do for Gravane in that moment, so I turned my attention back to the mystery that might reveal something about... something.

I poked Incapacitor's face. I half expected the body to dissolve to dust when I did, or at least to powder and collapse around the end of my stick, but no. Still solid, still pliable. Not desiccated at all then. I'd read that wrong. But something was missing from the corpse. Other than life, obviously. I mean... huh.

I'd been so focussed on the body I hadn't looked at Incapacitor's cybernetics. Not all the tell-tales were out. A few pieces still glittered, working tech about his person. Some of it, though, was as dead as Incapacitor himself. What was the difference between the two types? Maybe... I couldn't tell without taking the tech apart, but perhaps some had been wired into Incapacitor's nervous system, drawing power from him. Others would surely have independent power sources. When the host died, they would keep on ticking; whatever had killed Incapacitor hadn't affected them. I poked a few of them with my poking stick. Nothing happened. As tests go it was neither rigorous nor all that conclusive but somehow, I still felt it proved some-thing.

Incapacitor had not been drained of moisture but in some manner, he'd been drained of something altogether more vital. But it hadn't affected his tech.

My train of thought was interrupted by a thunder-ous crack. The roof of the prison finally gave up its last. Collapsing in on itself and sending a gout of dust and debris high into the sky. Small chunks of it spattered down around us. I dived under the cover of a stout tree and let the solid rain abate.

"That's that, then," said Gravane.

"I guess so. It didn't represent the Academy's finest hour. But it might still have been useful to keep around."

"Do you think Kayda made it out?"

"If anyone could get out, I'm sure she could. And did."

Gravane nodded sharply. "Do you still need time with your corpse, or can we get moving?"

I stared at the Welatak's body for a moment. With a lab and proper gear, there would be more to learn, but as it was? "Let's move on."

"Where to? The Academy?"

"I can't think of anywhere else to go," I admitted. "But keep your eyes peeled. Titan is still out there somewhere."

"And Kayda."

Fair point. "Yes, her too."

What was bothering me, but didn't seem to have occurred to Gravane yet... where was the response from the Academy? A failure this catastrophic must have sounded literal alarms at the main campus, and even if somehow they hadn't, we'd been making enough of a racket that someone should have noticed. So where was the army of superheroes I'd expected to come riding over the hill? Flying. You know what I meant. It was, I judged, about a half-hour walk from Tartarus to the Academy proper, perhaps longer through jungle. Where was everyone?

Gravane and I set off into the jungle. I had a lot on my mind.

# # #

I led us away from the direct line to campus, opting instead for what I hoped was a wider arc back to safety. "Titan ignored us the first time, but I don't know if I want to push our luck and stumble across him again," I whispered to Gravane. "Unless... I worry we should head straight back to campus and warn them about him."

"If the alarms, the sound of their prison collapsing, and the plume of dust don't put them on alert," Gravane noted dryly, "there is little hope for them."

He had a point.

Gravane offered to carry me again, but I vetoed the suggestion. The dense jungle made flying below the thick canopy too dangerous, particularly in the dark; night had well and truly fallen while I was inside Tartarus. Flying above the canopy would get us spotted in an instant. Also, frankly, I remained a little freaked out from my first flying experience.

At least the canopy was pleasingly roof-like; it kept us hidden and kept me safe from a panic attack. About the sky, anyway. I concentrated on my breathing, on placing my feet on the uneven jungle floor, on peering into the darkness, trying to judge our route. With each step, I strained for any sign that we were discovered. Every rustle in the undergrowth, every time an unseen critter started or stopped making a noise. Every time Gravane stepped on a twig. Every time, I was convinced Titan had found us. Or Laugh Riot. Or both.

Night in the Jungle of Justice is not a quiet time.

At least it wasn't cold. My flimsy prison uniform was not designed as outdoor wear. It kept me decent, but wouldn't have protected me from harsh elements, and didn't do much good against the jungle itself. Not for the first time, my sleeve caught on some prickly plant or other. Yanking free of an earlier plant already cost me a tear on the other sleeve, this time I stopped and carefully unpicked myself from the tree branch. As I did, I caught a sound. Voices. Close by and getting closer.

I hissed at Gravane to get him to stop, his glow would give us away in the dark. Put a finger to my lips, then cupped my ear. He nodded and stopped to listen too.

I couldn't make out the words, but the tone was clear: annoyance. The voice didn't sound like Laugh Riot's, or how I imagined Titan spoke, but that could just be me leaping to assumptions.

Another voice answered. Also not Laugh Riot. Who else was out here with us?

Gravane stepped up to me and pointed up. I hesitated but nodded. Gravane picked me up and flew us both into the cover of the low branches of a nearby tree. We waited, in silence.

A whir of servos, the stomping of metal feet, and the flash of spotlights announced their approach even before they crashed through the trees. Steel Spartan looked around the clearing, servos buzzing. "This doesn't look right at all. Are you sure we shouldn't be heading more in that kind of direction?" he asked, pointing off towards where Tartarus had been.

"This right," Bloodshock said, though he didn't sound confident.

Channis plucked leaves from her shoulder fur. "I didn't come to the Academy to go slinking around a jungle at night."

"We need to warn them," I whispered to Gravane.

Gravane put a hand on my arm before I could move. "That one there used to work for Doctor Gravestone," he whispered, "It is probable he moved his allegiance to Kayda when I was incarcerated."

Gravane was pointing to Penumbra, who had added several sprays of leaves to his normally black uniform, presumably in a largely unsuccessful attempt at camouflage.

"My contact was adamant, if we met her outside Tartarus tonight, she can tell us who murdered Veritas," Penumbra said.

"Still say was Grey," Bloodshock muttered.

"If that explosion *was* Tartarus," Channis said, "I don't know if meeting Penumbra's contact outside it is even possible."

"Or it's more possible," Spartan said. "It's inside that would be trickier."

"Penumbra's contact... it's Laugh Riot," I whispered. She wasn't lying. She could tell them who killed Veritas, but I doubted most of them would like the answer. Why were they out here? Laugh Riot couldn't have known about Titan before she went in, so these people were either hired muscle to help her break Gravane out, or patsies to blame for his escape. All bets were off now, though, and they didn't deserve what had happened to Incapacitor. "We still have to warn them."

Before I could move, though, Bloodshock and Channis collapsed, as though they were puppets with their strings cut. Steel Spartan slumped, and I suspected it was only his armour keeping him upright.

Penumbra goggled. "Guys? Guys?" He knelt by Channis, took her pulse. He scanned the trees as he did, head whipping back and forth, looking for an explanation for his friends' state. The answer, when it came, arrived from above.

Titan crashed through the canopy, landing with a sound like thunder, right next to Penumbra. Titan swung, and knocked Penumbra back, propelling him like a bullet from a gun. Penumbra struck a tree trunk with an audible crack and slid to the ground.

Titan leaned down and put one filthy hand on Channis's face. The Cholbren shuddered, limbs twitching, then was suddenly very still. In the glow of Steel Spartan's head-lights, Channis's skin grew pale and she… diminished.

Behind me, Gravane gasped. I snapped a glance at him; he was glowing again, that black-red of Gravestone's power.

"We have to stop this," I said.

But it was already too late for Channis. Titan rose, leaving the Cholbren nothing more than a lifeless husk at his feet. As he stood, Gravane's aura blinked out.

"Monster," Penumbra spat. He pulled himself up, hold-ing onto the tree for support. "You killed her."

"Yes," said Titan, his voice rasping from disuse.

"You will find me less easy prey," Penumbra said. He grabbed at a thick branch on the tree he'd fallen next to. He heaved and seemed surprised when the branch didn't snap off in his hands.

"No," said Titan. He launched himself across the clear-ing, reaching out to Penumbra.

I didn't see what happened next, because Gravane grabbed me and launched us away.

"No, take us back, we have to help them," I said.

"We can't help them."

"Take us back Gravane."

He tightened his grip. "No."

I had no sense of direction for our flight. Gravane kept

us low, and trees whipped past, slapping us with branches. I picked up more bruises, and my prison uniform more tears before Gravane landed us.

"Damn you, Gravane, we could have saved them," I said.

"We *couldn't*. I was trying to summon my power from the moment of his arrival. The attempt was futile, it seemed. It kept slipping through my fingers until Titan fed on that Cholbren, and then again on Penumbra. Whatever else Titan does, he stops powers. If we had interfered, he would still have fed on them. Then he would have fed on us. I saved your life, Grey. You're welcome."

I wanted to refute him. Wanted to protest. But he was right. Bitterly, silently, I led us on into the jungle.

# # #

We pushed through the dense foliage. Don't ask me what any of it was. Trees. Bushes. That kind of thing. The problem, it turned out, was that it was easy to lose your sense of direction when you couldn't see where you were going or where you had come from. It had already been more than the half-hour I'd estimated for the journey. Were we close to our destination? I had no idea. I wasn't even sure we were still heading the correct way.

"I can still fly up and look," Gravane offered, not for the first time.

"No, you've done quite enough with your powers already. We have to keep them as our last resort, right?"

"If this is about my powers driving me mad, you should know, I feel fine. Lost. But fine."

Off in the distance, there was a rumble of starship engines launching. Not from the direction we were heading but not far adrift. It was the third time something had launched as we walked, each one providing a much-needed bearing. But they were bothering me. Launches were rare at the Academy, one every few weeks, not counting the hum of the mail pods. Why so many launches in rapid succession, and where were they going? What the heck was going on?

"Do you hear that?" Gravane asked.

"The starship? Sure."

"No, not that. It sounds like water, up ahead. A river. Is the water here safe to drink?"

I didn't know. I'd skimmed the welcome file at the start of the first year, but hadn't paid too much attention to the jungle facts. I knew there were classes based out in the jungle too, and some sort of annual orienteering competition, but for reasons which I hope are apparent by now, I'd never partaken of either. I had, however, visited the Academy's water treatment plant; it had the decency to have a roof. I had to assume it was treating the water for something. "Best not," I said.

"This was exactly the sort of thing I prepared my bug-out bag for," Gravane grumbled, pushing aside another frond.

He stopped. "Oh wow."

I came up to join him. We were at the edge of a clearing. Luminescent vines twisted around the trees giving the whole place a green and gold aura, warm, natural. On the far side of the clearing, the ground rose in a cliff, perhaps ten meters high, wreathed in branches and more of the glowing vines. It was dominated by a waterfall, water crashing into a pool that took up most of the cleaning, running off in a river to the east, towards the coast. The water was clear and inviting but could well have been a petri dish of virulent diseases for all I knew. Still, despite that, I couldn't help but echo Gravane. "Wow."

"There's something metallic, man-made, up there at the top of the cliff," Gravane said, pointing. "I'm going to take a look; it might be a comm station."

"Wait!"

Gravane had already powered up, flying towards the cliff-top, his energy field rippling around him. Was it clearer than before? Was he pulling more power? Giving into Gravestone? He could have landed at the top of the cliff, released his power again, but he chose to hover instead, floating far above the small lake.

"No," he called back down to me. "It's some kind of science station, I think. Environmental sensors by the look of it. Still, it must link up to the Academy systems somehow, I wonder if we can tap that to communicate with them."

"We don't need to. We just need to get ourselves to the Academy. Can you see it? Are we close?" I hadn't wanted him to use his powers, but now he had it seemed a shame not to take advantage.

"Yes. We're not far now. It's that way." He pointed. A straight line in that direction meant climbing the cliff, but that didn't look too hard, depending on how secure those branches on it were.

"That's weird," Gravane added. "Hey! Has there been trouble with the jungle recently?"

"What do you mean?"

"There's a swath of dead trees, off over that way, quite a big area. Looks kind of grey and lifeless. No offence."

I'd not heard anything about a problem in the jungle, and while on one level someone might have told me and I hadn't registered it, I'd been preoccupied this year, after all, at the same time... grey and lifeless. That reminded me of Incapacitor.

"Gravane, I think you'd better come down."

He sighed theatrically. "Fine," he said, and drifted back towards me, across the lake.

A burst of bright white energy struck him in the square

223

of his back. He cried out in pain, and his aura winked out. Gravane fell into the water with an inelegant splash. He surfaced, spluttering, moments later.

"Gravestone! What are you doing here?" I knew that voice. There, hovering above the clearing, blazing white-hot light against the night sky, was Pilvi.

#

Gravane exploded out of the water, his aura spiking as he fired a beam of energy directly at Pilvi. She was more than ready though and seemed to evade the attack with little more than a sway of her shoulders. The two squared off against each other, Gravestone's hand wreathed in his dark energy, while Pilvi's eyes glowed like the sun.

"I don't know what this is all about, but I know you're behind it," Pilvi declared.

"Idiot child, I am the victim here, but I will not allow your lack of comprehension to decide my fate," Gravestone countered.

Oh for— "Will the pair of you just calm down and let's talk this over," I shouted. "We don't have time for this crossover nonsense."

Both turned their gaze towards me. Pilvi looked shocked, Gravestone looked furious.

"Both of you. Down here, now." I pointed at the ground next to me.

"Grey? What are you..." Pilvi spared one cautious glance at Gravestone, then flew to join me. "When did you get back on planet? They've been saying some pretty bad things about you. Do you know anything about the explosion at Tartarus? What am I saying, of course you're mixed up in it." She gave me a quick hug, before stepping back and returning her focus to Gravestone. Gravane. It was too easy to slip.

Gravane for his part shrugged and floated down to join us. He landed on the other side of me from Pilvi. He gave me a very deliberate long look, then released his power, and his aura vanished. "Ms. Rissanen, isn't it? A pleasure to see you again," he said.

"Cut the posturing, Mirabor. Pilvi, what's going on at the Academy? Säde, sorry." One of these days I'd remember to use her codename.

For a moment, she didn't answer, just kept staring at Gravane, eyes burning. Then she frowned, shook her head and blinked. Her eyes returned to their unpowered shade as she turned her attention to me. "Yes. Sorry, Grey. I just— never mind. They're evacuating. At the campus. There was some sort of alarm, and they summoned everybody to the quad. Captain Hawk sent Doctor Phenomenal away first, leading all the Welatak and amphibious students and staff out to sea. Then he started selecting students to—" She shook her head, "no, that's not right, he had a list, clearly prepared in advance. He read off names of students and a few staff and all of the visitors, boarded them on Academy ships and sent them up to the Academy training station."

Hawk must be really frightened of Titan. That he had a list prepared, he must be keeping that to hand. And sending the more vulnerable students to safety? It was a delaying tactic, but it wasn't facing the threat head-on.

"Did he just send Skills students?" Gravane asked. I was a little surprised that he knew about Academy factions, but thinking about it, I'd always suspected he had monitored me during my first year.

"If you think I'm telling you anything, you have another thing coming," Pilvi said through clenched teeth.

"Why do you ask, Gravane?" I said.

"I have the inkling of a theory. I hope it isn't true, but I suspect it may be."

I nodded. "Pilvi? Who was Hawk sending topside?"

She shook her head again. "No, it wasn't just Skills students. The rest were all first-year Powers students." She frowned. "That's not entirely true either, on the second and third ships, I think he sent up a few Powers students from later years."

Gravane nodded. "Yes. I see."

"What do you see, Gravane?" I asked.

"In a moment, let Ms. Rissanen complete her story."

"Is there more to it?"

"A little," she admitted, grudgingly. "When we heard the explosion from Tartarus, a few of us tried to investigate, but Captain Hawk was ahead of us. Staff members were guarding all the exits, turning people back, shooting down drones, if you can believe it. Apogee himself turned me away. There were no ifs or buts, we weren't allowed out to investigate. But that didn't stop the rumours in the crowd. There are enough clairvoyant, empathic, and precognitive students that rumours started to circulate; that there had been a breakout. That something was coming for us, and Hawk was scared. I overheard one of them mention Gravestone. I had to investigate."

"Nice to know you care," Gravane said with a bow.

Pilvi's eyes ignited again. "Step carefully, Gravestone. You try to be funny when Grey isn't around and I—"

"Pilvi!" I said, shocked.

"Säde," she corrected. "Let's all call me what he made me."

"Finish your story, how did you break out to investigate?" I said, trying to distract her more than anything.

"Hawk had hired the Brontom to help work the perimeter. I hadn't realised at first, but when I tried to get away the second time, I did a full circuit and found them patrolling one of the approaches. I knew Sergeant Nine would still try to stop me, but I gambled Sev—Probability Kid wouldn't. I bided my time, looked for an opening, and went for it. I was right. I got out, flew around until I spotted this *perseensuti* and thought I'd do the galaxy a favour."

"Charming," Gravane said, with a tight, mocking smile.

"Will you two cut it out. Okay, spill. What's your theory?"

"One last question, Ms... Säde. The Powers students that were evacuated, were they perchance students who were, in theory, powerful but still struggled to control their abilities?"

"Oh, come on, Gravane, how would Säde know that?"

But Pilvi nodded sharply. "As it happens, yes."

"Then it is clear to me that your Captain Hawk is attempting to achieve two contradictory goals simultaneously. First, he is protecting the weakest of his students, commendable, I suppose, but secondly, he is trying to deny Titan a... hmm, shall we say, a tasty meal?"

"Oh, no."

"Yes. After what we experienced when Titan fed upon Penumbra and the others, I think we have seen enough now to realise we were both wrong about the suppression field in Tartarus. It wasn't what was keeping Titan contained, it was Titan attempting to escape, trying to feed on whoever was trapped in there with him. Once Incapacitor and Kayda removed Titan's physical restraints, I suspect Incapacitor had just enough energy for Titan to power up and escape Tartarus. Incapacitor did not survive the transaction. Since escaping, and murdering those four students—"

"Which four?" Säde asked.

Gravane ignored her. "Titan has been subsisting by draining the very jungle around us, but I doubt that will keep him fed for long. He needs a real meal for that. Your army of superhero students? May be precisely what Titan is looking for."

"Hawk is trying to starve him out."

"Yes. It won't work. But the alternative is facing and killing Titan, and for some reason, your headmaster has been unwilling or unable to do that for... how long did you say Titan was trapped in Tartarus?"

"Twenty years."

"Quite. Well, I suspect we are all dead then, sooner or later."

"If he's right, and this Titan feeds on powers, we represent quite a meal, between us," Pilvi said. "We'd better move, predators usually evolve ways to find their prey."

"She is right, of course," Gravane added, "but it does rather raise the question of which direction to run. If we head to your Academy, we can be sure Titan will arrive there, sooner rather than later. If we travel away from it, Titan might be tempted by the larger meal of the Academy, giving us, perhaps, a chance to find a way to stay alive."

"Or he could come for the easier target first," Pilvi objected. "Come on Grey, you can't listen to this psychopath."

She was right, and I was worried. Gravane claimed it had taken him months to become Gravestone before, but he'd had his powers back less than an hour, and he already sounded different. But then, I didn't know the 'real' Gravane at all, did I? "We make for the Academy," I said, flatly.

"Good. We can be there in minutes if we fly. Grey, I can carry you," Pilvi said.

"Expending energy and moving above the tree line will both increase our chances of being—" Gravane didn't get a chance to finish his thought.

Instead, there was a rush of air, an explosion of motion.

I blinked and for a moment caught an after image on my eyelids, an explosion of light from Pilvi, as Laugh Riot burst out of the jungle and, at full extension, punched her across the jaw.

Laugh Riot's momentum carried her out over the lake, her feet not lingering long enough to break the surface tension, and she circled back towards us. She laughed throughout her arc, only pausing as she breathlessly slowed when she reached the shore again. She threw a hug around Gravane, this time he returned it enthusiastically.

While they reunited, I dashed over to where Pilvi lay, dazed but still conscious. I helped her up, she stood unsteadily at first but then found her balance. She put a hand to her jaw, winced in pain. She started to speak, but I shook my head. There was a real chance her jaw was broken after that.

Instead, "Where did you spring from, Laugh Riot?" I said.

This time it was Doctor Gravestone who laughed. "She has been following us, almost since the moment we escaped Tartarus. Did you truly not notice her? My word, Grey, you really are not an outdoorsman, are you?"

"I'm so glad to have you back," Laugh Riot said. "My Mirabor. The real you. Is it time to kill *this* fake, at least?"

Gravestone smiled. "I think, perhaps, yes." He rose into the air, his aura enveloping him with black-red energy.

Laugh Riot took up a sprinter's starting pose, the air crackled around her. "Say when."

Pilvi's hair ignited with light, her eyes blazed, and though she wisely chose not to join the banter, I could tell she wanted to.

What were they all thinking? "Stop it, all of you, what were we just talking about?" This would be like a beacon to attract Titan.

Pilvi's hair flickered and went out. Gravestone gave a startled yelp and tumbled to earth. Laugh Riot launched herself forward but looked confused when she made it to no more than jogging speed.

"Too late," I said, "Titan's here."

CHAPTER 19
MENDING BRIDGES

Pilvi tugged urgently at my elbow. She was right, it was time to go. The crashing sounds that marked Titan's approach were already too close and only getting closer.

"We head to the Academy," I told Gravane. "Quickly. Come on."

He took a step towards me.

"We leave them and the Academy to Titan. We're safer alone," Laugh Riot said.

Gravane stopped, looked at Kayda, then back at me. "Grey..." he said, an expression of desperate indecision painted across his face. Come with us, or abandon us? Gravane or Gravestone? He didn't have the excuse of the lure of his powers in the moment. Gravane claimed he didn't want to be Gravestone, that he understood the mistakes he'd made. This was his chance to reclaim his life, to redeem those mistakes.

His face set in a grim mask. I wondered if I'd ever see Gravane again.

"You're right, my love, lead on," Doctor Gravestone said to Laugh Riot.

They fled into the jungle, away from Titan, but also away from us, away from the Academy.

Pilvi stared at me with wide-eyed sympathy. She put a hand on my elbow again.

I nodded. "He's made his choice. Let's go."

Exit stage left, pursued by a supervillain.

# # #

I followed Pilvi. She knew a lot more about the Academy Jungle than I did. Her hair remained her natural blond, her eyes their natural blue. Either Titan was following us, or the area of his drain effect was wider than I realised.

Pilvi had reached the same conclusion. "Don't think we can make the Academy before he catches us," she said. Her words were awkward as she spoke without trying to move her jaw. She winced in pain, more than once.

"Right," I said. Despite myself, the vision of Incapacitor's withered corpse swam across my mind. I didn't plan on dying like that. "So, we make a stand?"

"Maybe," Pilvi said. A fierce and capable fighter if the need arose, our Pilvi, but too smart to throw her life away if there were alternatives. Her face lit up. "There!" she said, pointing at a small patch of ferns.

"Where?" I said, looking past the ferns. There was nothing more remarkable that way, just more jungle, and the ferns themselves were too sparse to hide in and too thin to protect us. "I don't get it."

Pilvi shot me a look, too pained for a lengthy explanation. Instead, she gave me a shove towards the ferns, and when I tried to go around them, she nudged me again.

She had clearly lost her mind. Titan could be right behind us, and she thought these flimsy leaves would—*oh*.

Within the perimeter of the plants, it was clear that the leaves were much thicker than I'd thought. They were broad, long and sharp-edged, and if they weren't made of steel, they were tough and strong. They'd make surprisingly good cover.

"It's a Notme Tree," she said, by way of explanation. "It emits a low-level psychic buzz that makes you look elsewhere. Easy to overcome if you know about it, but if not, you will almost always dismiss it as not what you wanted. I'm hoping it can block whatever Titan is using to track us."

"I never knew the Academy had psychic plants," I said. "Your jaw is feeling better?"

"No," she grimaced, "but I knew you wouldn't stop asking unless I told you."

We sat in silence after that, listening to the sounds of the jungle around us. Was Titan's crashing receding? The more normal sounds of the jungle returning? I hoped so.

"Pilvi, I've been meaning to apologise," I said, keeping my voice low.

She furrowed her brow quizzically.

"Way back at the start of term, I was a bit of an ass to you. I know I upset you. I'm sorry." It felt good to get that off my chest.

"When?" she asked.

"The morning after Veritas's murder. You came to offer help, I snapped at you and blamed you for avoiding us. You didn't deserve it."

"Oh." Pilvi hesitated. "But I kind of did. I *should* have been there. I *was* avoiding you. All of you."

"Don't talk," I said. "It's okay. Mind your jaw."

She shook her head. "Talking won't make my jaw worse. It just hurts. You need to understand, I've been... I've been going through some stuff."

"Pilvi?"

"When I first got my powers, I was excited. Couldn't wait to use them to help protect people on Nymanteles. We needed them. My powers. And using them was a joy, I can't explain how... exhilarating they are when I let loose. I didn't get over the rush until term ended and I was heading home to see my folks. That's when I realised.

When I remembered where these powers came from. The Ascension Machine. It gave powers to Gravane too. And his bodyguard, after a fashion."

"And Kayda Buchanan, Laugh Riot," I added.

"Who?"

"The woman who punched you. I think she also killed Veritas."

"Oh. Great. Well, I'm glad I didn't know about her too. Gravane's powers warped his mind, the more he used them, the crazier he got, right? And the price Gravane's bodyguard paid?" She shuddered. "I got to thinking... how did that start? Did it start with the same exhilaration I was feeling? If I kept using these powers, would I lose myself too? I couldn't risk it. When I got home, I spent one night with my family, and then I took off, went into the wilds. To keep them safe. To protect my family and Kaarina. From me, if I lost control. I tried not using my powers. But they're part of me now. It's like trying not to blink. So, instead, I trained. Tested myself. Looked for any signs that I was losing myself to them."

She stopped then, and I thought her story was done, but after a couple of minutes, she continued.

"I knew I had to come back to the Academy. The safest place for me, if I lost control, was to be surrounded by other heroes who could stop me. Other powered heroes. It hurt me, but that meant I couldn't be around you, Seventhirtyfour or any of the others. The best way to keep you safe was to keep you distant. So, I didn't meet up in the bar at the start of term. I wasn't there to support Avrim. I'm so sorry, Grey. You were right, you see."

I hugged her, being careful not to nudge her jaw. "I can't believe you were going through all that, alone, and I didn't know."

"How could you?"

"We're friends, Pilvi, I should have seen... but I was too wrapped up..."

"In a murder case, for another one of our friends," Pilvi said calmly. "It's not like you had nothing to distract you."

"Still."

"I'm feeling better now. It was seeing Kaarina, here at the Academy, that started putting me right. She got me to admit what was going on. Pointed out that the only crazy thing I'd done was push my friends and family away. And it wasn't too late to fix that. I've been mending bridges since. I thought I'd missed my chance with you, though, I'm glad to see you back. Even if..." She gestured broadly at our situation.

"Yes, well, I do seem to specialise in complicating the lives of those around me," I said.

She gave a short laugh, that quickly collapsed into a cringe of pain. "Seeing Gravane again, kind of set me off. I think I may have over-reacted. Where did the two of you spring from anyway?"

I brought her up to speed, giving her jaw a chance to rest. There were gaps in the story neither of us could fill in. I suspected that Penumbra had attacked Lucy's boyfriend but how did my DNA turn up on the scene? It probably wasn't important but did suggest that Laugh Riot had at least one more accomplice at the Academy that we knew nothing about.

"One other thing does strike me as odd," Pilvi said, as my story wound down. "The names all align a bit too well. Pluto, Tartarus, Titan? They're all a bit on point."

"That occurred to me too. I can totally see Doc Pluto creating a prison called Tartarus, but I do wonder if Titan was called Titan when they threw him in there. Hopefully, Dez can answer that one, if she ever did find out about the mysterious missing faculty member."

"Oh! Yes, she did. She told the rest of us. But the missing staff member can't have been Titan. Dez's theory is that she was a female Cholbren called Moon Tiger."

"Hmm," I hmmed. "That's not an exact match for Titan, I'll grant you. But this all ties back to that incident in the first year of the Academy. If he wasn't the teacher, he must have been one of the students."

"Grey?"

I looked up from my musing. Pilvi's hair sparkled with light.

"Let's get out of here," she said.

# # #

Our Notme hiding place was less than five minutes from the Academy, so now we had a chance to run, Pilvi wasted no time about it. I followed, glad that between the tree cover and my adrenaline, even being outside wasn't enough to stop me.

Pilvi slowed and bit her lip as we neared the edge of the greenery. "On second thought, let's make sure we get the friendliest reception we can." We circled the perimeter for another couple of minutes. When finally we broke cover, we were looking at the backs of two of the lab blocks. Between them, four Brontom clone warriors stood guard, body armour over their superhero uniforms, stun bolters at the ready. Or more precisely, three Brontom clone warriors and—

"Seventhirtyfour!" I shouted in delight, dashing towards them.

Seventhirtyfour lowered his stun bolter. "Grey?" he said, mouth agape. "Grey!"

Sergeant Nine, on the other hand, or, I guess technically, on *one* of the other hands, raised his bolter, pointed it at my head and barked, "Advance and be recognised."

I put my hands up, slowed to a walk. "It's only me, Sergeant," I said.

"Us," Pilvi corrected. She came to walk beside me.

"Stand still, no sudden moves," Nine said. "Two, search them. Three, Four, keep them covered. They are not to breach perimeter until I give the word."

Triple Threat and Seventhirtyfour pointed their weapons at us, although Seventhirtyfour gave us a grin and offered a thumbs up with a spare hand.

Twin Strike holstered her sidearm and came towards us. "Sorry about this," she said. She efficiently and thoroughly patted down first me, then Pilvi.

"Nothing, Sarge," she called back once finished. "They're both injured. Girl's got a broken jaw, I think. Permission to treat?"

Sergeant Nine, held up a hand for her to wait. He tapped his wristpad to open a comm line. "Sergeant Nine reporting perimeter contact in quadrant delta. Two humans, appear to be the student, Säde, and the fugitive, Grey." He paused, listening to a reply I couldn't make out. "Roger that, will detain for your arrival."

He nodded to Twin Strike. "Go ahead."

She held two of her hands either side of Pilvi's head. "May I? This may feel a little strange, at first, but should help," she said.

"Sure," said Pilvi.

Twin Strike's hands glowed with a soft green glow, matching her skin tone. It cast Pilvi's face into strange shadows. There was a peculiar sound like a crunch in reverse; Twin Strike hands stop glowing, and she put them down. "There. How does that feel?"

Pilvi worked her jaw. "Wow. Much better, thanks. No pain at all."

"Good."

"And yet you still wouldn't do that for me when I was in the Med Centre," Triple Threat grumbled. It sounded like an old argument.

"I told you, I wasn't sure what would happen if I healed you while you were stretched."

Something else was bothering me, though. "Wait, you're called Twin Strike, but you have healing powers? Do you also zap people with, say, acid and cold?"

Twin Strike looked confused. "No, I only have my healing ability. It's always felt enough for me. May I?" She offered her hands to heal my scrapes, bruises and possible concussion.

"Oh, yes please," I said. "I'm not criticising the power, I'm sure it's amazingly useful. It's more the name. Twin *Strike*."

Twin Strike's hands passed her glowing hands over my face, arms and chest.

"Grey, is this really the time?" Pilvi asked.

I shrugged feeling suddenly refreshed. "No. No, I guess not."

#

We didn't have long to wait before three figures flew over one of the lab blocks to join Nine's patrol. Captain Hawk, in his black and gold uniform, cape swirling impressively as he came in for a landing, flanked by Apogee on his left and a Zalex teacher I didn't know on his right. The Zalex's jet pack fired noisily as he settled towards the rear of the group.

Hawk strode past Nine without a word, coming to a halt only when he reached me. He looked me up and down, his expression... complicated.

"Four hours," he said. "I put you in Tartarus and within four hours, you have brought down something which has protected this place for twenty years. You have placed everyone here in terrible danger. I trust you appreciate that?"

"With respect, headmaster, you and I have vastly different views of the last four hours. You threw me in prison with Mirabor Gravane without warning me, a man who has a history of wanting me dead. In the process your lax security let two of Gravane's accomplices in there with me." I mean, some of that last bit was my fault, but I wasn't giving him a breath to butt in on that point. "Those criminals attacked me, then freed not just Gravane, but a homicidal prisoner you've kept locked up in there for two *decades.* A prisoner who you've told nobody about in all that time, I might add. That guy then brought the roof down on my head. By my count, I could have died three or four times in those four hours, so, no, I'm not going to let you try and guilt me for *your* mess."

Apogee and the Zalex gave each other worried glances during all this. The Brontom generally maintained stony expressions, except Seventhirtyfour who looked horrified.

Hawk spluttered and found his voice again. "Have you finished?"

"Actually, no. Despite all this, I've tried to keep Gravane from turning into Gravestone again, but eventually failed, because, why? Oh yes, one of the super-powered villains you let roam around your high-security prison was Gravestone's *girlfriend.* And oh, did I mention, the person who murdered Veritas? So, yeah, I managed to solve that while all this was going on."

I was getting a little hyper, I could hear it in my voice, but I couldn't seem to control it. My nerves were beyond frayed, I was exhausted, dehydrated and, yeah, scared. You bet I was.

Apogee stepped in to defuse the situation. "Stand

down, Grey. We can talk all this over once the crisis has passed. Sounds like we all owe you an apology, at the very least. Tell us, who all is out there in the jungle? Tangent, Gravestone and... two others?"

I took a breath, tried to control the shaking in my hands. I'd been keeping things under control pretty well, I thought, but now the danger, fear, anger, that I'd been keeping a lid on, it was all bubbling up again unbidden. And something else, a sensation I couldn't name, a strange sense of detachment, almost euphoria swelling in my chest. *What the hell?*

"Grey?" Apogee said. Behind him, I saw Seventhirtyfour take a worried step towards me.

"Sorry, Professor Gale. Yes. Well, no." I shook my head to try and unscatter my thoughts. "First, if Tangent was the name of your prisoner, he seems to be going by Titan now. Second, yes, there were two more in the prison, but Titan killed one of them—a Welatak tech specialist called Incapacitor. Titan also killed four students out in the jungle. Bloodshock, Penumbra, Channis and Steel Spartan." I didn't want to get into Penumbra's complicated role in everything. "That leaves... somewhere out in the jungle, you have Titan, Doctor Gravestone and Laugh Riot."

"Laugh Riot?" Apogee asked, his voice pitched to be as calming as he could.

I shook my head again. Her identity was as complicated as mine was in my first year. "Her real name is Kayda Buchanan, she has speed powers that she got from the Ascension Machine on Nymanteles. But she's been posing as a student called Fusillade since the start of term." I thought about Fusillade and her powers. "I guess her explosions were sonic booms she created with her speed."

Apogee put a hand on my shoulder. "Thank you, Grey. You've done good work, son. We can take it from here."

"We aren't going to fight again, then?" I said, with a still slightly hyper laugh.

"No, I think we got that out of our system back on Tamban Station. Relax. Recover. Catch up with your friends." He turned to Captain Hawk. "Sir, I suggest you continue with the evacuation. It's still our best plan for keeping people safe. If Tangent, sorry, Titan, is getting this close we don't have time to get everybody up to the Academy Station. I suggest organising the remaining students into groups and taking them deep into the jungle. I'll handle Titan."

"I should send some people with you," Captain Hawk said.

Apogee took to the air, the metallic parts of his uniform glittering in the light from the campus. "The more people we send, the more he can drain. The more powerful he gets. I can keep my distance, keep him distracted. Don't worry, I can handle it. I did before, I can again."

He didn't wait for Hawk to respond, just disappeared out over the jungle in a burst of acceleration.

I watched him go.

Calmer now, if still scared. My fingers tingled; my shoulders shook. I could let them handle it. Sorted.

Captain Hawk fell into discussion with Sergeant Nine and the Zalex teacher. I tuned them out, trying to get a little quiet in my head.

Seventhirtyfour broke ranks and came over to me. I could tell from his voice he was excited and pleased to see me. It was such a relief to see him after all this. And yet... I couldn't focus on his words. Something was still...

"Here," said Seventhirtyfour and thrust something into my hands. I looked down. It was a grapnel gun. Not my specific one, but the same model, a PS 10N. It felt cold but comfortable in my hand.

The moment crystalised. I wasn't done. I knew it. I felt the familiar weight of the grapnel gun in my hand. I thought about Professor Gale's theory. About his paradox.

I looked up at my best friend, the Brontom clone warrior, Seventhirtyfour. I knew he'd have my back.

"The thing is," I said, and was surprised at how steady and confident my voice sounded, "I don't think this is Apogee's story."

CHAPTER 20
STUDENT UNION

"You have that look again," Seventhirtyfour rumbled. "What are you planning?"

I could feel it. An idea brewing, fingertips fizzing, mind racing. I grinned. "I don't know yet, it's still cooking. But chances are, I'm going to need everybody. That includes you. Come on, let's sneak away while Nine's distracted."

Seventhirtyfour shook his head. "I'm sorry, Grey, no."

Oh. Reality came crashing down on my giddiness. "I need you, buddy, more than Nine needs you standing guard."

He laughed. "Oh, I'm coming, no fear. But it's time I stood up to the Sergeant. I'm not sneaking away."

My knees wobbled in relief. "Good. Do that."

I checked the sky. An Academy shuttle descended towards the spaceport, to start the next wave of evacuees.

"Pilvi?" I called her over. "Gather everybody. Meet me on the beach. Quick as you can. I think time may be running out."

She nodded and blasted into the sky in a bolt of white light.

I caught up with Seventhirtyfour.

He hadn't spoken to Nine yet, in fact, both Seventhirtyfour and Sergeant Nine were waiting patiently while Captain Hawk took a call from Apogee.

"...swathes of the jungle just dead. He's cutting through

it like a scythe, but I can see the carnage in his wake, makes it easy to follow him," Apogee said.

"How long do we have? How far from the campus is he?" Hawk asked. Our headmaster cultivated an air of unflappability, but the stress in his voice shattered that illusion.

"He's changed direction; he's heading on a... well... a tangent, towards the coast. He's close, though. If he turns back towards you, he could be there in ten minutes."

"He must be following Gravane and Laugh Riot," I muttered. Captain Hawk shot me an annoyed look.

"Say again, I didn't catch that," Apogee said.

"Sorry, Professor, it's Grey. I said he must be going after Gravane and Laugh Riot. The last time I saw them, they were running towards the sea too."

"That tracks. Captain, should I engage now?"

We all looked at Captain Hawk, but the headmaster seemed caught by indecision.

"What can you tell us about Titan's abilities?" I asked. "How's his swimming? Does he breathe underwater? If not, we could try dropping him in the ocean."

"No," said Hawk, but so softly, Apogee spoke over him.

"He was a typical brick. Strong. Tough. He doesn't breathe underwater, no, but he flies. Even if I could blow him out to sea, which isn't certain, he wouldn't stay there long."

Captain Hawk turned his back to us and stepped away, taking his comm with him. "You are free to engage, Apogee, but keep your distance. We can't have him draining you. The more you can slow him down, the more time we have to evacuate students."

"Roger that."

"Good hunting. Be careful. Hawk out."

Hawk drifted off the ground, his cape swirling around

him. "Sergeant, maintain the perimeter. Grey, report to Professor Croft at the spaceport."

I didn't reply. I didn't think he was handling the current crisis very well, but I still respected him too much to flat out lie to him. Unless things got much worse.

He soared skywards; I didn't watch him go.

"You heard the man, Brontom," Sergeant Nine called out. "Two, I want a check of our proximity alarms, keep in contact at all times."

"Yes, Sarge." She jogged towards the treeline, stun bolter up, ready for a fight.

"Three, Four, hold this position, while I make sure the fugitive," he gave me a pointed look, "doesn't deviate from his orders."

"Yes, Sarge," said Triple Threat.

Seventhirtyfour squared himself up, unkinking the stoop he normally affected around the other Brontom. "Sergeant, I need to request leave to attend to a personal matter."

Nine clamped his upper left hand on my shoulder. "We are in an active theatre, soldier, permission denied."

"With respect, sarge, I checked my orders, I have never been assigned to your unit. I respect your rank and authority and will follow any order you give me that does not interfere with my primary assignment. In this case, however, I believe my standing orders supersede yours."

Nine's grip tightened painfully, his fingers digging into my flesh. I think he'd forgotten what he was holding. "Ng," I said, to remind him. He didn't let go.

"Are you trying to *lawyer* me, solider?"

"No, sarge. Merely outlining my position."

"Stand your post, Four." He was barely containing himself now. Heat radiated from his hand, through my shoulder. Could I smell burning prison shirt?

"I am trying to, Sergeant. My posting is to the Justice Academy. I have orders to take advantage of available learning opportunities to become a space alien superhero. Your order contradicts mine, in that it requires me to act as a Brontom Clone Warrior, not as a superhero."

"You *are* a Brontom Clone Warrior, Four. From vat to vat."

"Yes, Sergeant. Which is why standing guard here is a wasted learning opportunity. If it helps, order me to guard the fugitive."

"Stand your post, Four, or face the consequences. You know what happens to clones who desert in the face of the enemy."

"I do." For a moment, it looked like Seventhirtyfour might relent. "But I am afraid, I must do what I must. And so must you, Sergeant."

Three looked aghast. Sergeant Nine released his vice-grip on me and stomped over to join her at the barricade.

"What... what can Sergeant Nine do to you?" I asked in a hushed voice, while I massaged my shoulder.

Seventhirtyfour stood ramrod straight and paced away from the other Brontom. "I... I'd rather not talk about it, Grey. One crisis at a time."

I shut up, and we hurried off.

We made one stop before heading to the beach. Not for vanity, but if I was going into combat, I needed something sturdier than my ragged prisoner gear.

Nobody was guarding the Academy Outfitters right then, so I spoofed the lock and raided their stock. I grabbed dark blue trousers and a long-sleeved shirt, wrapped a belt around my waist and clipped the grapnel gun to it. I found black boots with nice grippy soles, important for parkour. Finally, I added a high-collared stab vest over the top, for a little extra protection.

Seventhirtyfour grinned.

"What?" I asked.

"It's not a bad basis for a superhero outfit," he said.

"Oh, don't be daft." But I caught myself in the mirror. It needed work, but yes, not bad.

Securely clad in my much-less-draughty new outfit, we headed for the beach.

# # #

Pilvi had done what I'd asked her quickly and efficiently. By the time Seventhirtyfour and I reached the beach, the whole gang was there. Pilvi, Seventhirtyfour, Lucy... no, we were in superhero mode, let's get those names right. Säde, Probability Kid, Sky Diamond, Gadget Dude, Dez and me. Not everyone, of course, there was an Avrim-shaped hole in the group.

"Thank you all for coming," I said as I strode across the beach towards them. Sand crunched underfoot, and I concentrated on that, rather than looking up at the wide-open sky. The night was moonless, which helped a little, making it feel like I had a vast dark ceiling overhead.

"Grey!" Gadget Dude said in surprised delight.

Säde shushed him.

"What's up, boss? Where have you been hiding? Do you know you're on the run for attacking Lucy's wet boyfriend?" asked Dez.

Sky Diamond swatted Dez, then smiled at me, pushing her hair behind her ears. She hadn't brought David, I noticed. *Focus.*

"It's great to see you all. I've got some explaining to do, I know, but I'm afraid there's no time for much detail."

Dez rolled her eyes. "There never is."

"Here's the quick version: Doctor Gravestone is here on the Academy world. He was locked up in Tartarus. Kayda Buchanan, who has been posing as Fusillade since the start of the year murdered Veritas and arranged the attack on David to frame me so she could get into Tartarus to break Gravestone out." They all looked like they had questions, but I held up a hand to forestall them. "In the process, they have also released a prisoner called Titan, whose abilities include blocking people's powers and draining their life force. The Academy staff are running scared over Titan, hence the evacuation. I don't blame them. But *our* priority has to be catching Kayda, who goes by Laugh Riot now. We promised Avrim we would catch Veritas's murderer, and that's just what I plan to do."

"Where?" asked Gadget Dude.

"When she planned Gravestone's escape, she must have arranged some way off-planet. She couldn't use the Academy spaceport or the prison landing pad. Gravestone and Laugh Riot have visited here before, last year, they landed on a beach about a ten-minute run from here. I figure Laugh Riot would arrange a pick-up site she knew, and when we last saw her, she was running towards the coast."

I checked the sky again. It was empty for the moment. The only ships I'd seen since we parted company with Laugh Riot had been Academy ones. We still had time. I hoped we still had time.

"You all know what Gravestone is capable of. Laugh Riot is a speedster. I don't know who will be on the ship coming to pick them up. We should be ready for anything, but I do know she was working with a Germile brute called Big Bang."

"What are we waiting for?" Dez asked. "Lead on, boss."

I wouldn't ask them if they wanted to stay back. They all knew they had that option, but they would be offended if I voiced it. I still checked each of their faces. I saw some nerves, certainly, but mostly I was met with grim determination.

"Let's go," I said.

# # #

Engines roared overhead. It was a bigger ship than the last time I'd run this beach, still only a shuttle though. We were cutting it fine, but we still had time to get to them before they could lift off.

"Sky Diamond," I called, gesturing as we ran. "Can you keep that thing on the ground?"

"If I can get close enough to touch it, yeah."

"Then we will make sure you can," Seventhirtyfour said. We were all a little winded from our beach run, all except the Brontom.

The ship vanished below the next dune, a spray of sand erupted as it thumped into a heavy landing, the whine of antigrav and thrusters protesting the mistreatment.

We paused for a beat, lined up at the top of the dune. If there had been a camera handy, it would have been the perfect moment for an epic group shot. There wasn't, though, which was a shame.

In the cove below us, the ship settled into a landing, steam rising from its hull, metal pinging as it cooled. Across from us, at the far edge of the cove, Gravestone and Laugh Riot waited for the dust to settle. They hadn't noticed us yet. Time to put that to rights.

The team needed no cue from me. Säde burst with white light as she accelerated downhill. The rest of us pounded down the dune behind her.

Gravestone spotted us then. I saw him point, and in a blink, Laugh Riot was by the shuttle's entrance. Fast as she was, though, she couldn't board the shuttle until its entry ramp extended and the hatch opened. We had seconds before that happened; it must have seemed like forever to her, living at her speed.

Fortunately, Säde was able to provide her with a distraction from the wait in the form of a blast of sunbolts. Laugh Riot side-stepped easily enough, but Säde didn't stop to engage, she had her sights firmly set on Gravestone. For his part, Gravane's red-black aura ignited with a flash and he rose to meet her. The pair spiralled upwards around each other; flashes of energy lit the dark sky.

"Leave my boyfriend alone, you bitch," Laugh Riot shrieked at Säde, but she was trapped on the ground and couldn't interfere.

Seventhirtyfour, Probability Kid, coughed politely. "I would rather you didn't use such language about my friend," he said. His mask was up already, but now he pressed the other stud on his collar, to engage his Psionic Crown.

"You're not going to fly away from me, are you, big guy?" Laugh Riot asked with a chuckle.

Probability Kid shook his head. "You have my full attention."

Laugh Riot sprung towards him, faster than I could see. One moment she was there, the next... she was staggering away from the Brontom, nose bleeding. "What... how did you...?" She put a hand up to her face.

Probability Kid shrugged. "Beginners luck? Care to try again?"

As Laugh Riot plunged forward, Seventhirtyfour swung with his lower left and upper right arms. In a blur of motion, I saw an after-image of Laugh Riot ducking under one blow, but the other connected with the top of her head, pummelling her face-first into the sand. She spat out beach. "What the actual hell?" she said.

The Brontom laughed his rumbling laugh. "What can I say? Four-armed is forewarned." His Crown let him use what he called Battle Precognition; he could sense and react to Laugh Riot's actions even before she knew she was going to make them.

"PK, no. No puns," Dez said. She slithered past, keeping low to the sand, to meet the end of the shuttle's now-extended ramp. Gadget Dude bounded up behind her, though he spoiled her approbation by chuckling at Seventhirtyfour's joke.

"Actually, in the Combat Banter class I took last year," Probability Kid pointed out, as he thumped Laugh Riot again, "they said puns were acceptable banter for ice-breakers."

I was last into the fight. I was busy keeping an eye on Sky Diamond as she sneaked up to the shuttle. Not that I was worried for her, but I needed to know when she was in position. We had to keep the shuttle grounded. She put one hand on the hull of the ship and frowned in concentration. A beat, and then she gave me a thumbs up. I accelerated, joining Dez and Gadget Dude for whatever came out of the shuttle.

The hatch irised open to reveal a bald Germile dressed in dark blue fatigues. Or most of a Germile, anyway. I'd thought Bolsta was big, but this guy more than filled the shuttle's hatch with his massive frame. He had to bend his elbows to duck low enough to get through, and even then, he could only fit one shoulder at a time. "These kids on our side?" he growled at Laugh Riot.

"Definitely not."

"Their mistake."

He reached out to grab Dez, but she was too quick for him, instead, she jumped onto and scaled his arm, skittering up to sit on his broad shoulders. She slapped the side of his head with her tail.

"Get off me," the Germile growled, planting one hand firmly on the ramp so he could reach up and grab at her with the other.

Gadget Dude delved into his belt and pulled out a pair of goggles and a small black sphere. He slipped the goggles over his eyes and tapped the Germile on his elbow. "Excuse," Gadget Dude said, holding up the ball to the Germile's saucer-like eyes.

I looked away before the bright flash blinded me.

It all seemed to be going very well, so why did I feel so nervous?

Laugh Riot switched tactic. She couldn't get close to Probability Kid without him tagging her, so instead, she stayed back and scooped handfuls of sand to throw at his face. The effect was like a sandblasting jet. Probability Kid covered his face with two of his arms. He could still use his Battle Precognition and his two spare arms to defend himself, but the constant abrasion had already worn through his suit in a couple of spots. Brontom skin was tough, but he wouldn't stand up long to a sandblasting.

I ran at Laugh Riot and took my best shot. She evaded me with arrogant ease, taking her eye off Probability Kid long enough to give me a savage kick to the stomach, launching me across the sand to slam heavily into the side of the shuttle.

I lost track of the fight for a moment, as I blinked the random colours from my vision.

When my sight cleared, it looked like we were winning. PK had used my distraction to close on Laugh Riot and grab her. She beat at his shoulders at superspeed, but so far, he seemed unperturbed. Gadget Dude and Dez had the Germile... if not contained, then at least distracted. Why then were alarm bells ringing in my head? Where was Pilvi? Against my better judgement, I scanned the sky, retreating under the cover of the shuttle's wing, just in case. I could see two dots spinning around each other, light flashing around them. They were too far for me to make out details, but both combatants still seemed to be fighting, so that wasn't it, either. I—

Wait. There was something else up there too. Not just Säde and Gravestone. Another pair of figures heading towards them. Who was... oh no. We had somebody's attention, and who else could it be?

"Guys," I said. "We might want to speed things up, we have incoming."

Laugh Riot stopped pounding Probability Kid. Her eyes widened as, I assume, she reached the same conclusion I had. "Big Bang, time to do your thing," she shouted at the Germile.

Big Bang had dislodged Dez; he tossed her to the ground at his feet. "You're in range, Kayda," he said.

"Just do it!"

The Germile shifted his weight to his legs, standing awkwardly upright, stretching his arms wide.

"Take cover," I shouted. I wasn't sure from what, but it wasn't going to be good. I scrambled to put as much of the shuttle between us as I could.

He brought his hands together. I'm not sure I'd characterise the sound as a 'bang', but it was certainly 'big'.

A pressure wave ripped across the beach, scattering Dez, Gadget Dude, Probability Kid and Laugh Riot. They tumbled like leaves in the wind, fetching up against the far dune. Dazed or unconscious, I couldn't tell.

"Now, where was that other one?" Big Bang said. He put his fists to the ground again and shuffled around to look for me. Germile are strong, tough and fast in a straight line, but their gorilla-like stance meant they weren't as nimble on turning. It was the only advantage I had, so I would have to work with that.

Behind him, the shuttle hatch closed, and the ramp raised again. Much faster than it had lowered, its motors whining in protest.

I circled him, warily. I drew my grapnel gun and pointed it at him. I didn't think it would do me any good against him, but I felt better having it in hand.

"I should warn you," I said, "I think the display of powers around here has caught the attention of a dude called Titan. I don't know if Kayda mentioned him to you, but he's not on either of our sides, and it would be in both of our interests to be out of here before he arrives."

"Thanks for telling me. Stand still and I'll see what I can do."

"Hah. A generous offer, but maybe not."

I caught a shadow of movement from behind Big Bang. Lucy, one had still against the hull of the shuttle, her jewelled headband glittering. She put a finger to her lips and then pointed at the ramp.

I blinked to acknowledge her, not wanting to draw attention by nodding.

Bing Bang took advantage of my momentary distraction and aimed a causal swipe in my direction. He put no great speed or power behind it, and I ducked under it easily enough, backpedalling as I did. "Just letting you know I'm still here," he growled, grinning at me.

"You're not so forgettable, don't put yourself down like that."

"I'll put you down instead." He raised one meaty hand high and slapped down at me. I evaded that one too, what bothered me was I seemed to be losing the verbal sparring, which was the part I felt I should be winning.

Above me, the sounds of Säde versus Gravestone

were getting closer again. Weird splashes of light strobed across the battlefield as first Säde blasted Gravestone, then he returned the favour. Lucy had dipped back out of sight again, letting me scamper around behind Big Bang, manoeuvring him back towards the shuttle. To get him exactly where I wanted him was going to take finesse or pain. And I didn't have time for finesse.

I stepped into Big Bang's reach, pointing my grapnel right at this face. "Stand down," I said, giving him everything to focus on.

"No," he said. To make his point, he shifted his weight to his back legs and raised his whole body and arms until he towered above me, ready to smash me with one almighty two-fisted blow. This was going to hurt.

The shuttle's ramp motor's screeched. Big Bang tried to turn to see why, but he was too slow and cumbersome. The ramp scythed open, caught Big Bang across his back, and flattened him into the sand. It pinned him there. He was strong as all get out, but he lacked the appropriate leverage to apply it.

"Yes! Sky Diamond, you're amazing." I wasn't smashed. What a relief.

"My pleasure, boss," she said. "There's still a pilot in there, fighting my control. Care to grab him so I can help with the others?"

"Sure thing." I bounced up onto the entry ramp, enjoying Big Bang's grunt of irritation as I added my weight to his load.

The shuttle hatch irised open. A Cholbren in a flight suit stood on the other side, hands raised, trying to smile, mostly looking embarrassed. "I surrender," he said, "I'm just a pilot. I have no stake in whatever this fight is about. Who are you people?"

"We're superheroes."

"Sure. Obviously. Shall I move away from the ship so you can hijack it, Mr. Superhero?"

"Much obliged." I checked inside the shuttle to make sure nobody else was hiding back there.

By the time I got out, Lucy was already helping Seventhirtyfour to his feet again. Dez was sitting on the dune looking crestfallen, while Gadget Dude was securing suppression cuffs to Laugh Riot's wrists. For her part, she looked groggy and annoyed.

"Well done, team," I said. "Dez, keep an eye on Laugh Riot. Probability Kid, if you see any way to help Säde, take it. Gadget Dude, Sky Diamond, I need you in the shuttle. Quickly."

Gadget Dude threw me a quick salute, then dashed over, Lucy on his heels. I led them into the shuttle's cockpit.

"Gadget Dude, can you rig something that would let Lucy control the shuttle remotely?" I looked out of the window, the four figures in the sky were closer. "And, like, now, if possible?"

"That's not how my powers work, Grey," Lucy objected.

"I know. But if anyone can find a way around that, it's Gadget Dude. What do you say? Can you do it?"

"Can try," he said and dived under the console.

"I thought you just wanted me to fly us back to the campus," Lucy said.

"That only helps short term, there's still Titan to think about. If we can get him in the shuttle, and you can throw the shuttle into space... we have him trapped. That gives us time to find another solution. Keeps everyone safe."

She nodded. "I'll try."

I put a hand on her arm. "I believe in you, Lucy."

She looked me in the eye, for a long moment. "Grey, I—"

Gadget Dude reappeared from under the console, a chunk of the shuttle's flight control unit trailed wires from between his hands. "Can try this!"

From outside on the beach, Seventhirtyfour shouted, "Grey, I think you need to see this!"

"Come on," I said, and ran back down the ramp, Gadget Dude and Lucy close behind.

In the sky above the beach, Gravestone and Säde were all but upon us. Their descent seemed more of a fall than a flight. Gravestone's hand lit with his red-black energy but spluttered out before he could aim it at anyone.

I pointed back towards the Academy and yelled at the others, "We need to get everyone away from here and back to campus before—"

Gravestone fell from the sky, Säde had a hold of him and used him to soften her landing. There was no glow from Pilvi's eyes or hair.

"Titan's here," she said.

CHAPTER 21
GREY'S GAMBIT

The Cholbren pilot, still sauntering away from us, collapsed as though his strings had been cut. He slumped to the ground, unconscious.

"Can someone—" I looked over to Seventhirtyfour, and even as I did, Dez and Gadget Dude both fell. "Damn. Seventhirtyfour, can you grab... Damn." This wasn't going to work. Too many people needed carrying out of here, not enough people to carry. "Okay, Sky Diamond, can you help Gadget Dude? Don't forget that flight unit. Big Bang, if you want to live, grab Gravane and run to the campus. That's not a threat, that's a warning. Titan's coming, and you do not want a piece of that. If we stand and fight, we're all dead."

I glanced at the sky. I could see Titan clearly now, and Apogee behind him. Titan was heading straight for us, but it looked like he was struggling; Apogee must be holding him back, but he wasn't strong enough to hold Titan forever.

"Laugh Riot, same deal. It's too late to go your own way now. Get to the campus and turn yourself in."

"Take these cuffs off first," she said.

"No."

She didn't seem happy, but she went. Big Bang scooped up Gravane and followed her.

"Probability Kid, Säde, get Dez, Gadget Dude and the

pilot guy out of here, and make sure nobody takes off Laugh Riot's cuffs."

"What about you?" Seventhirtyfour rumbled. He stooped and lifted Dez to his shoulder, before jogging up the dune to where the pilot had fallen. He still had his natural Brontom physical strength. However Titan's ability worked it seemed to turn off superpowers first in those that had them.

"I have a plan. It's dangerous, but it could work. Lucy? Get far enough clear that your powers work, then rev up the shuttle, if you can. When I signal Titan's aboard, don't hesitate, power that thing into space with everything it's got."

"Whatever you need. I trust you."

My chest felt like it swelled to twice its size.

A whip-crack sounded above us, as Titan broke through the air barrier Apogee had wrapped him in. He'd be on us in seconds.

"Go!" I shouted. They ran. Seventhirtyfour and Lucy looked back at me as they did, but I shooed them away.

And just like that, I was alone on a beach under the stars. I was far too preoccupied to have a panic attack.

I wasn't alone for long. Titan landed at the edge of the cove with a heavy thump that swayed the trees around him before they began to discolour and wither. Leaves turned grey and brittle, shattered into dust in the breeze.

We studied each other. His long, ragged hair was past his shoulders, his beard full and unkempt. Both dark brown streaked with grey. He was big. Bigger, I think, than when I saw him fly past me in Tartarus. He seemed more... filled out. The scraps of his restraints had fallen away, leaving him standing in his tattered uniform, a black bodysuit with a large white T emblem on his chest. His hands and feet were bare. What he saw in me? Who knows?

Somehow, I was surprised when he spoke. A raspy throaty voice, ragged from disuse, but still strong enough to cut through the night air. "I saw you in Tartarus," he said.

"That's right."

"How long were you in there?"

"Not long. A couple of hours. I—"

He cut me off. "Hours? Just before my escape? That's not a coincidence."

"No, I—"

"Were you with that Welatak I ate? Was he a friend of yours?"

"No, he—"

"I thought draining him would taste like fish. It didn't."

I said nothing, he'd only cut me off again.

"Are you expecting me to let you live? Because I didn't attack you before?"

"Nope."

He gave a hacking, sawing noise that I think might have been a laugh. I don't think he'd done it in a while. "Good. Before, I needed *out* more than I needed *to eat*. Not true now. I've been starved for twenty years, tonight I feast."

I pulled my grapnel gun, left-handed, awkwardly. "Tonight, I stop you."

He hacked out a laugh again. "I might have been locked away for years, but I still recognise that thing. You can't hurt me with it."

I took a step back up the ramp of the shuttle, carefully, tripping now would be fatal. And embarrassing. While he was focussed on the hand with the gun, I brought my other up in what I hoped looked like a bracing action. Instead, I tapped on my wristpad and opened a comm to Lucy.

Titan took a step forward, then another, quicker and quicker as he ran at me across the sand. He was up to a full run by the time he'd crossed half the distance to me. The ground seemed to shake with each step. No. The vibration I felt through the ramp was the thrum of the shuttle's engines powering up. That much of the plan seemed to be working.

Titan reached towards me with one hand as he ran, and suddenly, my knees weren't quite enough to hold me upright. I sagged. Put my free hand on the hatch frame to steady myself.

Titan looked surprised and delighted. "You're stronger than you—"

Two meters from the bottom of the ramp, he slammed into an invisible wall with enough force to send him reeling, and me onto my ass on the shuttle deck.

Apogee floated above us; I could see his silhouette against the night sky through the shuttle hatch. The starlight glittered on his golden gauntlets and boots.

"Grey. I don't know how you're still standing, but... get out of here." Apogee's voice was strained. I realised he was trying to hold Titan in place again, wrapping the escaped prisoner in powerful winds. Titan was fighting back, though, and the battle was taking its toll. Apogee was being drawn closer.

"Professor, no, stay back. I have a plan," I shouted.

"Not your... responsibility... Grey. Ours. Mine. We should have... found a way. It should never... have come... to this. Gah."

"Give it up, Si," Titan roared. "I've gone easy on you, but that only goes so far."

"I can't let you do this," Apogee said, grimly. He extended his hand, fingers spread, towards Titan. Apogee clenched his fist, then jerked it back in a pulling motion.

Titan choked out a cough as a fine red mist erupted from his mouth. He gagged, trying to flail, but he was still pinned.

"I've just ripped all of the air from your lungs," Apogee told him, sadly. "I don't like doing it, it can cause permanent damage. You left me no choice. I'm truly sorry. Without oxygen, you will fall unconscious in less than a minute. I'll see about getting you healed when we put you back in your cell. I'm sorry, old friend."

Titan's fingers twitched.

Strength flooded back into my limbs. I was able to stand without leaning on the edge of the hatch. I could lift my grapnel gun again. Was it over?

No.

Titan was still conscious, and the expression on his face was not panic, or defeat.

Exactly what I was looking at dawned on me. In Tartarus, Titan's power drain was able to reach up ten levels of the prison. Fifty meters, at least. Apogee was already much closer than that. Perhaps he was stronger than Titan's power drain. Perhaps Titan could choose who to affect with it. Either way, Apogee's powers had never fallen to Titan's influence.

Until then.

Titan must have focused all his power on Apogee, freeing me, but...

Apogee fell like a stone. He was too close to the ground when it happened; Apogee's cry of pain was punctuated by the crunch of bones snapping.

Titan gasped. Then he rose from the ground, hovered just above the sand. His back was to me, I couldn't see his face, but he almost radiated hatred. "Twenty years. Twenty years at the bottom of that pit. I was alone and hungry for twenty years. You think I'm going to forgive that? You think I'm going to forget that? We were friends, once. I let you live. But you had to push it, didn't you, Si? You had to make a big deal of the deaths of a couple of Polifan. You threw me in a hole, all I did was feel a little hungry. Well, I'm still hungry, Si. And now it's time for you to feed me."

He floated towards Apogee, one had outstretched. Already, Apogee's skin looked paler, waxy.

For a moment there, I'd thought I might not have to use my plan. I'd really rather hoped. But there was only one way this crossover could end, wasn't there?

"Hey, asshole," I said and fired my grapnel. It snared him. I pushed the button to retract the cable, yanking Titan towards me in the shuttle.

I got lucky. (Is that the right word? Let's go with it anyway). I got lucky. Titan must have been so used to people trying to get away from him, I don't think it occurred to him that anyone would ever try to pull him closer. Even as he passed through the hatch into the cabin of the shuttle, I shouted, "Now, Lucy."

The shuttle hatch snapped shut, and the ship leapt into the air. The acceleration was so fast it overwhelmed the internal antigrav, and Titan and I tumbled back against the hatch.

We accelerated into the stars.

# # #

I don't think I blacked out for more than a few seconds.

Consciousness, when it returned, found me slumped awkwardly at the foot of one of the cabin's acceleration couches. Gravity was back doing its thing in the proper direction again, at least.

"You wanted to die? Is that it?" Titan stood hunched over in the back of the cabin by the hatch.

"Not especially," I said, awkwardly unfolding myself, pulling up to sit on the couch. At least I was inside again. My world was nicely contained: the passenger cabin held eight of the couches against the side bulkheads, the hatch to the outside at one end, the open hatch to the cockpit at the other, a storage cupboard to its left, the fresher on the right. The cockpit stood conspicuously empty but had a spectacular view of deep space out of the window. Oh, yeah. The passenger cabin also had a supervillain. Mustn't forget that.

He extended a hand and a wave of weakness flooded through me. My skin felt cold, tight, I couldn't catch my breath. Vicious cramps stabbed me in the legs and arms. "Kill me... you kill... yourself," I said, rasping between snatched breaths.

Titan stalked up to me, closed his hand around my throat and pulled me out of my seat. He didn't even seem to strain at my dead weight, hanging limply in his grip. I couldn't move, lacked the strength to resist, to fight back, I couldn't even raise my hands to claw at his wrist. I couldn't raise my voice to tell him he was dooming himself. Didn't he understand the brilliance of my plan? Couldn't he see?

My eyelids drooped closed. I didn't even have the energy to keep them open. I couldn't breathe. My heart thumped. I waited. For the next beat. It didn't come.

He let go.

I fell like a wet towel. I lay twisted on the deck of the shuttle, let sweet, sweet air fill my lungs again, thrilled at the sound of my heartbeat. Pins and needles attacked every inch of my skin, but I was still alive.

"Tell me," said Titan.

"Have a look in the cockpit. It's impossible to fly this thing from the inside anymore." I paused to gasp for air again. My head still spun. "Where we go and how we get there is in the hands of someone else. Say hello, Sky Diamond." I held up my wrist pad.

"Hello," said Lucy over the still open comm channel.

I lowered my arm, tapped my wristpad. "If you want

to go anywhere, ever again, you keep her on your side, by keeping me not-dead."

Titan knelt and growled at my wristpad. "Put us down now, or I will rip your little boyfriend into bloody chunks."

"Sorry, Titan, that's not going to work," I said. "Mostly because I know Sky Diamond will do what's right to protect everyone at the Academy by keeping you away from there. But also because I muted the call before your very-predictable threat."

I felt strong enough to move again, so I did, shuffling back to put some distance between us, before propping myself up against one of the couches again. Getting up into it still seemed like too much effort, but the effects of Titan's drain seemed to be passing. Eventually, I might even dare to stand up.

"Also, not her boyfriend," I added.

"So that's it? You think you beat me?" said Titan.

I shook my head. "No. But I have faith. There are people down on the ground who can use the time I've bought to find a way to beat you. I'm just doing my bit."

"Then perhaps I won't give them that time." He stepped over me and strode to the storage cupboard and pulled it open. "I bet there's a spacesuit in here. I fly fast enough, I bet I can get back planetside before the air runs out."

I tapped the unmute button on my wristpad. "You might be right, except you've not heard about the new spin drives on these shuttles, right?"

He ignored me, pulled a suit from the cabinet.

"I get it," I said, "you've been out of the loop for two decades. There's been a big jump in drive tech while you've been away. Sky Diamond, please activate the spin drive, take us into deep space, two light-years from the Academy."

"Are you sure?" Lucy asked over the comm.

"Yep. We don't want Titan just stepping out."

"Plotting course," she said.

"Don't you dare," Titan said.

I shrugged apologetically, showed him the Mute indicator on my wristpad. "Oops"

The shuttle performed a tight barrel roll, while antigrav kept our feet firmly on the deck plate. The stars out of the cockpit window swirled in a tight spiral, shifting slightly as we repositioned.

Titan didn't know the spin drive wasn't real, but when we stopped spinning, the starfield had changed. We were pointing in a different direction, but as long as the Academy planet wasn't visible out of the window, he couldn't be *sure*.

"Thanks, Sky Diamond."

Lucy waited a few seconds before she responded, faking a comms delay. Nice touch, even if comms delays weren't a thing in the age of Hyperwave relays. "Spin jump complete. Stay safe, Grey."

"I'll give regular updates, so you know Titan's still playing nice."

A few seconds delay. "Roger that. Looking forwards to it."

"You're lying," Titan said flatly.

"Often and well," I said. "But not about this. Don't believe me? Put on the suit and head outside. Even if you can fly at light speed, and I'm fairly certain you can't... it's two years to the closest habitable planet. I promise there's not enough oxygen in those emergency suits to last that long. Even assuming you pick the correct direction."

Sure, he could just open the airlock and look outside, but the longer he took to figure that out, the further away Sky Diamond could *actually* get us, hopefully making it a moot point.

Titan stared at the suit in his hands. He let it drop to the deck. "I should just tear this whole ship apart. I'm not going back into Tartarus. Or anything like it. I won't."

"Maybe there's another solution," I offered. Though after his murders, I didn't believe it.

"There is one thing you didn't think of you smart-mouthed ass," he said.

I declined to ask what. I was pretty sure I wouldn't like his answer.

He answered anyway. "I may have to keep you alive, to keep your girlfriend sweet, but it doesn't mean I can't feed." He gestured once more.

Agony swept through me again. A ragged scream tore itself from my throat.

Yeah, I am so smart.

#

He could have broken me like a twig at any time, but he didn't even get out of his chair, just waved a hand at me and watched me twist. He'd give me time to recover, then repeated the process. It must have been hours. It felt like weeks.

I had wondered why Captain Hawk would lock somebody up for twenty years. I didn't wonder any more. If Titan were even a fraction of this before they'd locked him up, I knew exactly why Hawk wanted to keep him away from people. So did I. And if he was amusing himself with me, I took heart that at least he wasn't taking out his anger on Sky Diamond or Gadget Dude or... anyone else.

I grabbed a little sleep when I could. Not the most comfortable rest ever, but today had been non-stop and even without Titan's ministrations taking their toll. I needed some shut-eye.

Titan gave me chances to check in with Lucy. I did my

best not to communicate quite how bad a shape I was in; I didn't want them rushing to the rescue before they were properly ready to. While I could endure, I would. Every second could be important.

# # #

He left me alone longer than before, but I still braced for the next onslaught, curled up on the deck in front of one of the acceleration couches.

Instead, I heard his heavy tread on the deck, and he slid into one of the couches opposite me.

"Tell me what I missed," he said.

I didn't respond.

"I've been kept underground for two decades. You may be thinking I learned patience. I didn't. I exhausted it. Talk to me or scream, it's all the same to me."

I shifted to an upright sitting position again. Tried to stare a hole through his head.

"What was it your little girlfriend called you? Grey? Talk to me, Grey."

"Drop dead."

"You want me to hurt you? Is that it? You think that's how you win? Kid, you're crazier than I am."

"I already won."

"Ha. How do you figure that?"

"You broke out of one cell; I've put you straight back in another." I gestured at the steel box around us.

He leaned forward and grabbed my chin. His hands were dirty, his long, ragged nails scratched my cheek. Up close, he smelled foul, baked-in sweat and grime gave his skin a sharp pungent odour. "You think I'm staying here?" he asked. "Doubtful. If Simon is still around, then I bet Henry is too. No way he leaves one of his students in here with me. Not again. Sooner or later Captain Hawk will come flying to the rescue, and I will be waiting. They won't beat me this time. I'm stronger than ever. Ready for them."

I jerked my chin out of his grip. Enough of feeling defeated on the floor. Time to stand up for myself and my friends. I pulled myself upright, my legs wobbled, but held. I took a step away from him, stretched, assessed the damage. After each of his assaults, life had returned to my limbs more slowly. I was still mobile for now. If I could get away from his influence, I might even recover a measure of my strength.

I looked back. Titan was watching me, his expression hard to read. Was he amused by my feeble show of defiance? Maybe. Anxious to talk after twenty years of solitary confinement? Possibly. Angry? Definitely, the rage bubbled close to the surface, for sure. What he didn't look was worried. He was out of his cell and he wasn't going back. Time to puncture that confidence if I could.

"You asked what you missed?" I said.

"I did."

"You missed *everything*," I said gesturing widely. "I wasn't even born when you were sent to Tartarus. You think your ability to torture me makes you *strong*? You have no idea. Compared to my friends, I'm nothing. The weak link. I have friends who can build anything, find anything, they know what you're going to do before you do. You think beating Apogee was enough? Säde is twice as powerful and doesn't need to get close enough for you to affect her. Do you realise how many students there are at the Academy now? Thousands. That's thousands of ways to beat you. You can't see them all coming."

"Sounds like a feast to me. Each time I feed, I just get stronger. Even your little bit of power makes me harder to contain. A couple more bite-size snacks like that and a whole galaxy of superheroes couldn't contain me. A few thousand teenagers aren't going to be more than a bump in the road."

"They stopped you before."

"I'm better now."

"Better?"

"When they locked me up, they installed a way to keep way abilities suppressed. Within a year, I'd learned to overcome it. Within five, I replaced it. They thought their suppression field was still working, but I fed on everybody they put in there. They thought it was their trap? I made it *mine*. They wanted me weak? They made me strong. I hoarded every scrap of power I stole, made it part of myself. By the time other prisoners found their way to me, I was ready to break out. Your Welatak friend may have speeded the process along, but a year from now, two? I was out of there with or without his help."

"How very inspiring," I said. "A real tale of triumph over adversity. And yet, you bought your way into Tartarus with death, and paid for your escape with more murders. Forgive me if I don't cheer you on."

Titan lifted out of his chair, hovering above the deck, framed by the cockpit hatch behind him. "I thought I'd missed conversation. I was wrong. Time to go back to basics." He extended his hand and I brace for another assault.

The shuttle's engine note changed, and the stars outside shifted, as the shuttle began to rotate again.

The Academy's station, and Academy world behind it, swung into view.

"We're still... you *lied*," Titan said.

"Often and well."

The station grew in the window. We were coming into dock.

I straightened my shirt, checked my grapnel gun. I

didn't know what the plan was for when we docked, but whatever came next, things were coming to a head, and I was determined to be ready.

CHAPTER 22
TITAN'S TALE

Titan gripped me by the collar, keeping me close at his side. "I'm not walking off this ship without my hostage," he said, his voice a little muffled behind the breather he wore. He'd fished it out of the shuttle's supply locker. He hadn't provided me one, so I hoped the air on the station was good.

The airlock cycled, and the tell-tales all lit green. Titan nudged me towards the lock controls, and I pressed the open button.

I'd expected the cavalry. I was disappointed. Instead, we were met by an empty corridor. A pair of emergency lockers stood open and empty in the wall; no spare suits, tools or even heaters. Past the lockers, the walls were bare, except for handrails at waist and shoulder height, and a rather pleasing yellowy-brown paint job. The only other thing in the corridor was a security camera at the far end, sat above the next hatch. A little red light blinked on top of the camera, to ensure it would get seen.

"Let's go, then," Titan said, pushing me forwards. He kept himself floating off the ground, careful to touch nothing but me. If there were a trap to be stumbled on, it would be me to trigger it.

I stumbled along the corridor, one hand on a handrail to help keep my balance. At about the halfway point of the corridor, I sagged artfully against the wall. It was mostly artifice on my part. I was hardly in peak condition, but my strength was returning. If Titan didn't think to drain me again, I might be able to mount a brief defence before he murdered me. Go me.

He shoved me on, and I went. Lucy had docked the shuttle for a reason. Why? I could comm her and ask, of course, but with Titan right there, I'd hate to spoil any surprise they had planned.

The hatch at the end of the corridor opened into a reasonable facsimile of a generic Arrivals hall. It was fake, none of the vendor stalls had real products on display, the furniture and fittings showed more signs of damage and repair than you would expect in a real working station.

Titan's nails dug into my shoulder. "What is this place?" he asked.

"It's Academy Station. It's a training space. They use it when they want to train in real station conditions. Zero-G combat, tactical assaults, disaster drills, that kind of thing," I explained. No harm in him knowing, he could probably work it out for himself.

"Where is everyone?"

"It's all automated, there's nobody up here most of the year, not unless there's a class on." Although they had been evacuating people to here earlier. They must have re-evacuated them when they came up with the plan to put me and Titan on the station.

"Why did they bring us here?" Titan said.

It was a good question, but I had no more of an idea than he had. I didn't answer, and he didn't press me for one.

By habit, I scanned for alternative exits. I'd not been up to Academy Station before, but by all accounts, it had been designed to copy typical station design as much as possible, to give an authentic training experience. It meant that there would be conduits and maintenance corridors, nooks and crannies I could make use of if I could get away. Indeed, I saw several, more or less in the places I expected them to be. The closest to where we stood... *huh*. Someone had drawn the number 729 on it with fluorescent green paint. It looked fresh.

"Whatever surprise they have planned for me, I'm not standing still for it," Titan rasped. "Get moving."

He pushed me, and I moved across the hall to another hatch. This led to the central lift bank for the station, but Titan nudged us away from them, towards a stairwell.

We passed another panel in the wall, this one painted with the number 731.

"Up or down?" I asked. If I had to guess he'd choose—

"Up."

Yeah. He'd spent twenty years at the bottom of Tartarus. He was conditioned to think of *up* as being *out*. And for all this boiling anger, he was still mostly trying to find a way out. I made a big show of struggling up the stairs, but up I went. If I could make that connection, I reckoned Probability Kid could too, even without his precognitive talents. I checked the next access panel we passed. The number was drawn smaller on this one, but there it was, 732. We were going in the right direction.

Titan took us off at the next level. Four corridors stretched off the landing, Titan shoved me towards the closest. In my mental map of a typical station, we should have been on a shopping level, with offices and support areas on the outer ring, but we seemed to have skipped several levels, as the doors lining this corridor looked to be traveller accommodation.

As we passed the third pair of doors, a light flickered on it. Titan punched the door, not waiting to see what the light was. The result: the steel door split like paper, but the light still flickered. It scanned up and down the door frame, expanded to a line, which spun and resolved into a holographic image of a human teenager. It took me a moment to realise who it was, if he hadn't been wearing the same costume as Titan, I'm not sure I would have ever clicked.

"You look better clean-shaven," I said.

Titan growled at me. "If your friends think an old photograph is going to distract me, they're wrong."

I shrugged. I had no idea what the plan was. It looked like Dez had finally unearthed an old archive picture of Titan, back when he was still calling himself Tangent. Gadget Dude would have been the one to rig the projector.

Two doors down, another holoprojection flickered into life.

Titan took a step towards it; I don't think he noticed he'd stopped flying. Or that he'd let go of me.

This image was a young version of Apogee. I recognised him immediately, and not just because of the costume, his grin was the same. I hoped he was okay. There had been no chance to check on him when I attacked Titan on the beach. If I'd acted soon enough, Professor Gale should have recovered, I had to hope.

"We were friends," Titan said, almost to himself. "Me and Si, we did everything together. Took the same classes, played on the same Power Ball team, chased the same girls. They always chose him, but that didn't bother me. Too often. We figured we'd be an unstoppable team after graduation. Apogee and Tangent."

Another hologram on another door, three doors down.

"I know what they're game is now," Titan said. "It won't work. I won't look." He took a step forwards all the same, right over an access panel in the floor with the number 734 painted on it.

I followed him, hesitated by the panel. It wasn't properly secured. If Titan were distracted enough, I could slip inside and away. It would be a narrow fit, but I could make it. The bulkier Titan, on the other hand, would have to rip the floor apart to follow. Not a coincidence; it was exactly what Seventhirtyfour wanted me to do.

Still, I hesitated.

"Who is she?" I asked. Titan had stopped before the next image, a pretty Polifan girl.

"I'd been using my ability for months, you see," Titan said. "I didn't know I had it. Didn't know it was my doing. Most people were worried it was some airborne disease that hadn't shown up on the scans when they built the Academy. Lots of students and some teachers, just feeling under the weather. I thought I was immune. I was feeling better than ever. It wasn't just me; Si didn't get sick either.

"We went flying. Me, Si, Veritas and Sparrow." He reached a hand to the girl as he said her name. "We got back a few days later to find the sickness had eased while we were away. It was only temporary though; it soon came back. I don't think anyone else made the connection. Just me."

"You realised you were the reason people were getting sick," I said, softly. I wanted to keep him talking, not catch his attention.

"Yeah." He walked a little further up the corridor, to the next image on the next door. I took advantage of his distraction to kneel and open the panel. But I still couldn't bring myself to leave.

"I learned to control it. And people got better. Everybody was relieved, there were some big parties to celebrate. But I wasn't celebrating. I felt hollow, empty. My power had given me a buzz, and now I'd stopped using it, it was like there was a... a black hole inside me, eating away at me. I had to feed it something, or it would con-sume me.

"Powers students were the best. If I fed on them, they'd survive, and nobody was any the wiser. Skills and Tech students, if I fed on them, I could kill them, and I didn't want that. It was an accident. You see? That first one was an accident. I didn't know my ability could kill.

"Hawk found me before I could hide the body. I con-vinced him it had been an accident. He was easy to con-vince. He didn't want his new school to fail before it had flown. A murder could have shut him down. But a tragic accident? Lessons to be learned, safeguards to be put in place? He could survive that. So, an accident it was. And I was more careful how I fed."

"Captain Hawk knew?" I asked. Kicked myself, I wasn't supposed to be drawing his attention.

Titan cast a look over his shoulder but can't have noticed the open panel at my feet. "Oh yes. That's why he blames himself for what happened after. He had a chance to stop it, but he didn't take it. Their deaths were on his hands as much as mine. He's an idiot. And a good man. Maybe that's the same thing. Couldn't stop me before, couldn't kill me after."

And he clung to the Academy as the one good thing to come out of his mistake for two decades afterwards.

"The end was almost embarrassingly predictable," Titan said, turning back to Sparrow's hologram. More holograms lit up further down the corridor, but Titan seemed stuck on this one. "She succumbed to Si's charms. It was only a fleeting affair, I'm sure, Si never stayed with his conquests long. I learned on the morning of that flight lesson.

"I was jealous. I admit it. Si was perfect. He was a god-dam hero, he had the powers, he got the girl. He deserved it all. But I'd be damned if he'd win the race too. I couldn't get what I wanted, but I was going to get *that*. But I needed a boost. I wasn't fast enough by myself. But if I stole a little power. Just sipped a little? Get the edge I needed?"

He reached into the hologram, closing a hand around the projector. Crushing it in his fist. "I took her all. One moment she was bright, vibrant, magnificent, wings beating like thunder, laughing as she pulled away from me. The next second she was an empty husk, plummeting to the ground. And I was stronger. Faster. Now I could win."

I'd heard enough. I understood now. I didn't need to hear the rest.

"They all turned against me. Even Si. I needed more power to defend myself." Titan said.

I crossed my arms over my chest and dropped into the shaft.

CHAPTER 23
SUPERHERO SCIENCE

I dropped as far and as fast as I could, rattling down the chute, picking up a scrape or two on my descent. I needed to put some distance between us, get as far out of Titan's reach as I could. Fortunately, Seventhirtyfour had chosen the escape route well, the service duct had a slight incline, so I was more sliding down it than plummeting to my doom. My speed still picked up faster than I liked. I applied a little pressure to the sides of the chute to peel off a little acceleration, slapped the wall in front of me to steal a little more. A quick descent was in my favour, but I wouldn't completely sacrifice control for speed.

I landed heavily four floors below where I'd started. Still well within Titan's field of control, but hopefully outside of his ability to target me specifically.

Looking down past my body, I'd landed on another access to this system of conduits. The hatch hadn't snapped open when I landed on it, but the impact had bent the catches almost to breaking point. A well-aimed kick finished the job and I dropped down into the corridor below.

I tapped the comm control on my wristpad. "Sky Diamond, you still there?"

"I'm here, Grey. We're here." I'd never been happier to hear anyone's voice. "Are you okay?"

"A little strung out. Titan's not the best of company, but

281

I'm okay, yeah. Thanks for getting me out of there. Do you have a plan for what comes next?"

"Hi, Grey, it's me, Seventhirtyfour. I'm sending a holo-overlay to your wrist pad." My comm chimed, and I tapped the screen. A holographic green arrow flickered above my wrist, pointing down the corridor. "Follow that, and it will lead you to the last escape pod on the station. We used the rest to recall the evacuees to the Academy."

"Right," I said, breaking into a jog. I checked the arrow as I ran, it remained oriented on my route however my arm moved.

Captain Hawk's voice joined the call. "Once you are safely away, we can deal with Tangent. I owe you an apology, Mr. Grey, for putting you in danger. And thanks, for giving us this opportunity to put it right."

The arrow pointed me left at the next junction, and then down a flight of stairs. "Deal with Titan, how, headmaster?"

"We have several options. The simplest involves control of life support. There were several Tech students among the evacuees, they rigged the life support systems on the station before they left. We can fill the place with anaesthetic gas, knock Tangent... Titan out."

"Won't work. He's wearing a breather from the shuttle's emergency supplies." Another flight of stairs, another corridor. The arrow grew bigger as I got closer.

"Good to know. Then we can increase the artificial gravity on the station. Pin him in one place. We can send in drones to apply suppression cuffs," said Hawk.

I ran past a row of empty escape pod bays. The final bay was my destination; its pod doors stood open, and my chance to get to freedom lay before me.

I hesitated.

"How quickly can you adjust the gravity for the whole

station?" I asked.

"It will take a few minutes. To restrain someone as strong as Titan—"

"Then that won't work either. Or well, it might, but if I'm any judge as soon as Titan realises what's happening, he will break out of the station. He's determined not to go back to prison, and he's willing to risk space to avoid it. He's tough and he's got that breath mask... I'm not sure I'd bet against him making planetfall." I raided the pod's emergency supplies for water and a meal bag. It had been too long since I'd eaten, and I was ravenous.

But I didn't hit the launch button.

"What else?" I said around a mouthful of meal bag.

"The station's self-destruct—" Hawk began.

"Then you better be sure it would kill him instantly, or he's aiming for planetfall again. Look, these are all great plans, but you haven't seen Titan, not as he is now. I've spent time up close with him. He is dangerous and motivated. Right now, we have him contained, but if he perceives a threat, or even if he's left alone too long, he's going to decide the risk is worth it and attempt to come back to the planet. He could die in the attempt, which is a victory of sorts I guess, but what if he doesn't? If he does make it back, what then? We've lost the chance to lock him down without putting others at risk."

"So, what do you suggest, Mr. Grey?" Hawk asked.

"Doing this remotely is too much of an unknown quantity. We can't take the chance. Whatever we do needs to be done eyes-on. That means I have to stay." I climbed back out of the escape pod and into the corridor.

"Grey, no!" Lucy and Seventhirtyfour blurted simultaneously.

"It has to be me, guys. For whatever reason, I seem to be less vulnerable to his drain than most. His aura felled

Dez and Gadget Dude instantly; me, I seem to be able to resist unless he uses it on me directly. If he doesn't see me, he won't be able to drain me. And we're on a space station. This is my home turf. If you can rig me a new overlay so I can track his relative position? Trust me, he won't see me."

"I'm inclined to agree with your friends," said Captain Hawk. "Even if we accept the premise that you need to be a witness to Titan's fall, it doesn't provide us with a solution to effecting it."

"Too late," I said. There was a launch button on the control panel outside the pod too. I pushed it without hesitation. The hatch slammed shut and the pod launched, exploding away from the station.

"Grey," Lucy whispered

"I'll be okay. Guys, you must have twenty years of data on Titan from Tartarus. Sure, he may be stronger than the last time you caught him, but you did catch him before, and this time we have more information. And, frankly, more people to work on the problem. You have an entire Academy of students many of whom are certified geniuses. Stop just protecting them and start *using* them. Put all those minds on it, we'll find a solution in no time. Just, whatever it is, it needs to be quick, it needs to surprise him and... ideally, it kind of needs to be fool proof."

There was a long pause from my comm. A long, worrying pause.

"We're on it, Grey," rumbled Seventhirtyfour.

"Great. In the meantime, I'm going to see what our friend is up to."

I muted the comm and headed back into the station.

# # #

My first stop was at an information board. I pulled up basic station schematics, just to get a sense of where

everything was. The map was incomplete; I was in a training area, so the information available on this console was
restricted to what students were allowed to know. It didn't
include places off-limits to students, or, I guessed, places
that contained surprises for them. There was enough
though. Enough to see that the designers of this place had
done a reasonable job of mirroring a "real" station's archi-
tecture. It was smaller, with enough missing elements that
I couldn't just navigate it on instinct, but there looked to
be enough similarities in infrastructure that I should be
able to move around it with confidence. Confidence that
I wouldn't get lost anyway. I downloaded the map to my
wristpad, but I'd rather find my own way around.

First order of priority was placing Titan. While I waited
for somebody to upload a tracking app to my wristpad, I
worked my way back towards where I'd last seen him. I
stuck to narrow service corridors where I could. When I
had to use the more public areas, I crossed each one cautiously, checking any shadow that looked capable of con-
cealing Titan before daring to move. I made it back to the
stairwell Titan had pushed me up without getting spotted,
and there I waited, one level below, straining to hear any
sign of him moving about.

That moment of quiet was my first chance to appreciate quite how eerie the training station was. The one constant on any normal space station is the sound of other
people. Even in the quiet areas, there would be sounds
of activity nearby. Ringing metal as somewhere somebody dropped something. The sound of footsteps on deck
plates. Idle chatter. Security guards asking each other
where that devilishly handsome teenager could have gotten to. That kind of thing. Here, nothing. It wasn't silent by
any means, but the background hum of technology had no
organic counterpoint.

I'd set my wristpad to silent, so the notification of the availability of the tracking app came as a slight vibration. I opened it, and a subdued blue arrow appeared. I moved my arm about, watching the arrow, triangulating Titan's position. It looked like he'd backtracked into the fake Arrivals area we'd passed through earlier. I suspected he wanted to be close to the shuttle, either because he thought I might go back to it, or because he had visions of sheltering in it if Hawk had planned to mess with the station systems.

I could work with that.

I went to the level above, found a service duct near the lift bank. This one narrow enough that I had to slither on my belly to make any progress. A little effort to fold my way around a corner and was able to drop half a level to reach another access point to the outside. I eased the cover away, setting it gently down to the left of the opening, then pulled myself out to perch on a narrow shelf behind replicas of a pair of colourful advertising holograms. I was a little more exposed than I would have liked, but it gave me a good view of the whole hall. If Titan were to spot me, he'd need to look up, which I've noted before is not a thing that many humans do, and peer through two brightly-lit animated displays. As hiding places went it wasn't infallible, but it was good enough.

Below me, Titan was taking out his frustrations on... well, everything. He crushed one vendor stall with a single kick, before working his way along a series of couches, throwing them at the walls.

All the while, he ranted. His general theme seemed to be revenge against Hawk, Apogee, the Academy, and occasionally even me. His voice muffled by the breathing mask he still wore, he yelled at the cameras, "Hawk! Come face me, you coward! I know you're listening. I'm coming for your precious students, and I will bring your whole stupid school down for what you did to me. Face me, if you think you can stop me."

He picked up another couch, but instead of throwing this one, he tore it in two with his bare hands, roaring.

He didn't seem in danger of calming down.

What could we do with him long term? We couldn't let him roam free among civilised folks. That much was clear from his story. He was psychotic, petty and powerful. I'd had no sense of remorse from him for the murder of the girl he claimed he'd been interested in. I'm sure even if he were to get his revenge, it wouldn't sate him, he'd be off murdering other people before long. At the same time though, I couldn't help but feel sorry for him. He had endured solitary confinement for two decades. Really, he was saner than he had any right to be.

Was there a middle ground? How could there be? While he had his abilities, he was too much of a threat. Even if we could find a way to permanently remove his powers, would he be safe to release into the community? I didn't envy the person who would have to make that choice. Presumably, someone from the Galactic Patrol?

Below, Titan hefted another bench; holding one end he spun like a hammer thrower. He released at speed, catapulting the bench upwards. Directly towards me.

I dropped flat, hugging my ledge. The bench exploded against the wall above me, about where my head had been the instant before. Shrapnel pinged off my stab vest. I tensed reflexively, and my left leg lost its brace against the wall, it slipped off the ledge and flailed in open air. My balance shifted, I began to roll, away from the ledge as gravity grabbed for me.

Knuckles white on the lip of the duct I'd come through, I pushed back with my right foot, bracing, straining to hold myself rigid.

Below me Titan stalked through the wreckage. The holo-advert still covered my hiding place. All I had to do was not fall on Titan's head and...

My right hand cramped, complaining at the abuse, my grip faltered. No. My centre of mass shifted again, but my left foot found a solid surface. A ceiling beam below me. It was enough. I braced again, shifted my balance, stabilised.

Sheepishly, I shuffled into a more secure position.

I must have watched Titan for an hour before he wound down. By the time he'd finished, the place was unrecognisable chaos. Not one bit of furniture at ground level was intact; it was all scattered and broken.

Eventually, Titan slumped to the ground in the middle of his mess and stared out of the window. Academy world shone below us. He stared at it with such intensity, he must be willing himself there. I wondered how long before he attempted to make the trip. My instinct was that it wouldn't be long.

My wristpad comm buzzed again. They had an update for me. I retreated up the conduit so I could speak in safety.

In a station this quiet, any sound I made was likely to carry, and I didn't want Titan to know where I was. I found a quiet office space, sat behind the desk and tapped my wristpad to accept the call.

"Hi, Grey, it's Pilvi." Her tone was business-like and emotionless. Not giddy with victory, but not devoid of hope either. "You're on with me, Gadget Dude, Professor Alembic and Blue Claw."

"Hi, Pilvi. Everyone. What do you have for me?"

"A lot of untested theories," she said. "This kind of analysis takes time, there's a lot of data to sift through, collected over years by Tartarus's systems, but my impression is there is some time crunch here?"

"There is. I've just been watching Titan tantrum for an hour. I don't think he has a great deal of patience left. My gut tells me he's going to make the leap, soon."

"That's not good." A different voice. "My apologies for cutting in. This is Blue Claw. Part of what my team is doing is assessing Titan's chance of making it back to the Academy. Given what we can extrapolate about his levels of invulnerability and stamina, factored against his flight speed and his access to life support technology, we estimate there is an 83% probability that he would survive the trip. The effort would deplete his reserves, however, and he would need to feed immediately upon arrival."

"So, he'd be weaker? More vulnerable?"

Blue Claw hmm'ed. They didn't sound happy. "No. Well, perhaps. The balance of likelihood is that his hunger and his drain ability would be sharpened, its effects intensified. Like a wounded animal, we believe this depletion would make Titan more dangerous, not less."

"Wonderful. So, we should keep him on the station?"

"Our available data does support that stratagem, yes."

"Professor Alembic, here." I'd never met the Professor, didn't even know her species. I only knew that Pilvi liked her, that would do for me. "I'm representing the faculty in this discussion. Captain Hawk is not happy with you or your recklessness, Grey, that's the official position of the Academy. But, yes, as Blue Claw says, your decision to remain on station has proved to be sound. I wonder how much of that was instinct and how much was planning? Should you survive this encounter, well... let's focus on that for now."

"Yes, let's."

"I have been coordinating the analysis groups," the Professor continued. "We are focusing on two main approaches and have two potential solutions. Blue

Claw and their team have been looking at a biochemical approach to the problem, while Säde has been leading up the team looking at energy-based solutions."

"Gadget Dude make things."

"Ah, indeed. We do have a representative from the engineers here, also," Alembic conceded.

"Look, it's nice to know who does what, but have any of these teams got actual solutions to the problem for me." I knew I sounded tetchy, but I'd been having a bad day.

Blue Claw answered. "We have analysed the Tartarus data and identified the areas of Titan's brain which are most active when he uses his drain ability. We believe that if we can disrupt those neural pathways, he would be unable to call upon his draining power. Moreover, we hypothesise it would also interfere with Titan's motor control, making him easier to pacify."

"That does sound good. What are the downsides?"

"Simply? It might not work."

"Right."

"The chemicals you need should be available in the station's med bay. It's well-stocked, as accidents can happen on training missions. The most difficult part of this approach is administering the solution to Titan. Ideally, it should be injected directly into his spine, but we appreciate that may be challenging. It will be less efficacious, but any injection in the region of his head or neck has a chance of delivering sufficient neurotoxin to Titan's brain."

"This is a neurotoxin? Is it dangerous?"

"There is a small, but non-zero, chance of permanent brain damage to the subject."

"How small?"

"There are too many unknown quantities to be accurate. Our best guess is around 4%."

"Right." That seemed... acceptable. I didn't like how

easy that assessment was to make. I set off towards the station's med bay, keeping my steps as light as I could. "You said there were two potential solutions. That's one, what's the other?"

"Tartarus had a lot of information about the way Titan's power affects the world around him," Pilvi replied. "There is a notable difference in... pitch of the suppression field's signature at one point during Titan's incarceration. We think Titan must have overcome the prison's security systems and replaced their suppression field with his drain ability."

"Yes, he said as much to me," I said. "Sorry, I should have said. I'm a bit rattled and losing track of who knows what."

"Don't worry about it," said Pilvi. "In fact, it's good that we didn't know. Means we approached it from first principles. Titan didn't tamper with the existing system, he overwhelmed it. In time, I think Tartarus's system just burned out, but initially, at least, both Tartarus and Titan were vying for dominance, Titan eventually winning."

"So, he's powerful. We knew that."

"Yes, Grey, he's powerful." Now Pilvi was sounding tetchy too. We'd *all* been having a bad day. "If he can over-whelm one energy field, the principle should work in reverse."

"Okay, so we need to create a counter-signal. One more powerful than his?"

"That would be the ideal solution, but Gadget Dude and his team have looked at what you have up there, and that's not going to work. We have an alternative, though. Instead of going more powerful, we're going more focused. Part of Titan's power is wasted on range. We can have you build a transmitter that will create a signal on the same energetic wavelength as Titan's drain ability. A little destructive interference should deaden his drain ability and could even go some way to draining Titan himself."

The med bay was in a section of the station off-limits to students during training sessions. It wasn't on my map, but I could tell where it was by its absence. I could ask the ground team for the passcode, but I hadn't flexed my lock-picking in a while.

"If our winning tactic for this is focus over range... how close do I need to get?" I asked.

"You don't have to inject him with it, at least," Pilvi said, dryly. "Close, though. Five meters. Probably. Maybe a little closer. All of this is best guesses on an hour's worth of research."

"Understood. You've all done incredibly. Will I need to build this transmitter?"

"Can send pictures," Gadget Dude chimed in. "Team say can use to build." He sounded dubious, but then, he wasn't the schematics and plans sort of gadgeteer. Gadget Dude worked by instinct.

"You've seen the plans, Dude, do you think I can make it?"

"Grey fixes grapnel. Can do this."

"Appreciate the faith. Thanks. All of you, thank you. If we beat this guy, it will be down to your efforts."

This was met by a round of murmuring from the other end of the call. If it had sounded a mite more optimistic, I'd have been more cheerful.

"You'd better get to the Med Bay, Grey," Pilvi said. "You'll find the meds you need there for Blue Claw's solution, and there's an equipment locker on the same corridor that should have what you need for the transmitter. Hold on, I'll give you the access code to get into the Staff Area of the station."

"I looked around the gleaming, well-stocked Med Bay.

"No need," I said with a grin, "I'm already in."
Time to get to work.

CHAPTER 24
FINAL EXAMINATION

I watched Titan stalk up along the corridor. "Don't make me hunt you down, Grey. I know you're still here. I can feel you. Feed from you. Don't think the fact that I can't see you will keep you safe." He paused, staring into a dark corner where the corridor branched off. "Are you there, mouse? I know you're close."

I was. Closer than I liked. He'd rather surprised me as I'd been heading towards his location: he'd decided to start moving too. Now, he stood almost directly above me, as I lay flat on my back in the crawl space under his feet. I was close enough to tickle his toes if I were to suddenly be insane. Close enough to catch his stench again, certainly.

My fingers reached for the transmitter I had clipped to my belt. If I had built it correctly, if it worked, I was close enough to use it now. I craned my neck to find the closest exit from the crawlspace. It would take ten seconds at least to crawl to it, time enough for Titan to recover or escape. I was in range for the transmitter but using it now—I might blow my one chance at it. Instead, I kept my breathing shallow and watched Titan's shadow play on the grill above my face.

Titan's long claw-like toenails scritched the deck plate above me as he set into motion again. I allowed myself a breath of fresh air, then turned onto my stomach and crawled after him. Careful not to get too close, particularly as he crossed the crawlspace's access hatch, I followed along behind and beneath him.

Titan reached a stairwell, looked up, then down, chose to descend. He wasn't flying. Did that mean something? Was he conserving energy? If he were tapped out already, that could bode well... or ill, if Blue Claw's theory about Titan's hunger sharpening his powers held. I took a moment to note it on my wristpad. Any and all observations I made there were being fed back to the science team on the ground. If my attempt failed, perhaps I could still find some data that would help their next attempt.

Ah, optimism.

I slipped out of the hatch, and paused, listening intently. Titan was still heading down the stairs, towards the station hangar bays. Was he checking for transportation, or just looking for a way out? Either way, I could feel the clock ticking. If he left the station without me... well, he wouldn't. Somehow.

I ran up the stairs.

There was no easy concealment on the stairwell, no simple way to follow him directly. I hadn't spent ten years getting into every conceivable corner of half the space stations of the galaxy without learning a few unconventional options. This one was an old favourite; I'd used the same one last year when I'd tried to escape the Academy before. I really needed to stop doing that. It was time to accept that the Academy was where I belonged.

Assuming I survived.

I slid down the vent and crawled to the end. I eased the panel loose, pulled it into the vent with me. It was a bit of a risk, made my hidey-hole easier to spot, but if I needed to get out quickly, better the cover was gone.

Below me, the Academy's main docking bay stood empty. It was a good deal smaller than on a normal station, but apart from that, it had exactly what I expected. One side was protected by a force shield but was otherwise open to space. Real, solid, emergency doors would be set into the ceiling, they would drop immediately if the force shield failed. Assisted by mechanical rams if we lost force shields and gravity. The station would lose a big gulp of air in the time it took for the hatches to seal, but better than losing the whole station. At the centre of each of the other three walls, equipment stations offered repair tools, load lifters, and medical supplies. Bigger stations might have more, but three would be more than enough for the Academy. I doubted they could fit more than two ships in a hanger this size anyway. Two gantries swayed gently near the ceiling. The ladder to reach the closest gantry was a short jump away from my hiding place.

There were no ships present, of course. They'd used everything they had to get the evacuees back off the station, and not coincidentally deny Titan an easy out.

Speaking of Titan, he entered at ground level, striding across the deck, making straight for the opposite end of the hangar and the open space beyond. He'd abandoned the idea of looking for me, he wasn't even scanning the room in case I was lurking there. He was laser-focused on the starfield in front of him; with each step, he picked up his pace. By the time he reached the halfway point of the hangar, he was at a jog. I almost missed the shimmer of an enviro-field around him. Not as reliable or long-lasting as a spacesuit, they were emergency-use devices, creating a bubble of air, warmth and radiation shielding but they depleted in less than a minute. They were supposed to keep you alive long enough to get into a suit, not to be used in place of one. Would the shielding block my interference emitter? There was only one way to find out, and time was running out to test it.

I sighted the gantry with my grapnel gun and pulled the trigger. The claw latched on, and the cable went tight, and I launched myself out of my hiding space before Titan had time to do more than look up at the sound.

The arc of my swing was textbook; both my boots caught Titan squarely on the side of his head. Strong and heavy though he was, the impact was enough to rock him, and I somersaulted back away from him, bending my knees to take the sting out of the landing. I retracted the grapnel and the cable hissed and twisted around me until it snapped back.

"Forgetting something?" I asked. That combat banter would have lost me almost as many points as the swing had earned me.

"Grey," he said, doing no better, banter-wise.

He raised a hand, clawed fingers reached for me, and I felt a wave a weakness. Time for the big test. I pressed the stud on the casing of the transmitter.

Nothing happened.

"To think I've wasted all this time hunting for you. I should have come here first," Titan said. He curled his fingers slowly, closing to make a fist.

My head span, vision darkened. My whole body sagged; my eyelids drooped. The deck rose to meet me.

No, I was so sure...

I pressed the button on the transmitter again. Stabbed at it repeatedly, desperately, as the world slipped away.

Click.

Like a light bulb switching on, I went from the threshold of sleep to two coffees too many energetic in a snap. I sprang to my feet, even as Titan recoiled from me.

"What have you done?" he whispered, something that sounded like dread tinging his voice.

He seemed smaller, standing there in front of the stars,

298

his normal swagger fled. "Let's find out what you're really made of," I said and lunged at him.

He wasn't weak. He was still bigger and stronger than me, in fact, but if he'd ever bothered learning to be a skilled fighter, that edge had abandoned him in twenty years in jail. I was better than him. He blocked most of my blows, but now and then, one snuck past his guard. It was like hitting steel, but each blow seemed to sap his confidence further.

He fell back. "No, you can't," he said, blocking a kick to his head with both forearms. "I was so close. This time I win. I deserve it."

"You've killed people, threatened others. People I care about," I said, switching to hand strikes to keep him guessing. I tagged him with a punch to the nose, felt it crack under my blow.

"I'll find them—uff!—and make them—ah!—pay!" he said.

I almost fell for it. I was so busy concentrating on the fact that I was winning, driving him back, I almost forgot where I was driving him to.

We were within a half-dozen steps of the terminator now, open space stretching out to infinity, only the light of Academy world, visible beneath us now that we were so close to the edge, broke the vista. He was trying to get away from me. If he went out, I couldn't follow. It would buy him the distance he needed, and if he survived the trip, would let him feast on my fellow students below.

"No," I said.

He counter-punched, and I stepped inside his reach. I grabbed at him, pivoted on my hip and *heaved*. Professor Red Ninja would have been proud of my technique, but even with Titan's momentum working for me, it was like dead-lifting a 150-kilo grain sack. For a second, I thought he wouldn't budge, but then our centre of mass shifted, and over he went. Titan grabbed at me as he went over, one meaty hand on my shoulder, the other reaching for my belt.

We tumbled over each other, rolling across the deck. He released me, and I skidded away from him, feeling every irregularity in the deck plate as my face slid across them.

I lay there a moment, pained and tired. Too tired. Tried to lift my head, couldn't. No energy. Dimly, I reached for the shattered remains of the transmitter on my belt. Titan stood over me, the rest of the transmitter box crushed in his fist.

"Was this important?" he asked. He tossed the pieces at me, then turned back towards space and the Academy. He broke into a run.

"Wait! You can't!" I shouted.

He leapt out through the force shield, it crackled as he passed through. He hovered there, framed in the hangar bay doors, his ability to fly meant he was not bound to the whims of gravity.

He rotated, spinning back to face me, a smile slowly spreading across his face.

This is the moment. He dives out of sight, I've lost.

Instead, he floated back into the hangar, gliding to a halt just above me. "You're right," he admitted. "I can't. My reserves are too depleted. Even I don't like my odds of surviving the trip. I need a boost. A top-up." He reached down, picked me up by the throat, just as I'd seen him do with Incapacitor, back in Tartarus, when he'd drained Incapacitor dry to make good his escape. "You're just the smart-mouthed tonic I need. I wonder how far down you'll get before you freeze? Don't worry, I'll drain you before space kills you."

He drifted back towards the force field one last time. I fumbled weakly at his wrist with one hand.

Titan paused just before the force field. "I know you're a talker, aren't you Grey, I sense that about you. Since the vacuum will rob you of that ability first, any last words before I let it have you?"

I couldn't get the words out, his vice-grip was crushing my throat, I could feel the power in my limbs draining away. All I could manage was croaking out a gurgle.

Titan chuckled, loosened his grip, just a little. "Say again, I didn't quite catch that."

"I said," I said, "'Always have a backup.'"

I brought my other hand up and plunged three syringes of the neurotoxin into the flesh and muscle beneath his chin. One needle shattered on his tough skin, but the other two bit deeply.

He dropped me. I sprawled on the floor, unable to pick myself up.

Titan clawed at his throat, pulled the syringes free, but their payload was delivered. It was too late for him. Or me. Depending on what the toxin did.

His mouth moved, but no words came out, then he too fell to the deck with a startled gasp. He reached for me, hand clawing, but whether his drain worked or not, I could feel no more exhausted.

Titan convulsed, twisting on the deck beside me. He gurgled one last gasp, and then lay still. I couldn't even tell if he was still breathing.

It was over.

Go, team.

I let myself sleep.

CHAPTER 25
EXTRA CREDIT

I woke up to a flashlight beam in my face. I managed to get one arm draped across to shield my eyes from the light. It took a herculean effort, and I wasn't going to manage anything more dramatic any time soon.

"He's alive!" Lucy declared. The obvious delight in her voice lifted my spirits, at least.

"This one too," Gadget Dude said from over where Titan was in my mental map of the room. He sounded less thrilled.

"Get them both loaded onto float pallets," Captain Hawk said. "Make sure the cuffs are secure. On both of them."

"Hey," I tried to protest, but it was a feeble sound.

Two large green shapes with many arms between them loomed above me. They lifted me and placed me on a marginally more comfortable resting place. Cold metal bands locked around my wrists. Someone moved my arm from over my eyes. I cringed away from the bright light.

"Sorry about this," rumbled Two.

"S'okay." I kept my eyes firmly closed, trying and failing to will away a headache.

Technically, I was still a fugitive, escaped convict and suspected murderer. I rather hoped that most people understood what really happened now, but there were formalities to observe before you let murder suspects go free. A hearing of some sort. At least, I hoped that's why I was still in metaphorical chains.

I felt Lucy's hand in mine. It was soft, warm. She squeezed my hand, gently. It made me feel better.

It was also comforting that they spent a good deal more time securing Titan.

The shuttle took us back to campus, and I was allowed to return to my dorm room, though Prof Croft posted guards on my door and the roof of the block opposite, in case I tried the window.

I was shattered and collapsed into bed as soon as I got home.

Lucy stayed with me, sitting by my bed as I slept.

She was gone in the morning, but I felt stronger for her being there.

# # #

Professor Gale visited me later in the afternoon. His tweeds hung loosely on his frame, his skin was pallid, dark rings bruised around his eyes. He walked with a distinct stoop.

"Professor Gale. Take a seat, please." I waved him to my desk chair and sat on the edge of the bed. "I'm glad to see you. After what Titan did to you, I wasn't sure if... you were..."

"Dead? Yes, well, I think Apogee may be. The powers Titan stole from me are yet to return, and my physical reserves are, well, as you see."

"I'm sorry, Professor."

"It doesn't matter. Apogee may be gone, but I survived, more or less. I was getting a little old for the hero life anyway. It's why I accepted the headmaster's offer to teach here this year."

"Will you keep teaching then?" I asked.

"Perhaps. I need to take some time away to reflect. I may be back next year. For now, I plan to rest and recover. Whether Apogee's powers return or not, I think he is retired."

Unsure how to respond, I said nothing.

Gale clapped his hands. "You've no interest in an old man's woes, I expect. I came to thank you. If you hadn't intervened with Titan, I doubt I would be here at all. I've spoken to Captain Hawk on your behalf. There will need to be a formal decision made regarding your legal status, but in the meantime, I've convinced him that the guards are unnecessary. You are free to return to campus life, although until that decision is made you will not be able to leave the Academy grounds."

"Thanks, Professor. That won't be a problem."

He stood, reached out to shake my hand. "Good luck to you, Grey. You did good work against Titan. Perhaps it was your story to finish, after all. I will see you again, I'm sure."

"See you around, Professor."

# # #

Gravestone and Laugh Riot were shipped off to a Galactic Patrol detention centre. I didn't get to see them before they left, but what would I have said to them if I had? I don't know. I had a long talk with Mrs. Gravane about everything. It seemed that putting the suppression cuffs on Gravestone had not returned him to being Gravane, not this time. Perhaps I'd seen the last manifestation of his original personality, perhaps someday he would find his way to the fore again. I hoped so. He had saved me a couple of times in Tartarus. I made sure his mother knew. She smiled at that, but it was a tight smile.

She didn't tell me what happened when Gravane and Laugh Riot were shipped off-planet. I wouldn't find that out until much later.

As for Titan, he didn't wake up. Whatever that neurotoxin we'd concocted had done, he was in a coma and
seemed likely to stay that way. I didn't know how to feel
about that. I didn't ever set out to hurt people, even if they
were people trying to hurt (and worse) me. I might have
regretted the outcome, but I couldn't find it in myself to
regret my actions. If I hadn't intervened, he would either
have died in space or gone on to murder hundreds more.
Let that one rest more easily in my conscience.

He was taken to a secure medical facility for treatment
and holding, a remote facility, but with people to properly
look after him. Throwing him down another pit wouldn't
help. He needed care, not more isolation. I doubted he
could be redeemed, but he still deserved help. Don't we
all?

# # #

"Well, this is becoming quite the annual tradition,"
Captain Hawk said. He rested his elbows on his desk,
hands clasped in front of his chin. "And it wouldn't be a
meeting to untangle one of your messes, Mr. Grey, without
a Gravane on hand to try and intimidate me."

Senator Serrenessa Gravane, sat in the chair beside
mine, inclined her head. "A pleasure to be here, headmaster. I am merely present to ensure my client is fairly
treated."

"We have dropped the murder and attempted murder charges. Taking all circumstances into account, we
are also waiving charges associated with Grey's escape
from Tartarus," Hawk said. "I don't suppose that is enough
to stop him being your client and persuade you to with-
draw?"

"My remit, as directed by the Gravane Corporation, is

306

regrettably broader than the criminal charges wrongly laid against my client," Serrenessa demurred.

A frown tugged at Hawk's face. "I take it that's lawyer for 'No'?"

"In the current scenario, that is correct."

"Peachy."

Hawk sat back in his chair and glared at me. I tried to keep my expression neutral, but he must have seen something in my face. His eyes narrowed. "There is nothing amusing here, Mr. Grey. I do not think you appreciate how seriously you have endangered the Academy by your actions."

"I stopped Titan," I protested.

"According to Laugh Riot, you knew she was present and had plans to free Doctor Gravestone. Had you informed me, instead of trying to take this on yourself, she and her accomplice would not have gained access to Tartarus. Gravestone and Titan would not have been released. Your brother," he looked pointedly at my lawyer, "would still be himself and not be trapped in his Doctor Gravestone persona. A number of students and staff would still be alive."

"Hey, that's—" Serrenessa stopped me with a hand on my forearm.

"When we entrusted the care of my brother to your facility," she said, icily, "you neglected to mention that its only other occupant would be a violent super-powered murderer. A criminal whose very existence and incarceration you had been lying about for two decades. My client may be reckless and overconfident, but he acted to protect my brother. You, headmaster, were criminally negligent in your provision of care for Mirabor. You took him in knowing an attempt had already been made to free him; you assured us further attempts would be thwarted. I fail to see how you made any provisions to meet that assurance.

"Your illegal incarceration of the student Tangent, latterly Titan, contravenes a dozen laws specifying the treatment of convicts. Moreover, mass-murderer or not, at the time of his incarceration, you were not registered as a legal detention centre. That we all see how guilty Titan is, does not absolve you of effectively kidnapping and holding the man for twenty years. My client's misdemeanours are nothing compared to your *crimes*."

Captain Hawk wilted under her assault. "You're right. It's over."

I stared at Serrenessa. This was not how I'd expected the meeting to go. I'd thought it would be like the one at the end of the first year when Hawk had been pissed at me, but we'd talked him around and I'd got to stay. What Serrenessa was suggesting though, that was something else entirely. "Are you planning to arrest Captain Hawk?" I asked.

"I? No, indeed. I am a lawyer. That does not empower me to arrest or detain people, beyond the limited circumstances covered by a citizen's arrest. The headmaster's status as de facto governor of the world where the crime was committed..." her eyes sparkled, she bit her lip. "It would be a fascinating case to argue."

"Right." The Gravanes weren't all insane, but I was starting to think they were all at least a little odd. I looked from her to Hawk and back again. "So, what *are* you saying?"

"She's saying the Justice Academy is done," Hawk said, flatly. "Whatever happens to me, it's over. My inbox is overflowing with messages from students transferring elsewhere, from corporate partners withdrawing their sponsorship. It's a political quagmire and the Academy won't survive it."

"No!"

Serrenessa held up a hand to stop us both. "I think the Academy can be saved. The Gravane Corporation, despite everything, is willing to continue its association with the school. My mother has been impressed with Grey's advocacy of this establishment. If he does not plan to cut ties with it?"

"Definitely not."

She fished her pad from her bag, tapped a few notes on the screen. "Good. Then we will do our best to see the Academy survives. However."

Hawk threw up his hands. "However, my time as headmaster is done, right?"

"I'm afraid so. One thing we would have to insist upon is that you and all faculty members associated with the decision to illegally hold Titan must step down."

Hawk drew in a deep breath, let it out slowly. "So be it. For the Academy." He ran a hand down his face. He looked older all of a sudden.

Serrenessa squeezed my wrist. "From here on, our discussion will likely descend into minutia and administration. Don't feel you need to stay for it."

"Right."

Hawk looked at me. "Funny, when I called you in, I was considering kicking you out for good. Seems like the boot ended up on someone else's foot."

I stood up, paced to the door. "I'm sorry, sir. We haven't always agreed with each other, and I've done a lot of lying to you, but this is not how I wanted things to end."

"End, Mr. Grey? Perhaps. Perhaps not. Perhaps this is just our form of conflict before we inevitably team up and defeat the true villain. The crossover paradox."

"I'd like that," I said. Then I retreated from his office, leaving him alone with my lawyer.

# # #

Hawk was right about one thing. We may have saved the Academy, but that didn't mean people would stay. Over the next few days, the Academy spaceport was busier even than at the start of the year. Academy shuttles and private charters descended, scooped up students and staff, then departed.

I caught the Avenging Spider, on his way to catch a ship. "Tom, surely you're not leaving?"

"Not forever. I hope," he said, adjusting the weight of the bag on his shoulder. "But I've had a call from family on Yson, they need my help with some stuff. Poisonous vampires on the rampage, they're like little... it's not important. I promised to help. Things here? They're just a bit weird now. You're staying, I take it?"

"Yeah, despite..."

"Hey now, don't be like that. This isn't your fault. The Captain's mistakes were going to catch up with him eventually. You were just a lightning rod. Seems you have a gift for that."

"No, I know. It's not my fault, but I don't know that I'm entirely faultless, either. Seems like there's plenty of blame to go around." I didn't tell him about the scrawled messages, and other things that I'd found pushed under my dorm room door. There was a vocal, and odiferous, minority who were absolutely set on blaming me.

"You put your life on the line to save these people, Grey, nobody could have done more."

I extended a hand; he shook it enthusiastically. "Thanks, Tom. Good luck with those vampires."

"Good luck with your studies. Remember, proper care of your grapnel gun is vital."

"That's the truth," I grinned and waved him off to join the others heading off-world.

Not everyone left, of course. After the dust settled

almost half of the students and a third of the teaching staff remained. We lost Professor Red Ninja, he'd been at the Academy at the start, and whether he'd been involved with the Titan decision or not, his presence then was enough that he had to step down. Doctor Phenomenal left to do a book tour. Professors Croft and Alembic stayed, though Croft seemed subdued in her lectures. I think she blamed herself for not knowing what had been going on behind the scenes.

As I say, there was a lot of blame to go around.

We lost a lot of familiar faces, and the atmosphere at the Academy, for those that stayed behind, it was weird. The place felt like a ghost town. A second wave of departures followed over the next couple of weeks, people who had wanted the Academy to survive but couldn't handle the changes. More didn't return from the winter break.

Those hardy souls that returned were, who? The most dedicated? The most stubborn? The students with nowhere else to go?

Yeah.

It was a strange sort of victory.

# # #

Gadget Dude gathered us all in the spaceport at the end of the winter break. The Academy is far too tropical to ever get properly cold, but Lucy and I had still stood together for warmth. David had been among those who'd left the Academy. Lucy and I had grown closer after that. It felt right. We didn't want to put a label on it, yet, but, yes.

"Have you heard from Sergeant Nine?" Pilvi asked Seventhirtyfour.

"He and the team have been reassigned. With the Academy being politically hot right now, Brontom Command felt it better to keep a distance. And, if we're honest, probably best for Nine that he stays away. I did talk to Twin Strike; I think she might want to give the Academy another go. We may see her next year."

"It would be good to have her back," Dez said. "The way things have been going lately, anyone with healing powers is a distinct advantage."

"Has anyone said anything to you about your standing up to Nine?" I asked.

Seventhirtyfour's expression darkened. "No."

He was lying. I didn't know what that meant, but if Seventhirtyfour chose to lie to us, to me? He had his reasons. I wouldn't press him. Yet. I just hoped the fallout wasn't too serious.

Lucy must have felt me tense. She quickly changed the subject. "Pilvi, you went home for the holiday, didn't you?"

Pilvi grinned, broadly. "Oh, yes. It was marvellous. Lots of home-cooked farm-fresh food, plenty of time with the family. And with Kaarina. I'd missed her. We've agreed that we will try to keep a distance relationship going after all. The galaxy isn't *that* big."

"Getting smaller every day," Lucy said. She broke away from me to give Pilvi a congratulatory hug.

Dez hummed a few bars of a song I vaguely recognised. "Hey Gadget Dude, what did you want us here for? There's more alcohol in the Fortress of Epictude. The acoustics are better in there too."

"Wait," Gadget Dude said, craning his neck to look into arrivals. "Not long."

He was right. A few seconds later, the door from Arrivals parted.

Avrim spread his wings, I caught a hint of apple blossom from his wing scent: he was startled to see us, but happy.

"Guys!" he said. "I—it's great to see you."

Everybody mobbed him at that point, but I found myself hanging back, watching Avrim.

Once the initial burst of greetings ebbed, he caught my eye. "You found her killer?" he asked.

"I did. Though it was a team effort to take her down."

He nodded. "And why? Why did she kill Veritas?"

"She was here under false pretences. Planning a break-out from Tartarus. I think Laugh Riot couldn't risk letting her true identity or plan slip. A sane person would just have avoided your Aunt, but she chose a different path."

"Thank you, Grey, thank you all. I wish I could have been there. But I'm glad you saw justice done."

There was something hollow in his tone. I'd heard Avrim be sarcastic, droll, even pessimistic, but this was the first time I'd heard him sound cold. He wasn't over Veritas's death yet. That was clear. He was back, and hopefully on a path towards healing. We'd all be there to help him with it, as much as he wanted.

He smiled, though it didn't reach his eyes. "Let me go stow my things, and then I have a lot of catching up to do, with all of you. With my education. Can't think of a better place to start than the bar. I'll see you all there in ten?"

"Sounds good. I think we deserve a party," I said.

Lucy hugged me. "We really do," she said.

# # #

We limped towards the end of the school year. The Academy beaten, but not defeated. The atmosphere was strained but got better. By the time the end of year exams rolled around things almost felt like they were back to normal. Normal for the Academy, anyway. If you ignored all the empty seats in the lecture halls.

I'd finished my last exam, a practical lab session for Prof Croft's class, when my wristpad chimed. I checked my messages and found a summons to Professor Alembic's office. I didn't take any of her classes, so it was kind of odd.

"Professor? You wanted to see me?" I said, poking my head around her door frame.

"Sit down, Grey, please." Her tone was flat. Not unfriendly, but it had the distinct ring of bedside manner to it.

I sat. "What is it, Professor?"

"I've been reviewing your med scans, the ones we did after your return from Academy Station. The business with Titan."

"I remember it well," I said.

"Hmm, yes. Well, I believe I have finally solved one of the small outstanding mysteries from that period. I apologise it has taken so many months to get to, but as you can imagine, it has been a stressful and distracting year."

"What mystery?" I shifted uncomfortably in my chair. After everything that had happened, I'd hoped to end the year on a quiet note. There was something in her tone that made me think things might get loud again.

"As you know, most Skills and Tech students exposed to Titan's ability were rendered more or less immediately unconscious."

"I remember, vividly." I could still see Dez and Gadget Dude dropping bonelessly to the ground.

"Powers students were able to resist, somewhat, as their powers represent a wellspring of energy that Titan could tap before directly affecting their conscious mental energies. You were also able to resist, and we are all grateful for it, considering the outcome."

"It was a team effort," I demurred. Although her definition of all was a little suspect.

"You miss the point. Grey, I know that you are registered as a Skills student, but the only explanation I can provide for your ability to resist Titan is that you have been misclassified."

"Misclassified?" I echoed, feeling particularly stupid. She seemed to be saying... but that was impossible.

Alembic caught and held my gaze. "Grey, I'm afraid there can be no doubt. I've analysed the scans and compared them to the ones you had when you first joined the Academy. There are marked differences between the two. Sometime between joining the Academy and facing Titan for the first time, something changed."

The Ascension Machine. It had to be. I hadn't come away unscathed after all.

"You're telling me I'm a *Powers* student?"

AFTERWORD

This book was both much easier and much harder to write than the first. I had a clearer vision of Grey's world in my head this time around, and I had set up several plot points in The Ascension Machine that I knew would pay off here. Against that, I was writing this throughout 2020, which, I think we can all agree, was a pretty weird and stressful year. There were times I couldn't focus on writing at all, and other times when only the writing was keeping me sane. Still, Grey's disconnection from the friends he made in his first year, while it had always been my intent for this book, had a particular real-world resonance that was unsettling.

There were some big turning points in this book, which will help set Grey in the direction of the finale of this trilogy of adventures. And beyond? Time will tell.

Titan has been waiting to rise since before I finished the first chapter of The Ascension Machine. And the effects of his arrival are far-reaching. Some we've already seen, but the ripples have only just begun to form.

Likewise, the revelation that Grey has powers has been a long time coming. It was always part of the plan, and there are some clues about it, and what it means for the future lurking around in this book. A careful reading of The Crossover Paradox might even provide some clues to what his power is. Suffice to say, yes, Grey is now a Powers student. (Spoilers, I guess, but if you're reading the Afterword before the book, I can't be held responsible for that).

Am I allowed to tease my readers in the Afterword? I guess I just did. I promise that tease, and a few more surprises, will be resolved in book 3.

Before I end, assuming you haven't just skipped to the After Credits scene, a few thanks.

First, always, to my wife Marjo. Thank you.

To Geoff at Shadow Dragon Press for believing in me twice now. And Ian for his work on the cover, people said such nice things about the cover for the first one, I didn't hesitate about inviting him back for the second, and I genuinely believe he's outdone himself. Excellent author Brent A Harris for being my alpha reader on the book, go read his excellent Twist in Time series. Beta readers Bonnie Millani, Matt Hardy and Claire Buss, all writers whose work I admire and whose advice I trust.

And thank you to those who read, reviewed, or supported the production of these books. I appreciate you all.

As ever, follow me on Twitter as @storycastrob and you can find the StorycastRob podcast on i-tunes and Spotify, if you want to hear me read some of my works. If you want to learn more about Grey's universe, check out storycastrob.co.uk/JusticeAcademy

Well, there we go. The difficult second book. If you've read this far, thank you. I hope it was as much fun for you as it was for me. Grey's story has been tapping on my brain since I began writing the first book, six years ago now. We've a way to go yet...

Rob,
Finland,
November 13th, 2021

AFTER CREDITS

So, we should probably address this as well. You already know more about it than I do, I guess, particularly because Mrs. Gravane kept it from me for months. I guess that's fair, I don't always tell her everything I should, either. Again, I wasn't here for it, but this story isn't complete if we don't at least mention it.

# # #

The Patrol Cruiser shuddered, a dull clang reverberating through the hull.

"What was that?"

"Unknown, Captain," Hardy said, fingers tapping out commands on the flight console. "Velocity cut to effectively zero, systems failure flags on almost every board. We're still in deep space, there shouldn't be anything here, but I see a shadow on the gravitic field sensor web."

"A shadow? Show me." Captain Kenward pulled his console panel around in front of him, and Hardy flicked the scan to it.

"Whatever it is, sir, it's big. Several kilometers across. Close, and getting closer," Hardy said.

"It's coming towards us?"

"No, sir, we're moving towards it."

The Captain gestured through his control field to open a ship-wide hail. "All hands, brace, executing emergency engine burn in three... two... one... mark."

The engines bellowed, thundered, and the cruiser

319

shuddered.

"Ineffective, sir," Hardy said, "we're still moving toward it; estimated collision in thirty seconds."

"Increasing engine power," Kenward said.

"Sir," Hardy objected, his console bucking under his hands as the whole ship rattled in protest at the abuse. "Red flags on all systems." The sound of warning pings punctuated the thunder of the engines.

"Sir!"

Kenward roared in frustration. "Cutting engines."

After the tumult, the silence was almost as deafening. It stretched for a long moment before the warning alerts began chiming. Ten, twenty, countless shrill shrieks clamouring for attention.

"Impact in... sensors off-line. Based on earlier calculations, impact in—" Hardy was interrupted by the sound of the cruiser ringing like a bell. "Sir, I think we hit it."

Kenward nodded. "I shall see what I can do about fixing the mess I made of the systems. Officer Hardy, please secure the prisoners."

"Aye, sir."

Hardy pushed back from his console, stood, and sprinted towards the stern, ducking under a ceiling plate that had come loose until one edge bowed into the corridor. Steam vented from something damaged back behind it. A bright red warning light strobed, making the steam all-but opaque. He fought through until he reached the portside security section.

He thumbed the lock panel, and it beeped in recognition. The door slid partway open, juddered, stuck. There was just enough gap for Hardy to push through.

"Having a bit of bother, officer?" the female prisoner asked from her cell. She laughed.

"Officer, I know what's out there," said the male prisoner. "If you open our cells and remove these cuffs, I could be persuaded to put in a good word for you."

Hardy ignored them. Instead, he pulled up the diagnostics on the security panel. "Looks like the security fields will hold," Hardy said. "I'm afraid, you're going nowhere, Doc."

Doctor Gravestone smiled tightly, then pointed. "That glowing red spot on the outer hull would suggest otherwise. It is expanding at a rate I would find alarming if I were you. I'm afraid you don't know my associates. They can be quite persistent."

A large glob of molten metal ran down the wall, scorching and hissing as it fell.

Hardy dove for the door, but it was too late. Some sensor had registered the hull breach, the door slammed shut.

The breach expanded until it was a meter wide. Beyond it, a team of aliens that Hardy had never seen before worked their cutting tool. They looked a little like Frantium, but with flatter noses. Behind them, another of the beings stood watching. His uniform was much more ostentatious; if Hardy was any judge, he was an officer of some kind.

"I'm afraid my offer just expired," said Gravestone. "You are to be congratulated on outliving it. Admiral, please kill this man."

Admiral Denbree of the third Vadram battlefleet drew his pistol. "You have no authority over me, Gravane," he said.

He fired, anyway.